the last pages

To the VanderVechts,
Enjoy the adventure!

Lara

the last pages

LARA WHATLEY

WINSLET PRESS

WINSLET PRESS

The Last Pages
Copyright © 2014 by Lara Whatley

To learn more about Lara Whatley, visit her Web site:
www.larawhatley.com

ISBN-10: 0990353818
ISBN-13: 978-0990353812

This novel is a work of fiction. Names, characters, places, and incidents either are the product of the author's imagination or are used fictitiously. Any resemblance to actual events, locales, organizations, or persons living or dead is entirely coincidental and beyond the intent of either the author or the publisher.

Printed in the United States of America

First Edition: June 2014
14 12 11 10 9 8 7 6 5 4 3 2 1

TO:

My Family:
who put up with my ramblings.

My Friends:
who helped me along the way.

Winslet Press:
who made this possible.

And You:
for taking the time to read my blood, sweat, and tears,
and for joining me on this journey,
for this is only the beginning...

CHATER

The cows chewed softly and the barn was ready to be closed up. Kale loved the sweet smell of hay, and she lingered as long as possible. A barn swallow gracefully swooped from the rafters and out into the surrounding fields. The dust in the barn sent swirling patterns through the light rays of the setting sun. Kale grabbed an old three-legged stool and sat down. She was perfectly happy to sit and stroke a calf as its mother gobbled down her grain. When she bent towards the calf to scratch behind its large floppy ears, Kale brushed her braid of wavy golden chestnut hair over her shoulder again. The calf stared up at her with its dark, questioning eyes and she smiled down at it.

Something shifted in the corner of Kale's eye. She looked around, assuming it was a mouse. Suddenly, she spotted two eyes glowing from behind a barrel. The eyes were too big and blue to belong to a mouse, or even a cat for that matter. Suspecting that there was someone in their barn, Kale's heart pounded so heavily that it felt as if it was in her throat. By the position of the eyes, Kale could tell that whoever it was had yet to spot her. Slowly rising, she walked over to the barrel, her feet making no sound on the bed of hay. She walked towards the barrel and without warning, she spun around and demanded, "What are you doing here?" She smirked when she saw a harmless figure jolt in surprise. The barrel fell over, revealing the silhouette of someone crouching behind it. A boy stepped out from the shadows; his dirty face lit up by the sun. He lifted his glance towards her, and they sized each other up. Kale guessed that he was about her age, maybe older, and his unkempt appearance gave away his position.

Without warning, the boy darted out of the barn and down the road, disappearing in the evening shadows with ease. Kale ran after him. Her eyes franticly searched the shadow-riddled yard. After several long minutes, she finally accepted that he was gone.

Kale did not think of the encounter as completely unusual, as there were many runaways that passed through her town, but Kale could not help but wonder who this mysterious visitor was. She went back to the house and tried to fall asleep beside her mother, but questions ran through her head throughout the night until sunlight filtered through the dust-paned window, waking Kale from her restless slumber. She put a kettle on for her mother, grabbed her satchel, and slipped out to the market. A mist hung over the town, and the fields between the poor farm houses in Kale's community were covered in dew. A songbird whistled joyously from its perch in the nearby trees.

Kale wished to dance all the way into the city on a day like this, but she restrained herself in case anyone might observe her. Once inside the city gates, she strolled through the market for a while, marveling at all the pretty objects in the shop windows. All of which cost more money than she could acquire in a lifetime.

As she passed a cake store, Kale spotted someone poking around in the ally. Recognizing him as the very same boy she found in the barn the night before, Kale called out, but the boy darted away. She ran after him, winding through the streets in hot pursuit. He grew farther and farther away each time she turned a corner until finally she reached a fork in the road and could not see him anywhere. Kale searched the whole area until she was forced to give up, struck by the realization that he was gone, again.

Nearby, a street vendor recognized her.

"Hello Kale!" the old merchant called out from his stall.

Smiling, she walked over. "Do you know that boy?"

The man rubbed his greasy hands on a rag and shook his head. "No, I haven't seen him around. Why do you ask?"

Kale sighed. "I found him in our barn last night, and I was just wondering who he might be."

The man nodded. "Yes, well I can ask around for you. But tell your mother I said 'hello'."

Kale smiled.

"I will!" she called, heading back to the market. Finding nothing to suit her fancy, Kale slowly made her way back home. On the dirt track that meandered through the big stone gates, Kale smiled at the guards standing idly there. They smiled back and waved, recognizing her from her many other trips.

Back at the cottage, Kale's mother was now up and enjoying her breakfast tea. "Morning, Kale. Find any bargains in the market?"

Kale shook her head. "No, but Barty said to say 'hello'."

Her mother chuckled. "He is such a nice man. I need to remember to pay him a visit soon." She handed Kale a cup of tea. "Well, you should start on your chores now, I believe the cows need to be milked."

Kale nodded and downed her tea in a gulp. Placing it on the table, she headed out to the barn. Sliding open the large oak door, Kale slipped into the musty barn and was greeted by the lows and moos of cattle. Although she scanned the area carefully, there was no sign of the boy she saw earlier. Slightly disappointed, she grabbed her stool and started milking. Placing the bucket beneath the cow, Kale coaxed the milk to squirt inside. A lonely *meow* at her right heel almost scared Kale off her stool. She turned and laughed when she found Shadow, the barn cat, begging for milk. His large green eyes said more than words could, and Kale aimed the teat at the grey mound of fur. He skillfully caught the stream of milk in his mouth, swallowing it with pure pleasure.

When he was satisfied, Kale watched as he gracefully slunk off on his daily rounds to catch little rodents. The cow Kale milked swished her tail at a fly and batted Kale full on in the face.

She chuckled and swatted the cow's tail away. "What was that for?" The cow didn't answer and kept chewing her cud. Kale sighed. "What would you do if a mysterious boy showed up in your barn, Belle?"

The cow turned, her eyes large and questioning. "I want to find out who he is, but it isn't my business, really," Kale continued, dreamily. Losing interest, and realizing she clearly wasn't getting a treat, the cow swung her head back to her food.

"But I can't help wondering who he is! Why am I so interested, Belle?" The cow ignored her. "Ugh, I don't know either..."

Her mother's call from the house brought her back to the moment, and she quickly finished up. The cows knew the routine, and milking the rest did not take long.

Three large buckets of milk later, Kale slid the barn door all the way open and shooed the cows into the pasture. After locking the gate and tossing some water into the trough, she lugged the milk up to the house.

Kale made cheese throughout the rest of the day. She and her mother only paused to eat lunch and bring the cows back in. At nightfall, they surveyed the day's work. They had successfully made two generous packages of tender cheese that were ready to be cured and still had half a bucket of milk left over that could be consumed with their meals. Kale's mother patted her on the back. Exhausted, they both retired on the bed.

Will I see him again? Kale wondered before her eyes flitted shut.

I may.

CHAPTER

I t was Sunday. Kale rejoiced in her time off work and bounded out of the house to find something to do. Amy and James, the twins living in the house across the road, were playing in the dirt as usual.

Kale walked over and crouched beside them. "You two making mud pies again?"

A pudgy little boy looked up at her, and in a matter-of-fact voice stated, "No, we not maka mud pie! We maka brekast. Too early for maka mud pie, dat for dessert!"

Kale laughed. "Why, of course. Silly me." She picked up a stick to join the two rascals. "May I help?" Immersed in their play, the children smiled and nodded before delving back into their creation.

A familiar voice rang out from across the street, "Kale! Come to the house, Kale!" Sighing, Kale left the two children and ran towards the house. She reached their old cottage in no time, swinging herself inside by the doorframe. Her mother turned from the shelf, with two coppers in hand.

"Go buy a loaf from Sake. I'm sure she will still have something that is fresh." She placed the coppers in Kale's hand and kissed her daughter on her cheek.

Kale nodded and left the house, heading up the dirt beaten track once again towards upper and lower town. Normally she would be excited for the trip. Kale loved to look at all the beautiful things in the shop windows, but today the sky was grey and promising rain. The wall surrounding lower town was massive, made from huge blocks, puzzling Kale by how they could have gotten there. The cracks in the stone were covered in a thick green layer of spring moss, but the wall still provided a sense of security for the middle class families living in the closely packed buildings. There were guards positioned at the gates to lower town, but they saw her and nodded, allowing her to continue.

As she passed through the massive gate in the wall, Kale marveled at its thickness. This gate alone could pass for a tunnel. She placed her hand on the cold, smooth stone, running it along as she walked. Her soft pink skin was out of place against the dark forbidding stone. She was sure that if she whispered in this chamber, the stones would reflect her voice, repeating it like so many gossipy women, as if she had said something wrong.

Out in the open again, the noise of the street vendors hit her like a wave.

"Combs! Bone Combs! One for a six pence! Combs!"

"Come-and-git 'em! Hot fresh pies!"

"Buy my wool! Home spun wool!"

The clouds cleared somewhat, and an orangey glow reflected off of everything. The old woman, Sake, was at her bread stall, calling for her share of buyers. Kale reached her canvas-roofed sale table with no trouble, a feat only accomplishable by one who knew how to maneuver the packed streets.

"Hi, Sake. Mother sent me to buy our supper," Kale announced.

Sake seemed to light up at the sight of Kale, who would sometimes trade goods with her or do errands and deliveries.

"Of course," Sake responded. She bent beneath her table and stood up with a small loaf.

"I saved the best for you, though there was some man here earlier who was giving me a hard time for it, so I put it under the table." She grinned, revealing her rotten mouth that seemed to be full of more spaces than teeth. Kale gingerly took the loaf and wrapped it in her shawl. She then dumped a couple of coppers on the table.

"Thank you so…" she began, but there, in the corner of her eye, she saw him.

That boy again!

He slipped around the corner and disappeared.

He would not get away that easy this time!

"I'm sorry, Sake. I have to go," Kale mumbled her apology. As she took off, following the boy's trail.

Sake shook her head, muttering to herself, "That girl is going to get into trouble some day," and carefully placed the coppers in her pocket. "Not my place to judge, she and her poor ol' ma. Bless their souls."

Sake was not the only one watching Kale. In the shadows something shifted and unfurled two black wing-like limbs. One onlooker spotted the dark figure as it took off into the sky, but he shook his head incredulously and looked at the bottle in his hand.

"Gotta lay off the grog," he said. Dumping the bottle on the ground, he walked away.

CHAPTER

K ale took off down the alleyway in the direction the boy had taken and swung her head around franticly, trying to catch sight of where he went. She came to a split in the alley, but the boy was nowhere to be seen. Trusting her instincts, Kale dashed to the right.

There!

A fleeting shadow ran as fast as it could. Used to sprints, Kale urged her muscles faster, and in reward, noticed that she gained on him. The boy slowed to a jog.

Tired? Already?

Afraid that he would take off again when she grew close, Kale did not slow up until she was only a few feet away. They both stopped cold. Now that she was finally facing him without one of them running, she didn't know what to say.

They regarded each other for a while, and Kale noticed that he looked slightly suspicious yet somehow amused. His ruffled auburn hair glowed faintly red in the dim light, and it fell over his face at odd angles. He had so many freckles that, at a distance, his face looked tanned.

"So you finally caught me," he said.

Kale jerked in surprise of his voice. "What?"

He tipped his head like a quizzical puppy. "You have been trying to catch me, right? Well, here I am."

Kale's jaw dropped. "How did you know...I mean, I thought you were trying to get away, yet you sound like you wanted me to find you."

He grinned. "You could say that."

Kale frowned. *This boy is strangely cryptic. I still don't know who he is!*

"Why have you been following me? No one else seems to see you, and you show up where ever I am. What is going on?" Kale demanded.

"Can we go to the candle shop?" he asked, looking up through his bangs.

"Why?"

"So that no one will overhear us. I am temporarily living above the shop," he explained. Kale was hesitant, but she nodded. "Good, let's go." He turned, and then stopped. Looking her straight in the eye, he stated, "What you see and hear cannot be told to anyone. Understood?"

Suspicious, Kale could only nod.

Together they made it to the shop surprisingly fast, and they slipped in the door without anyone noticing. He lead Kale to the top floor of the shop where the shelves were more full of cobwebs than candles, and the broken window sent dappled light across the floor. Kale hesitated. There was no door or room visible here. She looked at him for an explanation and was surprised to find him looking back.

"Can I trust you?" he asked.

Kale paused. "What do you mean?"

He looked down and continued, "I can't let anyone know how to get into my hideout. Could you close your eyes while I open the door, and then I will lead you in?"

Kale's heart pounded. "I don't know if I want to. I mean I just met you, and I don't even know your name, and something could go wrong, and…"

He was still looking at her steadily. "This is important. If it is too hard for you, I can just knock you out."

Kale gasped, but he still looked serious. He looked down and then back at her. "Leon. My name's Leon."

Kale calmed a bit.

Leon, Latin for lion, hmm. A noble name for one living on the streets. At least I know he trusts me . . .somewhat. Kale's hesitation lifted. "I will try to keep my eyes closed."

He looked relieved. "Ok, close them then."

Kale squeezed her lids shut and stood very still. She could faintly hear the squeak of hinges, *or were they wheels?* Leon opened the door and checked to make sure she wasn't cheating. Quickly, he returned and grabbed her wrist, guiding her through the space and up two sets of stairs. Kale balanced herself during the ascent, wondering if the walls were closing in on her before they finally reached a landing.

"Don't open yet," he whispered. She nodded, and he pulled the door shut behind them, leaving Kale in complete darkness.

"Okay. You can open now," he said.

It took Kale a couple of minutes for her eyes to adjust, but she could almost make out the large beams that held up the shop roof. She guessed they were somewhere near the spot where the walls ended and the roof began.

"WELL, YOU KNOW WHO I AM. WHY HAVE YOU BEEN FOLLOW-ing me?" Leon broke the silence.

"Your name is hardly who you are, but why have *you* been following *me?*"

"I don't really know where to begin, and we don't have much time. All I can say right now is that I need your help. I had to find someone who would help me, and so I started to follow you. I knew that if I let you see me now and then, your curiosity would lead you to me."

"What do you mean? You wanted me to follow you? You were purposely letting me see you?"

He smiled, shrugging his shoulders. "I have to admit, you caught me off guard in the barn, but other than that, I know how to move unnoticed."

She still was not sure but resigned, "Ok, so I'm here. What do you need me for?"

Leon sighed. "You can't trust the king," he straightforwardly stated.

Kale frowned. "What?"

Is this how he always starts conversation, with a disrespect for our royalty?

Leon's eyes darkened with seriousness. "You can't trust the king. I am only staying here for a while, and I need a post in this town. A spy that is well connected; one that can get updates on the going-ons and then send word to me. You looked like a good candidate for that." He paused. "I have very good sources to believe he's involved in treason." He looked back at her, waiting to see if she was taking it all in.

Unimpressed, Kale continued, "Have you lost your mind? How am I supposed to believe you? The king has been good to us all these years after his brother's death. Besides, he's the king! How can *he* be involved in treason?"

His eyes showed no emotion. "You have to trust me. If you won't do it, I can find someone else. For my sake, don't tell anyone what you have heard. I am not asking much, just for you to send me notice of what is going on, just as if we were family or good friends."

"We are not friends! I don't even know you! What if I get into trouble because of you?" Kale hoped he would promise that she wouldn't.

He sighed and looked off into space. "I can't confirm anything, but I could use your help." Suddenly he stiffened, and his eyes shot towards the wall. Kale faintly heard the voices of men grow closer.

Leon whispered, "We have to go. Now. Are you in or not?"

Kale sighed. "I guess I could . . . I mean, it's not every day that I get confronted by strange boys with fanciful ideas of treason."

Kale did not notice if he smiled or not.

"Wonderful. We should go now," Leon blurted.

Kale held up a hand. "Wait, how do you travel?"

He waved her off. "I have my ways. Close your eyes."

When Kale opened them again, they were standing in the empty candle room.

"You know," Leon said, "you aren't supposed to see the door. It wouldn't be a hideout if you did."

Kale nodded. "How did you find it? I mean, if it is so well hidden."

Leon chuckled. "Purely by accident, actually. We should go, before someone spots us up here," he said, motioning towards the outside.

CHAPTER

Once they reached the end of the dirt-beaten track, a woman rushed up to greet them. As she grew closer, the loose ends of her bun, tucked into the kerchief around her head, grew visible, along with the smudges of hasty wiping on her simple garden dress.

"Mother!" Kale exclaimed with surprise. She didn't need to look at the figure slipping through the trees, away from the town, to know that Leon had left.

"Darling! Where have you been? I have been so worried." She swept Kale up into her arms. "When you didn't come home from the market, I thought, maybe... Oh, Darling!" Her mother's heart raced, and Kale sensed terror in her embrace.

Kale frowned and pulled away. "Mom, what happened?"

"It was a man, a big man with dark hair and eyes, and he, and..."

Seeing how shaken her mother was, Kale led her back to their cottage and sat her in a chair by the table. Filling a kettle from the water pail, she hung it on the stake over their fire and grabbed the brush from the lone shelf that held her possessions. She sat down and began to undo her mother's careful knot at the nape of her neck.

After the water boiled, Kale set out the tea for both of them and hesitantly asked, "What happened, Mother?"

Her mother looked up from her pewter cup and started to speak, paused, then continued, "A large man in a cloak came to the house today. He said he was here on account of the king, Lord bless his soul, but I thought to myself, why would the king send a man to this house today? We have paid our taxes, and they have collected the harvest from our fields already, so I started to worry. He walked into the house without invitation, which the king's knights never do, and leaned his sword on the wall. I hadn't even noticed a sword under his cloak. But he had one, and never had I seen such a weapon. It was neither beautiful nor shameful, but completely black, like his cloak, and I knew it was deadly at first glance. It almost glowed, Kale! Glowed black! I saw it shift as if a coal; it's dark surface swirling with some unknown power. Kale, I think I am going crazy. Never have I seen something like this in my humble life! I suddenly wanted to be as far from this man as I could get. Naturally , I prepared what little bread we had for him, and he ate in silence. His presence seemed to cool the room, yet he must have been chilled himself, as he never removed his hood. Rather peculiar, if I do say so myself. All I ever saw of his face was his dirty black locks which fell away from where his face *should* be, and occasionally the light reflected off his sharp, pale cheekbones, and long hooked nose. Then, he started talking, presumably in a friendly tone, but his voice was grating and cold. He asked a lot about you . . .your hobbies, where you go in the day, what you do… I wasn't sure why. Then he said something about you seeing a particular boy."

Kale sucked in her breath, but her mother took no notice and continued, "He got very serious, almost threatening, and he seemed to think that you should know about this . . . traitor! The boy had sneaked into one of the king's castle windows. Those walls are almost devoid of handholds, but he got in, and made it into the princess' bedroom. He was in the middle of rummaging around in her drawers for something, no one knows what, when a servant came in. The poor girl screamed and woke her mistress. The boy threw his knife at her, but the princess had already seen his face before he escaped out the window again. Of course, she alerted the guards, but he was gone into thin air!" Putting an arm on Kale's shoulder, her mother asked gently, "Am I upsetting you, dear?"

Kale hastily sat back in her seat and tried to cover up her pale face by taking a sip of tea. "Not at all, Mother. Continue. Your story is quite fascinating."

She inhaled and continued, "Well, there are posters all over the upper town for him, and someone said they spotted the very same boy with you. The king evidently heard about it, and told our Lord, Sir Irwen, to track down this traitor. The man in black told me all of this, but he was not done. He leaned in close to me, and for the first time, I saw his face. I tried not to scream, for what I saw was horrific. The man had a long grey scar starting at his left cheekbone, which crossed his eye, and ended just above his eyebrow. The skin around the scar was gathered, but the worst part was his eye. He didn't wear a patch, and so his eye was visible, all milky white and blind to the world, but it still moved with its twin, as if it could see. His good eye was black, not dark brown, or even grey, just all black but the whites of his eyes. He breathed on my face, and with a hint of a smirk, he brushed my hair behind my ear and whispered, 'If she sees him again, tell her to come by my place.' I closed my eyes to his horrific face, and when I opened them again, he was gone." Her mother shook again, but Kale was too numb to comfort her. They both sat in silence until it grew too dark to see. Wordlessly, Kale helped her mother to the bed they shared and laid her down. Curled up beside her, she waited for sleep, but it never came.

CHAPTER

K ale looked for Leon during her daily chores the next morning, but
she could not find him. She did not even get a glimpse of him in
the streets of lower town or hanging around the candle shop.

*Maybe he just decided that he had finished the job he came for and left to other towns
to conscript others.* Somehow, that thought made Kale feel like her life was
suddenly pale. She realized that, for a brief moment in time, she had something exciting, even dangerous, that she was part of. She followed some
mysterious creature and had been tempted to question the intentions of her
king. Feeling sort of empty, she headed back home and found her mother
already in bed. Slipping down beside her, she quickly fell asleep.

MEANWHILE, IN AN INN NOT FAR FROM TOWN, TWO FIGURES
met under the dim lamplight and in musky odors of the pub. Both were
cloaked, and there sat one lone drunkard that might notice them, but not
remember.

A kind of hissing voice issued from one of the figures, "You found the
girl?"

"Yes, she does not know anything, but she questions rumors of treason."
The man shifted, and the light revealed a lone scar running over one eye.

The other cloaked figure chuckled. "Yeessss. We knew she would." The
hissing paused. "She isss . . . the one?"

"Yes, she is definitely the one," the cloaked figure confirmed.

The first figure grinned, unseen by his partner, "Good."

KALE WOKE, HER HEART PUMPING OUT OF CONTROL. SHE WAS unable to scream because of the hand over her mouth. Trying to struggle, her mind swirled with fear.

The attacker whispered in her ear, his hot breath tickling her skin, "Stop it! You will wake your mother. We have to get out of here . . . fast!"

Leon.

Kale quickly nodded, and the hand was removed.

She immediately faced him, whispering as loud as she dared, "What is *wrong* with you?" She couldn't read his face for remorse, which angered her more.

He just whispered, "No time to explain. We need to go. Now!"

Kale stood and carefully stepped over her sleeping mother, still fuming at him for scaring her. "Why should I go with you? I just met you!"

Leon grabbed her arm and pulled her towards the door. "Just come now! I will explain later."

Kale shook him off, but before she could help herself, she blurted, "Fine! Let me get some stuff." From the shelf, she took some of the left-over bread from the day and two coppers. Her mother shifted in her sleep, and Kale felt sorry for her. Not wanting her to worry, Kale grabbed a scrap piece of cloth and began scribbling a message.

Leon noticed what she was doing, and in two quick steps grabbed the fabric and tossed it on the coals in the hearth, growling. "What are you thinking? If they find this, your mother might end up dead! It is better that she knows nothing."

Kale shuddered at the thought.

Why would someone do this?

She put her hand near her mother's face but pulled back as Leon motioned to her and hastily headed out the door. Kale glanced at the sleeping figure once more before hurrying after him.

Out in the cool night air, Kale's senses woke up. She hurried to catch up with the dark form sprinting towards the trees. "Wait up! I can't run that fast! I don't really want to go with you. Can you please tell me what is going on?"

He slowed a bit. Looking back, he called, "Hurry, we have to make it into the forest." Kale was still trying to make sense of what was going on, when two things happened at once. They reached the forest just as the alarm bell went off in the towns.

"Is that for us? What have we done?" Kale said. "What did *you* do?"

Leon shook his head and motioned for her to follow. Kale did, not wanting to be left behind in the dark forest, and they walked on for quite a while .

Leon slipped between the trees like a shadow, but Kale crashed along behind him as fast as she could without tripping over the many hidden logs and twigs. The trees seemed to grab her hair and clothing, trying to pull her back from whatever lay ahead. A cold wind rustled through the leaves on the forest floor. The intricate shadows cast by branches twisted and moved, creating scary shapes on the ground.

When the moon went down, Kale began to feel too tired to go on. Her heals ached, her muscles burned, and she was about to collapse on the ground when Leon stopped so abruptly that she almost ran into him.

"I think we will be safe this far from town for now. We can rest 'til morning and then start up again," he pronounced.

Kale plopped on the leaf-covered forest floor, thankful for the break. "Rest 'til morning and then continue? Where are we going, Leon?"

Leon sat on a stump, staring into space for too long.

What has made him like this? Kale shivered; the night air had grown cold now that they were not moving.

"Leon, why are we running?" Kale played with a leaf at her feet.

A muscle in Leon's jaw jerked. He ran a hand through his hair and huffed, "I overheard some men talking." He paused. "They were planning my arrest. I dismissed this, because I am hunted. But this was different. They went on to say that there was someone who had been helping me . . . but someone they could use to turn me in." Leon looked up at her. "They meant you." Kale's heart quickened. Leon continued, "When that bell went, it was because someone must have spotted me, and surely they will now go to your house to question you. But you're here. I knew that I had made a mistake in trying to get your help. I should have just asked one of my old, reliable friends. I'm sorry I caused you this trouble. I really am. I didn't think they would try this hard to catch me."

Kale was stunned for a moment, but then she started to boil. "You used me as a replacement to save your friends some trouble? You knew your friends, whoever they are, could do this job better than I! You never told me you were a criminal! You put my mother and me in danger, and now you are dragging me out here on this wild goose chase with you when you deserve to be hung! You—"

"Kale," Leon started. "I didn't know this would happen..." He paused, as if deciding something before continuing, almost resigned. "They are not trying to catch me because of any crime I did, despite my accident at that castle. I am a threat to them."

Kale looked up, her anger cooling slightly, her mind full of curiosity.

Leon continued, "There is a well-kept secret, a secret that one person managed to stumble upon; a secret that should never have seen the light. With it out, there is the danger of that one person spreading the word, causing the kingdom to crumble. So naturally, the easiest thing to do is to eliminate that one person."

Realization washed over Kale. "That one person is you? Isn't it?"

Leon nodded. "I never meant to figure it out; I just did. At first I wanted to find out if it was true, so I started sneaking around looking for evidence. That was when I accidentally killed the maid. I never meant to do that either. It just happened." He looked at her, and Kale could see the pain in his eyes. "I guessed what I never should have, and they want me dead for it. I found out enough evidence of the grisly truth, and knew I had to escape. I started posting spies in the towns that would send word to me, and I moved from one town to the next, always avoiding the places that were heavily guarded or too full of gossip to avoid suspicion. When I arrived in your town, my friends would not help me. They had heard the rumors, and they did not want to ruin their own reputations. I felt badly for them and started to look for others I could trust. That was when I found you."

Kale was dizzy with the information and didn't know what to believe. "So you are being chased because you found out some secret about the king?"

Leon shrugged. "In a way."

Suddenly hopeful that all was not lost and that she might actually return to her mother unharmed, Kale said, "Well, if only *you* know the secret, why can't I go back home? If anyone does find me, I won't know anything."

"Did any stranger confront you or your mother?"

Kale remembered her mother's story and sighed. "Yes, actually, a man in a black cloak came."

Leon shuddered involuntarily. His eyes seemed to glaze over as if he was seeing something that wasn't there. He reached gingerly to his neck, where a small scar was visible. Kale noticed and tipped her head inquiringly, but Leon shook his head. "It is just as I thought. The fact that they would take time to look for you means that, not only do they know who you are, but they think I told you what I found out. If you go back, you will wind up dead."

Kale looked horrified.

"These people won't take any chances; they can't have two"—he emphasized with his fingers—"criminals running around free. That is why I came to your house tonight. You had to join me." Leon paused. "…It is nice to have someone with me for a change." He caught her look and stopped.

Tears were filling up Kale's eyes, for she knew now that she would never be able to go back home, and never see her mother again. Any hope she once had now vanished, replaced by a dull coldness. Falling on the leaves weakly, she laid awake, her heart throbbing and wounded. Leon sighed and leaned against a tree. The hours passed in silence.

Neither of them had slept when dawn came. Pink clouds hugged the glowing horizon, and light streamed through the forest. A mist covered the low forest floor, and Kale found that it was not any warmer than the night before.

Leon looked at the sky and then rose stiffly to his feet. "We should go," he said without emotion. Kale stood and stretched. Her emotions were not as raw any more, but her mind, still numb, wondered about what was in store for them. Leon briefly covered up any of their traces in the leaves, and they started to walk on into the forest.

"We have to find someplace to stay immediately. We will rest until night-fall and then continue. It is not safe to travel in the day," Leon started. "I will try to find some supper." Kale stumbled on, unresponsive. Leon took the hint that she did not want to talk, and they walked on, side by side, yet so alone.

CHAPTER

T he sun was already above them when they reached the edge of a clearing. A large, lush valley lay before them; its floor covered in soft, new grass. Kale saw small cottages nestled closely together, surrounded by fields, barns, and pastures. Leon scanned the village briefly before he continued on to an earth-packed cart track leading into its center.

Kale caught up but looked hesitantly around, not sure what to think. "I thought we were avoiding people?"

Leon chuckled. "While you were overwhelmed about the realization that you were stuck with me, I was setting up false trails. It will take the guards time to find out which direction we took, so when we set out again tonight, they will be at least a day behind us." Leon smiled a bit. "Don't worry! I have done this before, remember? I happen to know an old friend who will be more than happy to give us a place to stay in his barn. I am sure his wife will feed us for some chores as well." He continued down the track, and Kale followed, slightly more confident now.

They reached the barn, and Leon slid open the old door. Its rough old wood squeaked and groaned in protest, as the dusty interior of the barn was revealed. Leon swiftly walked through the doors and headed to the back. Kale followed, not wanting to be left behind. Reaching a ladder nailed to the back wall, he climbed up into the loft. It was dark and musty, but full of loose hay and shafts of straw, creating a warm sheltered nook. Kale fell into the hay; exhaustion overtaking her.

Leon watched as she closed her eyes, and he sighed.

KALE SHIFTED, AND LEON GREW ALERT AGAIN. HE QUIETLY
climbed back down the ladder and after carefully shutting the barn door,
headed to an old stone house near the edge of the track. Rapping on the
door softly, Leon waited for a response. He could hear the shuffle of feet
within the house, and an old man with long stringy hair opened the door.
"No sales today, come back another ... Leon!" His face was transformed
by a smile. "What brings you to these parts?" he asked, his gruff voice
evidence of a long life.

Leon shrugged. "Sightseeing."

The old man winked. "Come on in, Laddie. I am guessing you will want
some lunch, eh?" He offered, opening the door wider.

Leon nodded. "I was hoping you would have some extra work for me to
earn my keep for the night."

The old man smiled. "No need for that! You are the son I never had.
Just remember to visit more often!" The little man scurried over to his
stove and rummaged through bottles and breadbaskets.

Leon smiled at the kindly man. "Thank you, but this time I have another
mouth to feed."

The man stopped for a second, placing a jam jar back on the shelf
before turning, "What, did you find an injured birdie along the way?" he
asked in mock jest.

Leon shook his head. "No, I brought a partner; she wanted to be in on
some of the things I see in my travels." Leon said, hoping that the man
clued in.

Pausing a moment, the old man scratched his head. "A girl, eh? Take
good care of her. I don't know why a lassie would like to see the world
though. Talked her into it, did ya?" he asked, smiling again.

Leon nodded. "Took some convincing. Not sure how she will get used
to life on the road though, you know. Homebody her whole life," he said,
winking.

The little old man chuckled and dumped two loaves of bread in Leon's
arms along with a small jar of jelly. "Should best move on at twilight, have
heard the rumors spreading," he cautioned.

Leon looked gratefully at the food and nodded, "Thanks for everything.
I will repay you someday." The old man just waved from the door, as Leon

headed back down to the barn.

KALE WOKE TO THE SMELL OF SWEET STRAWBERRY JAM, AND for a split second, she believed that it had all been just a nightmare. When her eyes came into focus and she spotted Leon, she sighed.

Leon looked hurt. "What? I brought food, but you look like I am last person you were hoping to see."

Kale shook her head. "It's not you. I just thought that I might have been dreaming this whole time, until I saw you and realized that it was actually happening." She sighed, sitting upright in the hay.

Leon slit his knife through one of the loaves of bread. "I know how you feel." He spread some jam on both halves and then handed one to Kale, who gratefully bit into it. Leon stashed the other loaf away in his sack. He turned his half around thoughtfully in his hands but didn't eat it. "I was nine," he said, staring at the bread as if it was suddenly very interesting.

Kale looked up. "What?"

"I was nine when I was first, officially, on my own," he clarified, taking a bite of the bread.

A wave of sympathy hit Kale. "But I thought you have only been running recently. I mean, that's what it sounded like."

Leon nodded. "I haven't been *running* my whole life, just wandering around. That is why I know the country pretty well and have friends who will take me in. I have always been a wanderer," he said in a somewhat matter-of-fact tone.

Kale looked down, suddenly feeling bad about her complaining, her homesickness, when Leon had been trying hard to make her comfortable... Leon, who had been homeless longer than she. "I'm sorry," she said sincerely.

Leon seemed to wake up. "What for? You didn't do anything, and it is my own fault you had to join me. I am the one who should be sorry." He looked towards the barn wall where the warm sun was streaming through the old boards. Kale noted that his hair glowed orange in the golden sunrays, and she could just make out his freckles. Leon grabbed his pack. "Anyways, the sun is setting. You slept quite a while, so we should probably move on," he suggested.

Kale stood slowly, sorry to leave their little haven, but she didn't complain. Before he reached the ladder, Leon turned suddenly and pulled a dagger out of his cloak, handing it to her gently. It was long for a dagger, with a well-used leather handle. To Kale's eyes that were only accustomed to butcher knives, it was a thing of beauty, deadly beauty. She stared at the weapon in her hand and started to slide it back towards Leon. He shook his head and closed her fingers around it. Before they went down, Leon stopped again and held up a finger. He rummaged around in a pouch until he pulled out a leather strap.

"Here, this will keep it covered," he said, holding out the thick leather band.

Kale stared at the oddly cut leather, not understanding what it was. Shaking her head and chuckling, Leon stepped closer to her. "Do you seriously not know how to use this?" He bent towards her and wrapped the leather around her waist. Kale raised her arms, watching as Leon tied a sturdy knot and slid her dagger into a little pouch at the side.

"There, now it is hidden, and we won't have any guards wondering why some pretty little lady is running around with a knife," he said, patting the blade.

Kale was still not sure she wanted to be a pretty lady running around with a knife. "I won't have cause to use it. Why don't you just keep it?" she asked, strongly hoping that what she said was true.

Leon shook his head. "No, it is better to be prepared for the worst and hope for the best. That was my first blade, and it saved me many times. If we should get split up, it might come in handy." Kale paled at that thought, but did not push the issue further.

As they set out once more, Leon made a quick stop at one of the houses and talked briefly with a man there. Kale noted that the man looked as if he had tears welling up in his eyes as he passed Leon some food and hugged him. Leon patted the man on the back and left to rejoin Kale.

"Who was that?" Kale asked, while the old man waved from his door.

"Just an old friend. He gave us some of his own food for the trip," Leon answered. Kale waved back at the old man as he disappeared into his house. "He also said he has been hearing too many rumors for us to stay here very long. We need to reach Florian before daybreak," he said, determined.

"Florian! That is more than a day's walk away!"

"We must reach it by morning. Come." Leon insisted, as he began walking briskly away from the town.

CHAPTER 2

They reached the forest once more, and Leon seemed to relax. Kale, somewhat refreshed from her sleep, found the going easier than the night before, but after a couple of hours, she grew tired again. The night was cold; her simple brown dress did nothing to protect her. The forest appeared uniform; they seemed to pass the same trees over and over again. Kale worried that they were going in circles. She hated being trapped in the bush, and she longed for a proper bed to sleep on. Wondering about what was happening back in town, Kale remembered her mother and wondered how she was faring, if she was alive. A tight knot grew in her stomach, but she pushed the thought away.

A breeze moved through the trees. She shivered and pulled her shawl tighter around herself. It was late in the night when they finally reached the walls of Florian. The city was vastly larger than any Kale had seen before, and even at nighttime, the sheer height of the walls astonished her. Leon motioned for Kale to wait, and he disappeared along the wall. The wind danced through the leaves at her ankles, lifting them up and on through the night. Kale felt nervous about being left alone in the dark; the shadows played weird tricks on her eyes.

When Leon finally returned, she followed him to a small wooden door farther along the wall, which might have been used for livestock. A round man with a lantern motioned for them to hurry. Kale wondered who he was, but she didn't ask any questions. Once they were through the opening, the pudgy man quickly slid the door shut, locked it, and rolled an empty barrel in front, concealing the door from prying eyes. The man then bobbed down the street, lantern swaying from his pudgy hand. Leon and Kale followed him wordlessly, as he made off through the foggy streets of Florian. The man darted inside an inn and was soon lost among the drunken crowd. Kale did not like the sight of this place, with its shabby walls and the broken inn sign reading "The Gallows" above the shop.

"Are we staying here?" she asked.

Leon nodded and hurried inside, clearly not preferring the place either. Deciding that the inn at least looked warm, Kale followed, not wanting to be left out in the dark, cold streets. Just as she passed through the doorframe, Kale's eyes drifted over a particular shadow in the streets. An inexplicable shiver ran down her spine, and she hurriedly stepped into the tavern.

Inside, Kale looked around the musty room and spotted Leon at the innkeeper's counter. She made her way over fallen drunkards and knocked over benches, barely daring to breathe because of the stench. Leon left after a heated discussion, dropping some coins on the counter before he joined Kale. "We have a room for the day. Then we will leave," he said. He showed her upstairs to the very end of a hall.

The room they rented was small and stuffy, with no window, but it had a couple of bed mats. Leon placed his bag on the mat and headed back towards the door.

"Eat something from the bag and get some rest. There is some business here that I need to attend to," Leon said vaguely before shutting the door as he left.

Kale grabbed a loaf from the bag and nibbled it thoughtfully. After she was full, her body collapsed onto one mat without complaint, too exhausted from walking all night to consider their sleeping arrangements.

LEON HEADED BACK DOWNSTAIRS, MAKING SURE KALE WAS not following him. At the bottom of the stairwell, there was a cloaked man waiting for him. The man whipped out a knife and pinned Leon against the wall. "What took you so long?" He growled savagely.

Leon wrenched the wrist away from his throat. "Careful now! It took longer than I thought." He walked calmly over to a table and sat down. The stranger sat too, but he didn't remove his hood. Underneath, Leon saw his black hair, one blind eye, and a scar running through it.

"The master is not happy. You know he does not like to wait," the man said.

Leon nodded. "I know. How could I forget?" His hand reached to the scar on his neck; he remembered the night that shadowed figure had taken a strange glowing weapon to his throat. It never healed properly and those flashbacks still haunted him.

Leon wondered how the weapon glowed; it must have had some sort of power in it. He knew magic should not exist, so he explained it away as a trick of the light. "But he will have to be patient a little longer. The girl is slow," Leon insisted.

The man looked around suspiciously, and then said, "Is she here?"

Leon nodded calmly. "Yes."

The dark man's eyes lit up at this, and Leon noticed. "You remember the deal," Leon whispered. "Oh, and the Shadow better stay out of it, as you promised."

The man nodded. "Of course, and you better remember our bargain, too. You have a fortnight to be there; if not, you go with her," he said, somewhat amused.

Leon gulped, but did not show fear. Satisfied, the cloaked man stood and left Leon sitting alone at the table. In the corner of the inn, another shadowy shape watched the encounter. He grinned as the man left, watching Leon carefully. "Yesssss, you will be there, won't you? Hopefully you remember our lassst encounter," he said to himself.

Leon spun when he heard the soft hissing whisper. The hair on the back of his neck stood on end, and he scanned the room quickly. When he didn't spot the figure he was looking for, he sighed softly and assured himself that his imagination was only getting the best of him.

Leon headed back to his room and found Kale fast asleep on her mat. His mind was troubled, unsure of what he should do. Angst overwhelmed him and he collapsed on his mat as well. Leon's dreams were plagued by nightmares of a strange hooded figure reaching out to him with a glowing knife. He scrambled away until he hit a wall. Just before the knife touched his skin, he spotted two glowing red eyes beneath the cloak.

CHAPTER

All through the day, Leon woke periodically, and each time Kale slept undisturbed, but when night fell again, he was itching to get a move on. He shook Kale gently until she groaned and pushed him away. He laughed, stood up and said, "Come on! We need to go."

Kale plunged her face into the mat and pulled her shawl over her head. "Can't we just stay here? I'm tired! No one will find us!"

Leon grabbed her arm and lifted her out of bed. "I don't think so. We have to move," he said, tossing over her dagger.

Kale groaned, but she grabbed her small pouch of food and followed him. It was dark again by the time they left through the little door in the wall and headed on towards the forest. The noises no longer spooked Kale, but the cold remained. "Where are we going now, Leon?" she asked hesitantly.

His voice carried a bit, as he had gotten ahead, but he paused for her to catch up. "We need to get to Bartleona. It is several days away."

Kale sighed. *More walking.* She hiked up her shawl around her bare shoulders, wishing that her homespun dress was thicker to shield her from the night chill. She couldn't help but notice that Leon was tense. She was just about to ask why, but decided against it. At every noise, he seemed to jump, and it wasn't until they were safely settled once again that he began to calm down.

The barn was larger than the last they stayed in, but it too, was filled with hay and the welcome sounds of animals. Kale crawled up to the loft and lay down on a pile of hay, comforted with the familiar. She curled up to keep warm, and soon was fast asleep. It seemed like she had only just dozed off when Leon woke her. Dusk had just fallen and it was time to move again.

Leon stopped to get some more food at a farmer's house before they continued.

He had only been talking to a woman at a farmhouse for a couple of minutes when an eerie silence swept over the place. Suddenly, there were shouts in the distance. From the jarred barn door, Kale saw four soldiers running towards them. Their shiny metal breastplates reflected the moonlight as their hobnail shoes smacked against the dirt beaten path. The torches they carried illuminated the soldiers' serious faces.

Kale's heart quickened. *They found us!*

Leon sprinted back to the barn, shouting, "Go! Run! I will meet you in the forest!"

Without hesitation, Kale raced toward the forest. She only sprinted a few yards when she heard the soldiers yell. Curiosity overcame her, and she spun around to watch as Leon turned to face them, drawing out his sword. It shone in the moonlight; its steel surface perfectly smooth and flawless.

Kale had never seen such a weapon. She noticed that the soldiers also carried swords, and she knew that one man against four was destined for failure. She gasped in fright as an image flashed through her head of Leon being chopped into pieces. Suddenly, Kale didn't want to watch any longer. She turned and didn't look back while only seeking refuge of the forest. She could hear steel hit steel and she shivered from the sound of the battle. There were a couple of cries, and then the slashing stopped.

Kale waited expectantly for proof that Leon survived, but to her dismay, she only heard the shouts of two soldiers. *They got him!* Kale stood stunned for a moment. Suddenly, she heard the footsteps of a soldier charging towards her. She jumped to attention and started to run away. Fearing for her life, she broke into a feverish sprint. Tripping over downed trees and lone boulders, twigs ripped her face as she fled. Kale heard the soldier gaining and started to panic. When she felt his firm hand on her shoulder, she prepared to face him and attack. She was in mid leap when she realized that it was Leon, badly scratched and completely surprised. He did a roll to the side to avoid her, and she landed where he was two seconds before.

"That was good!" Leon praised her.

Kale blushed. "Leon! You scared me half to death! First, I thought you died, and then I thought you were trying to kill me!" She sighed and continued, "Are you hurt? I thought they got you! How did you get away?"

Leon smiled. "Not too hurt, and I am alive. I don't even know myself how I got away... just that when the fighting was thick, I managed to slip away and run for the woods."

Kale laughed with relief. "The soldiers didn't notice?"

Leon shook his head. "No. They were too occupied with whacking the flour bags I hid behind, and the whole place seemed to fill up with smoke!" He chuckled.

Kale tried to imagine what that would have looked like, and a grin split across her face.

CHAPTER

Moods brightened, Kale and Leon continued their journey through the woods. The moon shined brightly through the trees, causing the leaves to look almost silver. The forest slept, cloaked in a warm peacefulness. Yet the crickets cheerfully chirped in the shadows trumping Kale and Leon's footsteps. They plodded along for a while longer, and Kale noticed that the going was suddenly easier. She scanned the ground and realized they reached a path in the woods. Thankful for the road, she continued hesitantly behind Leon for fear they were now an easy target.

It was getting towards the early hours of the day when they turned a corner in the path. There stood two bulky men in long, black cloaks, blocking their way. Leon and Kale stopped in their tracks, unsure of what to do. Before either of them could react, the first man reached out and wrapped his thick arm around Kale's neck; she felt a knifepoint at her hairline. She gasped and clawed at the man's arm, but he held tighter, cutting off her air supply. Leon growled and tried to leap at her captor, but the other man grabbed his right arm, twisting it behind his back. Leon groaned in pain and was forced to stop. The second man quickly pinned Leon's other arm behind him. Bright red and gold flashes leaped before Kale's eyes, and she went limp from lack of oxygen. The man holding her loosened a little, and she gulped up a lungful of air.

A dark shadow drifted out onto the path and spoke, "Hello, Leon." Leon looked up at the cloaked figure through his bangs, his chest heaving. He tried to wrench away his hands from behind him, but to no avail. Kale looked from the shadow man to Leon, stunned. This man was cloaked head to toe in a black robe; *surely Leon could not know someone this evil looking.*

"Don't remember me?" The shadowy figure drifted closer. Leon remained silent, his scar itching as the dark figure advanced and seemed to smile. "What about the girl?"

Kale fidgeted when the shadow thing turned towards her. An inexplicable chill overcame her, as he said, "Did Leon tell you why he isss here?" Kale was confused and frightened, but she shook her head, and the shadow-like being seemed to emit what might have been a chuckle.

"Leon agreed to bring you in," he hissed at her.

Leon struggled again. "No!" he shouted defiantly.

The shadowy figure emitted a cackling laugh. Mockingly, he continued, "Oh, you didn't tell her? How you agreed to exchange her for your pardon and a bagful of coinsss?"

Kale was horrified at this idea and looked at Leon, expecting his denial, but his eyes only held a fiery shame. "Why are *you* here? I never made this deal with you, The Shadow!" Leon shouted.

The Shadow paused and moved closer. "Oh, but you did, didn't you? Seeing that you made the deal with one who serves me." He paused, letting the words sink in before gesturing to the cloaked man who had his arm around Kale's throat. Only now, Leon looked up at the scar running through one blind eye.

"On my ordersss," the shadow finished.

Leon looked horrified. "He tricked me! He never said this was part of it. He promised you would not be involved!"

The Shadow laughed. "Yesss, but I always wasss. I planned to wait until you made it to the city yourselvesss, but you were too tempting. Why do you think I ordered the soldiers to retreat? I wanted to get you myself!"

Kale strained her neck to keep the knifepoint from puncturing her skin. "Leon?" she asked, begging him to tell her that it was not true.

He struggled to look up at her, but his eyes held bitter regret.

The Shadow looked at his two captives, satisfied. "Tie them up," he said dismissively. The large men obliged, tying Kale's arms in front of her, but leaving Leon's arms behind his back. He fought them with every ounce of energy he had, but Leon was no match for the two henchmen. When the men finally got them securely bound, they shoved Kale and Leon forwards. They fell to the ground, hard, and sat in silence as the shadowy figure circled them. Kale still could not process all that had happened, but Leon funneled his anger towards the figure, and glared at him vengefully.

The Shadow hissed in satisfaction. "Stupid boy, to think the king would actually take you in and pardon you. As for you, Little Darling, well, we have some ideasss." The figure paused by Kale. "And we've decided that you both will bring in some good money at the market in Bartleona as slavessss."

He paused for effect, and Leon groaned.

Leon and Kale both knew what this meant. Bartleona was infamous for its brutal slave trade. Once a slave in Bartleona, one's life could never be redeemed.

Kale turned ashen and looked down at the gravel in dismay. Leon noticed her face.

"No! I will promise the king what he wants—let her go. She doesn't know anything!" he pleaded.

The shadowy figure chuckled. "Begging for mercy? We shall see."

Despite her anger towards Leon, Kale loathed the shadowy figure more. She knew the king wanted Leon's head on a platter. Then it dawned on her. *Leon just offered his life in my place!*

CHAPTER

The large men led Leon and Kale over to a horse cart that was concealed in the foliage and dumped them in the back. The men undid the ropes from their wrists and quickly snapped on cuffs that were hooked to the wall of the cart, securing Kale and Leon in place.

"Just in case you get any ideas when we start moving," one of them said, in a gruff voice.

The shadowy figure climbed atop the black horse that was hitched to the cart, and the stallion started to walk. The bulky men trotted alongside the cart, silent. Leon tried to pull his chains out of the cart plank by bracing his legs against the wall and pulling with all his might. Kale noticed this and tried to wiggle the peg holding the chains in the wood loose, but it wouldn't budge.

"It's no use," Leon said. "The pegs are driven deep into dry wood. They won't come out." Kale leaned back against the cart wall, exhausted from the stress. She was aware of Leon watching her, and guessed what he was thinking. She sighed. "I don't know what to believe anymore," she admitted.

Leon nodded. "Me, neither."

Kale looked up at him. "What do you mean? I find out you are being hunted. Then I find out you were working with the people hunting you, to hand me over!" her voice grew with passion.

Leon remained silent.

Kale broke down as a tear trickled down her face. "What about my mother? What about me? What happens now?" she asked, spilling over with raw emotion.

Leon looked at her sadly. "I was tired of running, and they offered my pardon and money if I did what they said, and submitted to living under the king. I convinced myself that this would be better than life on the run, but there was one condition; I had to bring you in. I didn't know you, and they promised not to hurt you, so I agreed. It wasn't until afterwards that I realized the king might want my life regardless."

Kale's body grew limp with confusion.

"But I was tricked. The Shadow was clearly working with the man I made the deal with, a man who guaranteed he worked for the king. I would never dream of being involved with The Shadow." He paused and then thought out loud, "Now I am wondering if the king is under The Shadow's rule."-

Kale's head was swimming with new information. "How did I get involved in this deal in the first place?" she asked, searching for answers.

Leon sighed. "I can't tell you, or they would kill you."

Kale gasped, "What?! Why?"

Leon just shook his head, not answering.

"Someone makes a deal to bring me in, my life is at stake, and I get silence from *you*?" she cried.

Leon remained resolved. He did not take her bait.

Kale breathed in heavily, realizing that she would get nowhere with Leon. Defeated, she slunk back against the wall.

The cart left the road, continuing on a dirt path, and it started to bounce and jostle along. Kale tried to stay upright, but the cart knocked her off her knees over and over again. Leon was bracing himself in a corner, gritting his teeth each time a bump slammed them down into the hard, cart bottom. The two burly men in cloaks were forced to walk single file behind the cart on this narrow trail.

Kale followed Leon's example and wedged herself into a corner, using her legs to brace herself in place. Her spine jarred each time the cart slammed down, and soon she grew sore and bruised. Tired, but still upset and perplexed, she searched for answers. "So why did you fight the guards and keep me away from them for so long? Why didn't you just hand me in to them right away?"

The answer didn't come at once. "I'm not sure. I guess I was having second thoughts about the deal and what I had signed up for." He shook his head—ashamed. "I was so stupid not to see it before."

The cart hit a bump that knocked them both flat. Kale, thoroughly tired and bruised, remained on her back, and did not even attempt to get up. Leon wiggled back into sitting position, just as the cart rolled to a stop. The Shadow got down off the horse, leaving the cart for a moment. He walked up to the door of an old cottage, and rapping on it, began a conversation with the hobbled old woman who greeted him. She had long gray hair, and her hands were gnarled with age, hands that were so old and grey that they almost resembled claws. She wore peculiar attire, a long tattered blue cloak and strange wooden shoes.

Kale and Leon's chains were attached to pegs driven all the way through the side of the cart. They could be unlocked from the outside and slid through the wood, so that the prisoner could be moved without undoing the cuffs. The large men unlocked the pegs and lifted Leon and Kale from the cart. Placing them on the ground, they shoved them forward.

CHAPTER 11

A large old cottage, badly in need of repairs, nestled in the forest. If it was not for the sharp cruelty of the old wood, this part of the forest might have been beautiful. The dark green summer leaves split the light into dappled patterns on the soft forest floor, and a lone songbird whistled somewhere close by. The large men led their captives towards the house, causing Kale to feel like a dog on a leash. Both she and Leon were too tired to fight back, so when they arrived inside, they fell to the ground in exhaustion onto a small hay pallet on the floor. Their captors hooked the chains to a ring in the wall and left.

Kale tried to sleep but found it uncomfortable with her hands chained in front of her. The chain clanked around every time she moved. She noticed Leon trying to get comfortable as well, but he had his hands chained behind him. Finally, they both sat up and accepted that sleep was impossible.

The night seemed endless in the musty cottage, as neither of them could sleep, and there were many eerie noises filtered through the rooms. Once, Kale even thought she heard a human scream. The walls were lined with all sorts of strange objects. Some jars contained animal parts. Others, Kale shuddered to even guess. One jar in particular caused her skin to crawl. It was filled with small milky white spheres of all sizes. Kale stared at the jar, debating its contents, until one of the spheres swiveled around and stared at her.

Kale's heart leaped into her mouth, and she choked back a shriek as the rest of the eyeballs in the jar turned to look at her. She turned her face away, and tried to clear her mind of the horrific image. *How can those eyes move on their own?* Kale gathered up her courage and glanced around the shadowy room again, avoiding the staring shelf. *What kind of person would collect such a souvenir?* An image of the old woman popped unbidden into her head. *A witch?* Kale wondered. *No, that is impossible.*

Finally, the first rays of sunlight cracked through the dusty layers on the window. When the men came back to get them again, neither had slept, and they felt just as tired as they were before. The breeze in the forest cooled their faces as they left the cottage. Back in the cart, they were tossed a piece of stale bread, which quickly disappeared between them. The Shadow emerged from the house and walked over to the side of the cart and hissed, "We made good timing yesssterday, we may even make it to Bartleona… tonight!"

Kale's heart sank as The Shadow grinned and stretched out a pale hand to caress Kale's cheek. She flinched at his cold touch and felt Leon fuming beside her. She was happy for his company but still simmering inside at his betrayal. The Shadow mounted the black horse once more, and they set off again. Kale was not used to the light of day and was surprised by how bright and cheerful it was, in spite of their circumstances. The going became easy, and the cart stopped its continual jostling.

Before long, they came across a road with many other travelers going in the same direction. They reached the main road for Bartleona. Kale welcomed the familiar street sounds. For a moment, she thought she was in the market back home. Dogs barked, people talked, and children laughed as they played tag through the cobblestone streets. Whenever travelers grew near to the cart, they quickly skirted away at the sight of the shadowy figure, the forbidding men, and Kale and Leon. Kale felt ashamed every time someone spotted them in chains and shook their heads with scorn or walked away muttering, "Rebels." Leon watched sadly as a mother herded her children away from the cart, covering their eyes protectively.

The sun grew bright in the heat of the day, and the smell of sweaty people became overpowering. Kale's tongue grew dry, as she had not had any water in a while, and her lips started to crack. The going slowed as the travelers weakened beneath the sun. Kale noticed heat waves rising off the dirt road when a castle loomed ahead. The sun was beating down on her face and skin, and Kale could feel herself burning. Despite their predicament, she was eager to get out of the heat and indoors in Bartleona. Once they passed through the gate, the cool of the shade was immediate. The thick stonewalls were forbidding, yet somehow they calmed Kale.

Inside the castle walls, the cart took a couple of turns through the city before they reached the shambles. The houses here were shabby, and the only place that looked inhabited for the moment was the pub, and this, too, was badly in need of repairs. Soon they rolled to a stop in front of a jagged, aged wood building. The Shadow stepped down from his horse and knocked on the door. There was some shuffling inside and a couple of gruff yells. A fat, greasy man with unkempt hair stepped out the door. At the sight of The Shadow, he grinned a toothless smile, gleefully asking, "What ya got fo' me brutha?"

The Shadow simply nodded towards the cart. The pudgy man took awkward flight around to the back, rubbing his hands together in anticipation. He spotted Leon and nodded thoughtfully, but when his gaze shifted to Kale, the hunger that lit up his eyes caused her to shift uncomfortably. The pudgy man grinned giddily again and then toward The Shadow. "How much ya want fo' 'em?"

The Shadow moved around to the front and started to pat his horse's head, which did nothing but spook the poor beast.

"I came to you on the King's business. I will charge you nothing, if you make sure they do not escape, and they go to," he paused, "well, 'disciplined' masterssss." He did not turn from the horse.

The pudgy man almost danced with glee, but The Shadow held up a pale finger, "If you do not, Sam, I will be back."

Sam didn't seem notice that The Shadow had spoken for a second, and Kale saw The Shadow's finger twitch. Sam flinched and groaned, his muscles convulsing. When The Shadow lowered his hand, Sam bent over and wheezed, "I-I understand."

Kale's heart sped in response to what she witnessed. This was no ordinary man they had been traveling with. The Shadow nodded and mounted his horse. Without word, the two burly men, who Kale had almost forgotten about, unhitched her and Leon from the cart. When their chains were in the hands of Sam, the cart rolled down the road and out of sight.

CHAPTER

As Kale turned her head back towards the house, she almost jumped, for Sam's prodding eyes were staring her right in the face. He hooked their chains over a post near the house and started to circle them like a hungry dog. Leon stared stubbornly ahead, and didn't even flinch when Sam decided to target him first. He looked inside his ears and pulled back his eyelids, nodding and grinning the whole time.

He felt along his jaw and ruffed his hair looking for lice. When Sam tried to stick a grubby finger in Leon's mouth to look at the state of his teeth, Leon jerked his head back. Kale was worried for a second that the man would get angry, but instead Sam grew more excited. He tweaked Leon's cheek and chuckled. "Feisty one, eh? Bring a better price tha' way." Then he shook his head. "I gotta look a' em teeth tho' boy," he said, almost apologetically.

Leon grimaced, put up with it, and then spit after, to rid himself of Sam's grisly taste.

Satisfied, Sam then walked over to Kale. She tried to hold her head high, but she couldn't help shrinking back a bit when he approached her. Sam whistled. "Won't have any trouble findin' ya a buyer, will we?" He paced around her a couple of times, ran his hand through her hair, and looked at her eyes and ears. When he started to shove a finger towards her mouth, she quickly opened wide.

He looked, and nodded. Then, grabbing their chains, he led them into a shack adjoining the cottage. Kale almost gagged at the fumes that reached her nose once inside. Vomit and human waste were among the strongest smells, and Kale was very careful where she sat once they were chained

55

side by side to a wall. As her eyes adjusted to the gloomy atmosphere, she spotted other huddled shapes in the room. They were not alone.

The figure closest to Kale moved, lifting a dirty head from the ground. Kale's hair stood on end at the sight of the large cat-like eyes that shined back at her from behind a head full of grey matted hair. The woman's pale skin stretched tightly over her old bones, and Kale felt a pang of sympathy for the mess of a human being. A tear brimmed in the woman's eye, and she whispered, "So young…" When she reached out her gnarled hand, Kale readily grabbed it and tried to warm it in her own. Her heart throbbed, somehow thinking of her mother. How easy it would be for her to end up spending the rest of her days like this, thinking her daughter was dead, and crying her days out chained to a wall.

Kale leaned down next the woman and spoke softly, "How long have you been here?"

The woman sat up, and Kale was shocked to see how small and shriveled she was. Kale could hold her in her arms like a kitten.

The woman sighed. "A long time, dearie. Long before you would remember. We here," she gestured to the rest of the room, "are the ones that won't *sell.*"

Kale lowered her head. "Do you have a, um…" Kale started, finding it slightly awkward to ask the woman's name.

The woman smiled. "Call me Margaret. Marge for short," she said quietly.

"Marge. I'm Kale," she replied, gesturing to herself.

"What a pretty name," Margaret said.

Kale sighed, remembering sadly, "It is my mother's middle name…"

Margaret smiled understandingly. "You miss home?" she asked, putting a small hand on Kale's arm gently.

Kale nodded, but then shook her head, trying to compose herself. Still, tears welled up in her eyes.

"You can tell old Marge, dear. I won't tell a soul. My days are numbered anyways."

Kale hesitated, but then gave in, and Marge shuffled closer. Wiping a tear away with one finger, Kale started, "I am wanted and going to be sold as a slave all because of him!" she whispered angrily, pointing at Leon who appeared to have gone to sleep. "He did something awful to anger the king or something, and then came to me to get help. Then they wanted me too, so we ran and were caught, and now I can never go home! And my mother is probably dead! My mother..." she gasped back a sob. "I don't even know why this all is happening! Why would they want him, no, why would they want *me* so badly? It's not like I did anything wrong!" Her voice almost grew to a scream. "And he, he betrayed me! He brought me into this, and then practically handed me over! I was so stupid, not seeing the evil in him! He—" Marge cut in and laid a hand on her shoulder.

Her tears blurred her vision, and Kale allowed herself to fall to the ground, with her head in Marge's lap. She cried until she had no more tears left. The salt made her mouth dry, and Kale thought miserably of all the wrong and its effects. They sat in silence for a few moments, Kale thankful for this woman's willingness to listen to her. Margaret wiped away Kale's tears and gently combed her fingers through Kale's long, wavy hair. She hummed a lullaby, a strange song with a haunting tune. Kale was somehow soothed and moved into a deep and needed sleep. The tune was the last Kale remembered before she was met by the blazing sunlight of a new day. It was sale day.

CHAPTER

Rough hands grabbed her from her cramped position on the ground and lifted her to her feet. She was led outside in the blazing sunlight, blinded for a few moments. As her eyes re-adjusted to the outdoor light, she made out ten others that were brought out of the house. Spotting Leon just a few feet away calmed her; Kale didn't want to go alone. Despite what he may have done to her, Kale knew he would protect her now.

Sam came out of the house, whistling, as happy as a bee in a hive. A deep repulsion came over Kale. *How can he be so happy when he is throwing away lives, like old Marge back in that house?* Slung over Sam's arm was a type of chain. Kale wondered what it could be for, until she noticed that each length of chain had two cuffs attached side-by-side to it, and farther along the chain, a larger cuff, or collar. These were slave chains, used for transporting slaves, prisoners, or rebels. Today it would be used to hold the slaves. For sale.

Sam strolled up to the first slave, a young man who looked to be barely thirty, and hooked the cuff around his neck. Then, undoing the former chains the slave wore, Sam quickly replaced them with the cuffs attached to the collar. Moving around the group, Sam hooked every one up in this fashion.

When he reached Kale and snapped the collar around her neck, she almost yelped at the feeling of the cold metal on her skin. But it was more than that. The collar completed her hopelessness; it weighed her down and chilled her to the bone.

After Sam finished, she, Leon, and the others were promptly hooked in single file. Sam stood at the front and surveyed the sorry lot. He shook his head in dismay.

"No, this will never do," he said to himself. Hooking their chains to the post in his yard, Sam scurried back inside his house. He returned with a large bucket of water. Moving along the line, he poured it over their heads. The freezing water splashed over Kale's hair and down her neck. She gasped as it soaked her completely. It ran into her eyes and mouth, but since she was chained, she was unable to wipe it away. Sam scanned the line once more before nodding and then dragged them out towards the center of town.

Kale never felt so ashamed in her life. Adults and kids alike laughed at them as they passed. A couple of street boys even threw rocks, until Sam yelled and they scurried off into the shadows.

As it turned out, new slaves were actually pretty popular. A large crowd gathered around the auction ring. Kale saw more—and longer—chain lines of slaves being brought in from all over the country. She heard people chuckle as they passed by, and she realized that Sam must have been some-thing of a joke to the rest of the slave traders.

Sam signed up for his turn to use the auction ring and was lucky enough in the draw to go fifth. The heat of the day could've been brutal and waiting until the end was torture, for everyone. Besides, the first sales brought in the most money. No one wanted to be the last to be sold.

While they were waiting for him to sign up, the sun helped dry their drenched clothes. Kale closed her eyes and allowed herself to imagine for a moment that she was actually at home, in the airy fields near their barn. Sam's rough hand on her shoulder brought her back to reality. He pulled them over to a spot near the ring in the shade of a house and allowed them to sit.

"I got good slaves dis round. I might be able to git ma girl a doll. Ya, tha'd be nice," he mumbled to himself.

Tired, she watched as the first slave trader—a thin man with a long nose—stepped up into the slave ring with his lot. Kale immediately disliked this man, but it soon grew to hate when he slapped a small girl for being too frightened to step up into the ring. Kale watched in disbelief at the little money offered for these lives, as if more could make the sale seem more humane. All of his slaves slowly sold, and the next slave trader stepped up to the stand.

The day grew long before it was finally their turn. Kale's hands grew clammy, and her heart sped up. Two slaves were sold before Sam pushed Kale into the ring. When she stepped up onto the box and saw all the faces staring at her, her head started to swim.

She panicked, for once she was sold, there would be no going back. Looking franticly around for Leon, she spotted him behind her. His eyes met hers and he motioned forward, encouragingly. Kale nodded back and tried to be brave.

The second she found her place, Sam started the auction. "And now folks, this is a strong, willing girl, would be great for watching children—"

"Who would let that rat near children?" a lady from the crowd cried out.

Kale was hurt, but Sam was undeterred. "She is good for other jobs too. She could help in the kitchen, clean up the house, or wash your clothes. She would be a great help serving in an inn." Here Sam winked at the crowd, and a couple of them laughed and nudged each other. Sam continued, more confident now, "So who will start the bidding?" he asked.

A nasty looking man with sharp features called out in a gruff voice. "Ten!" he shouted, pounding his fist against the rail that surrounded the sale ring.

Kale looked the man up and down and decided she would like anything more than to be sold to him. She hoped it was unlikely that she would go to him, since his first bid was less than she could pay for a pig back home.

Sam smiled. "There's a ten, anyone for eleven? Eleven?"

A hand shot in the air.

"Eleven! Going for twelve!"

More hands.

"Thirteen, thirteen! Fifteen?"

The crowd went wild. Kale let herself smile at the attention she was getting. She glanced over at Leon and caught his sly grin.

Finally she was handed over to a stone-faced woman, and Kale realized that it was the same one who had first called out during the auctions. The woman yanked on her chains, causing her to jerk forward, and dragged her to a spot in the crowd.

"I want to see what the rest of the slaves sell for, then we can get you home to work," she muttered hoarsely to Kale.

Kale was not sure what to think of her new master, but she tried to hope for the best. At least she would get to see what would happen to Leon.

When it came to Leon's turn, he stood tall on the podium, not shrinking back under the accusing stares of the crowd. When the bidding started, he had no shortage of buyers either. Many people wanted him for the hard and dirty work.

He finally sold to a large, grimy looking man who immediately hit and almost winded Leon.

"If you do not listen to me, boy, you will get more of this!" the man shouted, completely unfazed by the onlookers.

Leon was unmoved, and this seemed to anger the man even more. He huffed and yanked on the chain, slamming Leon to his knees, but Leon reached his way back up and stood, boldly facing him. This threw the man into a rage, and he began to pummel Leon while dragging him along.

CHAPTER

K ale flinched and immediately felt relieved that she was sold to a
woman. She scolded herself when her heart told her that Leon
got what he deserved. Beside her, Kale could hear her new master
whispering disapprovingly to another buyer about this treatment of a slave.
She hoped that this meant the woman would be reasonable.

The hours went by as more and more slaves were sold. When the day
was finally over, Kale and her new master left the ring and headed down a
cobblestone street into the thick of the city. Her master pulled her along for
a while and then turned to her.

"I guess since you'll be living with me, you might as well know some
things before we reach the house. My name is Mary, and you will be helping
in the kitchen, as one of my kitchen maids died last week. You may also
help with my niece on occasions, and her name is Anastasia. What is your
name girl?" she asked simply.

"I'm Kale," she said quietly.

Mary nodded. "Fine name. How did you come to be a slave, girl? Born
as one? Criminal parents? Prisoner of war?" she asked.

Kale paused, as none of these actually described her correctly. Kale
chose the option that made her sound the most innocent, and then made
up a quick story. "My family and I were taken during a raid when I was
young," she whispered, trying to pull on some tears.

Mary sighed at this. "So many come here that way. Well, I hope I can
count on you. Promise you won't run off?"

Kale nodded enthusiastically. She wasn't lying either. A runaway slave
could end up charged and killed gruesomely.

"All right then, here you go." Mary pulled out the keys for the collar and cuffs and unlocked her. Kale gratefully rubbed her sore neck and wrists. At the sight of the bruises covering Kale's arms, Mary gasped. "Oh terrible! I shall have a word with Sam. Come inside!"

Kale felt relief overtake her, and when they reach the house, she thanked God that she didn't go to that other man.

The old house was somewhat charming with its wooden floors, old furniture, and little windows of genuine glass. Kale stared at the rippled glass and marveled at its beauty. Only in stories had she heard about these windows. There were tapestries on the walls, another rarity, and Kale gaped at the beautiful scenes depicted in vibrant colors. They were even more beautiful than the ones she used to marvel at in the church back home.

When she reached the kitchen, she tried to be friendly with the other staff, but they ignored her. All of them looked spent, and the only time one spoke was as she handed Kale an apron and told her to sweep the kitchen floor. By the end of the day, the kitchen, and most of the lower floor, had improved because of Kale's hard work. She went to bed sore and exhausted. Her hands were covered in blisters and splinters from the old, wooden broom. That night she was shown to a pallet on the floor, not unlike what she used to sleep on at home, and she soon drifted off.

Six hours later, Kale woke up to a small girl staring at her in the face intently. She sat up quickly, and managed, "Who are you?"

The girl stuck her nose in the air.

"My name is Anastasia," she said, punctuating each syllable. Kale took a mental note to avoid this girl.

"And you're the new slave?" Anastasia asked prudishly.

Kale was starting to dislike the child already. She looked like a perfect china doll: the blonde curls, dress and everything, *everything but her attitude.*

"Yes, and you should probably go and find your aunt," Kale pointed out. "She will not want you down here talking to us."

This statement was clearly true because Anastasia looked taken aback, but her face quickly hardened. She stuck out her tongue at Kale and then started to wail. She screamed and cried, pounding her fists into the floor so that real tears would come. Kale knew the girl was acting, but she did not want trouble with her new master, so she tried to get her to be quiet. She grabbed the girl and tried to cover her mouth just as she heard someone rushing down the stairs. When Mary walked in and found Anastasia crying, she practically had a fit. Running over and scooping the crying child into her arms, she coddled her. "Oh baby dear, what happened, Ann? Tell your auntie."

Ann smirked at Kale from over her aunt's shoulder, and then mustered the most pathetic voice Kale had ever heard. Kale had to bite her lip to keep from laughing at her.

"Oh, I came down for a drink. I was so thirsty, and that new maid said I wasn't allowed, and she tried to chase me away with a broom! She hit me with it, Auntie!" Anastasia wailed.

Mary immediately turned on Kale. "You must be very careful around my darling child. She *always* has my permission, which you didn't know, so I will let it go this time, but anything more like that from you, and you can speak with the police!"

Ann's eyes lit up at this, and Kale's heart fell. *Great, just great.*

"Yes, I understand," Kale sighed.

CHAPTER

T he rest of the day carried on without incident. Kale figured out her place, which was to clean the house and speak only when spoken to. The staff eventually warmed up to her, but conversation was brief. Kale got more accustomed to working in the kitchen and the life of a slave. Seasons passed unnoticed, with every day becoming exactly like the one before.

Her favorite time of the day was when she was allowed to go to the market on an errand. Sometimes she wondered about what had become of her mother... and of Leon. Whenever she thought of them, she immediately tried to shove the thought away, for it was always painful to think of home. A deep throbbing rose in her chest, and she found herself choking back a sob at the memories that flooded into her mind.

Home to Kale was another world, another time and place. It seemed like so long ago when she started following that unusual boy... Now she knew they had both changed, somehow grown up. Neither of them remained who they used to be. After all, she had been a slave in Bartleona for the whole of fall and winter now.

The Leon of her memories was not mysterious and intriguing, let alone romantic; he was a frightened and confused child. She had also been frightened and confused, but now she had overcome that. She knew she couldn't be tied to the past. So when she started noticing a handsome aristocrat who lived next door, Kale decided it was time to move on.

It was a chilly spring morning, and Kale took out the scraps from the kitchen. She wrapped her thin wool scarf tight around her shoulders and briskly walked to the back of the yard. The closely packed houses left almost no room between them, and the space behind was used as a gutter. People dumped their slop and waste into the back streets, and the mess seeped into the drainage systems within the city. Kale slowly poured the bucket into the gutter, so as to not slosh herself with the foul mess. The hair on the back of her neck raised, as she got the feeling that someone was watching her. Pictures flashed through her mind of The Shadow, and she spun around.

Leaning against the side of the house next door was a tall, friendly looking man, but Kale's nerves were on end, and she was tempted to bolt for the house. The man saw her fear.

"No, please don't go," he said kindly.

Kale stared at the man, looking him up and down. She was not sure if she should trust his dark eyes and friendly smile. Suddenly, she felt embarrassed; she knew how dirty she must look with her disheveled hair, rags, and bucket of slop. Kale smiled briefly, and, blushing, she darted into the house.

The next day, she left to run an errand in the market. Mary had dinner party plans and had sent her to purchase the food. She was at the meat stall when the same tall young man with dark hair and eyes walked up beside her and ordered some meat from the vendor. Kale felt her skin grow hot, and she shifted uncomfortably beside him. Kale quickly paid for her meat and was about to hurry away, when he gently put his hand on her arm.

"I'm sorry, but I couldn't help noticing that you worked for my neighbor. My name is Matthew. What is yours?" he asked gently.

Kale was caught in his warm smile. "My name is Kale," she whispered.

"I am sure I will see you around then, Kale," he said with a smile.

Kale's heart sped out of control. "Yeah, I guess," she mumbled, quickly moving to another food vendor.

Kale rushed home that night, unable to remove the color or grin from her face. Lying awake on her mat, she wondered what to make of these new feelings. Part of her was tempted to just let go and allow herself to feel whatever she wanted. The other part of her would not let go of the memory of Leon, and she felt somewhat nervous about trusting a boy – no matter how gentle, kind . . . or attractive he might be.

Matthew is not a boy, she reminded herself. *He's more mature.*

Her stomach fluttered out of control. Somehow the old latched ceiling above her seemed new and interesting. Her world suddenly transformed, as if she had just begun to actually "see". All at once, life became something colorful and exciting.

CHAPTER 16

Every day from then on, Kale tried to share a glance with Matthew, even a smile. She went out regularly to dump the slop, when usually she would try to avoid doing it, just to see if she could find him there again. Seeing him made each day brighter.

Matthew would sometimes take the garbage out when she was washing the clothes, so they could share a glance. Kale grew more and more interested in this new mysterious man. Thinking back to how she met Leon, she laughed at their similar interactions. Both had been illusive, which made them more attractive to Kale.

But one day, a man came to the door with a letter, a letter that had the name Kale printed neatly on it. Letters were almost unheard of, as few could write, and when they came, they were usually from the priest or the Lord of that city, and only for pressing matters. Kale's mother valued education and taught her daughter herself, so Kale was one of the few privileged enough to read and write. She recognized her name immediately. Before Kale could take the letter, Anastasia ran to the door and snatched it away. Her eyes grew wide, and she ran shouting down the hall, waving the letter in the air, to her aunt's room.

Kale was called up promptly, and Mary read the letter aloud to her. "Dear Kale, I will be in town today, and would like it if you could join me for the afternoon. Matthew."

Mary smiled surprisingly at Kale. "Sounds like you have attracted some interest!"

Kale tried not to grin, but she couldn't help it. *He likes me!* "May I go? I have been so faithful, and I will work twice as hard when I get back!" Kale started hopefully.

She was cut short as Anastasia piped up, "No, you can't. You must do the work now!"

Mary immediately snapped at Ann. "She can go!" Mary said. "I decide who goes where in this house!"

Kale could not believe her ears. *Was this the same woman who had condemned me at the sale or sided with that wicked child when I arrived?* Kale didn't miss shooting Ann a smug look.

Ann's jaw dropped, and she ran from the room crying while Kale struggled to find just the right words.

"Thank you," Kale managed. "I will do what I can to repay you."

Mary paused. "No need," she began. "Injustice lets people like us rule over people like you. It brings joy to see your face light up like this." But then she stopped herself. "Shoo, go on! You don't want to keep the poor man waiting," she said sternly.

Kale took off her apron, undid her long braid unlocking her golden chestnut curls, and then ran out the door and down the street. The market was busy; people were jam packed in the narrow streets. Kale realized it would be hard to find him in these crowds. She looked for him all over the town and was just about to give up when she finally had an idea.

Sure enough, Kale spotted him by the meat stall. He smiled when he saw her, and Kale walked over. "Meat, again?" she said with a grin.

Matthew laughed. "Thought it would be easier for you to find me here."

Kale nodded. "It was. What are we going to do today?"

"Well I thought it might be nice to get something to eat at the inn on the corner, and then maybe go for a walk outside town."

Kale's face lit up. "Perfect."

Together they walked to the inn, hand in hand. Kale sat down at a table while Matthew ordered. Once the meal was set down, and they had eaten a little, Kale grew more at ease.

In the dim light of the inn, they talked. Kale steered the conversation away from her past and tried to ask questions. With every passing minute, Kale grew to like Matthew more. His brown eyes seemed to soak in everything, and his smile warmed the room. His presence sent shivers of excitement down her spine.

When they had finished the meal, and it was late into the night, Kale heard a light rain start to fall on the roof. Matthew sighed. "I guess there's no walk for us tonight." Kale looked down, disappointed.

Matthew lifted her chin to look at him. "I cannot see you for the next while, but what about in two weeks from today? Then we can go on a walk for sure."

Kale smiled. "That would be nice."

They left the inn together. Matthew took her up to Mary's house, using his coat to shield her from the rain. The rain grew heavy now, rocking the trees and sending rivers through the streets. Thunder rolled, and lighting brightened up the dark grey-blue sky. Other town's people were running, drenched, in an unorganized fashion, trying to find shelter.

When they finally reached her doorstep, Matthew left her under the overhang. She waved at him, as he walked down the street before she went inside. As Kale gently closed the door, her shoes sloshing water onto the floor, she was surprised to meet a very angry little Ann.

Kale tried to scoot around her, but Ann stepped in her way.

"You are going to pay for what you did, Kale. You just wait and see!" Ann said, pointing a defiant finger in the air.

Kale was unnerved by the little girl, as she watched her stomp off down the hall, but she knew that Ann could easily get her trouble.

The rest of the house was asleep, and Kale wondered what Mary would think if she knew her precious little Ann was up this late. She tried to forget about Ann as she headed back to the kitchen. Quietly Kale lay down on her pallet, her heart throbbing.

This is going to be a long two weeks.

CHAPTER 11

For the next couple of days, Kale worked hard to occupy her mind. Despite many responsibilities, repetitiveness allowed her mind to wander. Once, as she passed a window, she spotted Matthew talking to another man. She stood there, watching him.

"What are you looking at?" asked one of the other kitchen helpers.

Embarrassed, Kale quickly looked down.

"Oh, nothing," she replied and got back to work, determined that she would ignore Matthew and just be satisfied with the fact that she would see him in another week. Throughout that time, Kale's life consisted of avoiding Ann, working hard, and trying to keep herself from daydreaming. She put extra effort into her work, often serving hours longer than the others, so that Mary would relieve her one more time.

The long-awaited night finally came, and Kale headed out to the market to meet Matthew. The shoppers were dwindling, slowly leaving for home as the last rays of sun sent rosy light over the cobblestoned streets. She found him at the inn this time. He greeted her with a smile and an outstretched hand.

Kale readily placed her hand in his. "I have been looking forward to that walk you promised."

Matthew nodded, smiling, and they walked out of town and through the walls. He nodded at the guards who smiled back and shouted, "Remember to be back before curfew!" Kale and Matthew nodded, heading down the path towards the woods.

There was a cool summer breeze rustling through the dense foliage. Moonlight streamed through the trees, creating a latticework of light on the forest floor. They walked silently together for a while. A twig snapped, and Kale suddenly had a flashback to when she and a very different boy were in a similar place. She pushed the thought away and started up a conversation. They talked about Matthew's work as a businessman, Kale's work in the house, and all the recent going-ons in Bartleona. Stopping beside a small river running through the woods, the conversation paused for a moment.

Kale watched thoughtfully as a trickle of water followed the path of the stream, leaping over stones and moss to whatever lay below. She briefly wished she could be like a drop of water, carefree and brave, leaping over anything that got in the way. When she turned back towards Matthew, he was looking at her intently. She was captivated by the warm look in his eyes, and for a moment, he leaned in and they kissed.

Kale was surprised; it was the first time she had kissed a man. She felt nervous at first, but then, at that very moment, Kale realized she loved Matthew. Kale melted into his arms. He held her gently, and she welcomed his warmth, the sense of security that she had not felt since she was last in her mother's arms as a child. When he finally pulled away, the moon was well overhead.

"We should go back now," Matthew whispered.

Kale nodded hesitantly. -

Together they walked back into town and up their street. Kale walked as slowly as she could, wishing the night would never end. When they finally reached the house, she reluctantly left him and went inside. At first, it was difficult for her to fall asleep, but when she did, she dreamt of a wedding… and she was the bride.

CHAPTER 18

The next morning as Kale swept, she passed by the kitchen door and heard some maids whispering. Kale paused by the doorframe and listened. She could tell by the voices, that one of them was Darleen, a tall fair maid with dark hair. The other was a fairly new girl named Angela, who was short and skinny, just a wisp of a human being.

"Do you think he actually likes her?" Angela asked quietly.

There was a pause before Darleen answered, "Yes, I believe so. The way they look at each other…"

Kale's face hardened. They were talking about her!

"Well, does she know?" Angela asked.

"Know?" Darlene paused. "Know about . . .*him?*"

"Yes, you know, his reputation with women. Actually, I heard that the longest he can keep one is a week!" Kale's heart started to pump as she heard the maids giggle.

Would he turn out to be another disappointment? Another broken trust?

Suddenly, the talking stopped inside the kitchen, and she froze.

Did they know I was listening?

Kale crept away and swept by the door. When the maids poked their heads out, they sighed, thinking Kale had just been working, and they continued with their gossip. Kale tried to convince herself that what she heard was just harmless chatter, used to pass the time, but somewhere in her mind, a seed of doubt began to grow.

CHAPTER

A strong wind blew through the city early that morning. Red and gold leaves occasionally flew over the walls from the forest. Kale pulled her shawl tight around her shoulders and clutched the wicker basket near her chest. Mary had realized how skilled Kale was at maneuvering the markets, so she assigned Kale to all of the errands there.

Making new friends and viewing the wares occupied Kale's time at the market, but the more she grew to like the city; the more she missed the one she loved back home. Today, the last leaves of fall broke loose in the wind. The grey sky promised snow, and folks were starting to spend more time indoors. Kale paid for some cheese and milk, and then she bought some bread. Staring down at the perfect loaf, Kale started to tear up; this day was exactly like the day she left. It had been a whole year since she had left home.

Feeling sentimental, Kale walked down the old cobblestone streets and stared blankly through the shop windows. In comparison, today the pretty things looked bleak and uninteresting; their perfect colors seeming fake, almost worthless.

Sighing, she left the upper class area and found herself wandering through the streets until she reached the shambles. Almost immediately, she recognized old Sam's hut, and walking up to it, Kale hesitantly knocked. Sam came to the door, as hyper and jolly as ever. When he spotted Kale, recognition swept over his pudgy features.

"What are ya doin' here? Didn't I sell you a while back?" he asked.

Kale nodded. "Yes, and I am still owned by the one I was sold to," she assured him.

Sam scratched his head. "Then what are you here for?"

Kale looked hopefully at him. "There was an old woman here a while ago. Margaret? I was hoping to see her," she said, suddenly realizing that there was nothing better she would like to do.

Sam looked at her thoughtfully. "It might do her some good. The old hag is sick and will probably be leaving soon… You may, if you like. Just for a short time."

"Thank you." Kale smiled.

Running inside, Kale found Margaret lying on her bed. Kale knelt by her side and laid a hand on her shoulder. "Marge, wake up." The small body shifted a little, and two cat-like eyes peered out from under a grey mat of hair. Kale smiled and collapsed beside the old woman. She pulled Margaret into a warm embrace. "I missed you. You have been the only one I could confide in."

Margaret squeezed Kale's hand. "I missed you too, young one." She broke out in a rasping cough, and had to let go.

"Darling, I am finally leaving this place," she admitted weakly, looking away from Kale for a moment.

Worried, Kale looked at Margaret. "You will live, Marge," she insisted.

The old lady shook her head sadly. "My time has come. I am going home to join my Savior," she said, somewhat hopefully.

Kale tried to hide her grief. She shook her head, trying everything to stop the inevitable. "Don't leave me here alone!" She grew desperate. "You are my only true friend."

Marge smiled up at Kale, caressing her cheek. "And you were mine," she said gently. "But now I must go."

Kale was stunned at what was happening, and she grew angry. "Then you can't leave! You have to stay! I will make you stay!" she insisted.

Marge shook her head. "I wish you could, darling, but no one can do that, you know it." She sighed. "Let me go."

Kale looked down at the shriveled woman who seemed to embrace the situation, and tears brimmed in the corners of her eyes. "I can't." She wrung her hands in desperation. "I have been fighting everything for the last year, I am not about to let you slip away from me."

Marge stroked her hair. "You have to, Kale. Just let go." Her cat-like eyes looked up at her. "Let me go."

And then Kale sobbed, her lungs heaving. She squeezed her eyes shut, sending tears down her cheeks.

"Sing to me Margaret, please," Kale pleaded.

Margaret held her hand and nodded slowly. Her voice was quiet and raspy, broken only by Kale's sobs at every pause, but everyone in the slave house seemed to listen to the words.

> *"Listen to the wind, the wind song of your heart.*
> *It blows through the hills and grasses.*
> *It will brush away regret and tears,*
> *And return to its home in the mountains.*
> *So listen to the wind song,*
> *That beautiful melody.*
> *It will blow ore the valley to bring you to me.*
> *As long as the wind blows, I hope you will know,*
> *That we will together go home—"*

A long deep sigh escaped Margaret's lips, and she went limp in Kale's arms. Tears pouring down her cheeks, Kale laid Margaret gently down on the hay so that she looked as if she were sleeping.

Bending down beside her, Kale whispered, "Thank you, for everything."

Kale spent a couple minutes with her eyes shut, letting herself drain the tears. Getting up slowly, she made her way back out of the hut and nodded to Sam. He watched her sadly as she passed before closing the door again.

The long walk back up into town seemed to take hours. Kale's heart was heavy, and she felt a deep emptiness. Just like a hole in her dress, that let the cold wind through. This was a hole that could be patched up, but never perfectly.

A shabby grey cat slunk by in the ally, its grey hair ruffed and tousled by the wind. Kale stared at it, tears streaming down her face. A voice entered her head,

"And you were mine." Margaret's loving face flashed through her mind.

"We will together go home."

CHAPTER 20

C hristmas came too fast, and everyone worked hard to prepare. Kale trudged through the snow to the market. The feast was supposed to be grand. The maids scoured the house from top to bottom, and everyone started to cheer up. There was something about Christmastime that just seemed to light up the air and fill everyone's heart with joy. Kale rarely saw Matthew as her work multiplied. There was going to be a grand ball at Mary's place. Kale could hear everyone talking about it.

The evening of the party, a soft snow fell, and street lanterns hung with wreaths lit up the blanketed streets. Kale watched longingly as the household members did up their hair and donned their beautiful dresses. Even Ann was dressed up for the occasion. Then Kale heard giggling behind her. She spun around and was surprised to find all of the staff dressed in beautiful dresses too, their hair done up in lavish knots.

"Well, aren't you going to get ready, Kale? The staff is invited to the Christmas party. I believe Matthew saw to that!" Darlene giggled.

A grin lit up Kale's face; Matthew wanted her to be at the party! Kale sprinted to the kitchen to find a beautiful, dark blue satin dress lain neatly there. She admired the handiwork of the seamstress, as she quickly slipped it on. Undoing her bun, she let her long chestnut hair fall to her shoulders. She admired her reflection in the hall's looking glass. Staring back at her was a tall, confident young woman. Kale was surprised by how much she had changed since she left home.

A bell rang, announcing the first guests, who were then escorted to the ballroom. Kale followed behind them timidly. She waited in the large, decorated room, absent-mindedly listening to the guests pleasantly making conversation. When the music started, and people began to dance, the room was too crowded for Kale to find Matthew. A dashing young man with sandy blonde hair asked her for a dance, and Kale agreed, gingerly placing her gloved hand in his. She smiled at the attention she was getting from all the young bachelors, and when she got a snooty look from a jealous young lady, Kale almost laughed with glee.

Kale welcomed the chance to forget her position and have fun. When the music hit a high point, she was surprised to find herself flung into Matthew's arms. By the whispers across the room, Kale guessed that everyone knew how Matthew wanted the slaves to be a part of the dance, just so he could be with her. Then the music slowed, and they moved together, in perfect steps across the room.

When all the guests had left, Matthew kissed Kale goodbye before he departed as well. Kale called a hurried goodbye after him, but his carriage already pulled away into the snow.

CHAPTER

Winter blended into spring, and soon all the snow melted. Kale still had regular visits with Matthew, but they never interfered with her work.

One day, when Kale was sweeping the upper floor, she passed Ann's room and heard crying. Cautiously she pushed open the door and found Ann sprawled on her bed, sobbing.

"Go away!" Ann shouted.

Seeing the girl's pain, Kale softened somewhat and walked over. "What is wrong?" she asked gently.

Ann sat up, her eyes red. "You wouldn't understand. It's not like you have had any friends!" she said, wounded.

Kale ignored her. "I might be able to understand how you feel if you will explain to me what happened."

Ann went hysterical. "You could never know how I feel! You are just a mangy dirty slave! A dog! You don't have any feelings at all! How would you ever understand? You are worthless!"

At this, Kale broke down, remembering all the pain. Remembering her mother. Remembering Margaret.

"How dare you!" Kale sobbed. "I am *not* worthless. I do have feelings! Feelings that you would never understand! My only friend just left me, and now I am alone in this world. What would you do if you were taken from your home?" Kale stopped, many of her forgotten memories flooding her mind.

Ann went quiet, and both girls stared at each other through their tears, neither listening to the other. Suddenly Ann jumped up and ran down the stairs. Kale's heart stopped, as she wondered if she had pushed the girl too far.

Just then, she heard Mary calling for her. Kale walked down cautiously, trying to plan out a good story in her head. When she reached the study, Ann was in the arms of her aunt, still crying. "Is this true Kale? You threatened to take Ann from this home?"

Kale's jaw almost dropped, but she controlled herself. "She misunderstood me, Mary! I would never want Ann to be in danger!" she insisted. *Two can play this game Anastasia,* Kale thought to herself.

Mary nodded, and Kale relaxed.

"You hear that Ann, my child. Kale would never want to hurt you," Mary whispered to Ann.

With a nod from Mary, Kale gratefully left to start her chores. After a short time, Kale was surprised to see Ann standing boldly in front of her.

"Kale, I just want you to know that I am leaving. When you are in jail or dead, I will come back." With that, she gave a little laugh and trotted off, her pigtails bobbing.

Kale dismissed this as Ann's way of trying to scare her. Still, she was a little unnerved by the girl's words.

Later that day, as Kale talked with Matthew outside the house for a moment, they were met by a frantic Mary, tears streaming down her face.

"Ann! My child! She's gone!" she cried hysterically.

Kale remembered what Ann had said and bit her cheek in frustrating. She said a hurried goodbye to Matthew and briskly followed Mary into the house. Kale frantically searched everywhere a small child could fit. For an hour, she, Mary, and the staff combed the house from top to bottom. Not a cupboard was overlooked; the whole house was turned upside-down.

Finally, Kale accepted the inevitable. Ann was missing. As she walked near the living room entrance, Kale felt her body stiffen. There stood two uniformed soldiers talking with Mary. Mary spotted Kale's statue-like form, and in her hysteria called out to her. Kale sucked in her breath and stepped into the room.

"Did you find her, Kale?" Mary cried.

Kale shook her head, avoiding eye contact with the soldiers. Mary fell to the floor and began to weep. "I should never have let her out of my sight.

Especially after this morning, when she was so upset that—"

Kale knew what has just entered Mary's head, and her heart stopped. Mary rose from the floor. Her eyebrows furled as an accusing finger pointed at Kale. Mary's hair was now in a wild tangle from her crying, her appearance making her look insane.

"It was you! You threatened that you would take her from me this morning, and now you have! Where have you hidden her?"

"But, Mary!" Kale frantically worked to return some of Mary's sense. "You know I would never hurt anyone! Ann misunderstood me!"

Mary wouldn't hear it. "Soldiers! Arrest her this minute! *She* has done this!" she screamed, as her maids tried to calm her.

Kale shook her head in disbelief, her mind spun out of control. She stumbled back a bit. It all happened so fast. The soldiers grabbed her arms. She panicked and tried to break free.

She looked to the staff she had grown to be friends with, pleading for help, but they shook their heads. Kale knew they didn't want to risk their safety either.

Kale's emotions began to unravel as she cried out to Mary, "I have worked so hard for you! This has been a home to me. Ann just never liked me. Please don't send me away, Mary. Please don't send me from Matthew. I beg you!"

Mary wouldn't hear it. "Get that evil girl far away from me!" she shouted to the soldiers.

Tears streamed from Kale's eyes. As she left the house, she somehow knew, deep down, that she left Matthew behind forever.

And Matthew was there, watching. He watched as she was dragged down the street. His expression was not of concern, but of pity.

"Matthew!" Kale screamed. "I didn't do it!"

Matthew noticed the spectators gathering and immediately pulled his hat down over his eyes and slunk into the crowd. Although it was a short walk to the jail, Kale struggled the entire way, crying and screaming, pleading for someone to listen.

CHAPTER

he soldiers walked her into a cell and dumped her onto the floor, where she immediately curled up and continued sobbing. She looked up at the dirty ceiling of her cell through her tears and screamed, "Why?" to the world.

Why did I have to leave my home in the first place?

Why did Marge have to die?

Why did I ever have to meet Leon?

She shouted out all the injustices that she had to bear, and when she could think of nothing else, she pressed her tear-stained cheek against the cold stonewalls. Kale was suddenly reminded of the stone in her gate back home, but those stones seemed somehow much more friendly than the ones surrounding her here. She sighed, tears flowed again, and lying down on the floor, she rocked herself to sleep.

It was only a couple of hours before the sun cracked through the clouds, and a bird trilled outside. Its brilliant voice carried even through the thick stone walls of the jailhouse. When she woke, she found that someone had left a bowl of water and some bread under her iron door. Gratefully, Kale quickly scooped down the meal. She didn't know what would happen next. Would they give her a trial? Would she be allowed to live? Kale swirled a finger in the dust on the stone floors as she waited.

A dirty servant boy dressed in rags came by and took her dishes. He left, did a double take and then laughed. Kale looked up and frowned at the boy; the last thing she needed right then was another mocker. The boy leaned an elbow on the grail of her door and waited.

Kale was annoyed by him and angrily snapped. "Go away!"

Kale remembered that these were Ann's exact words only a couple of days earlier, and she felt childish.

The boy stayed, and when she took a closer look at the freckled face and reddish-brown hair, Kale gasped. She felt as if she was looking at a ghost from the past. Yes, he had changed, he was taller—and thicker—with a stronger jaw, and his eyes did not show the same fear that the boy in the barn did, but his smile gave it away.

"Leon?" Kale asked hesitantly, not sure what to make of her emotions.

"Yes?" he replied, almost joking.

Kale paused, unsure of what to say. She didn't expect to see him ever again and was not prepared for this surprise.

Leon broke the ice. "You woke me up last night, what with all your howling and screaming at the world. I had thought that you were the quiet type, so I was not sure what to think when you started to wail like that."

He shifted his weight and let his arm swing down from the grail. "Can't say I enjoyed it. Robbed me a couple of hours of my precious sleep."

"You do not know what I have been through!" Kale tried to explain.

"Must have taken a lot to land you in jail. What did you do this time?" Leon asked, grinning.

Kale knew he was just playing around, but she was still stung by the tactless comment. "Stole a child," she said.

Leon was taken aback at this. "What?" he asked, the smile gone from his face.

Kale smiled now. "Not really, but that is what I was accused for. How'd you land up here?"

Leon shook his head. "I was sold here, remember? A jailor bought me."

Kale remembered the man Leon was sold to and grimaced.

"Does he treat you well?" she asked.

Leon shook his head. "No, but your master did better?"

Kale didn't want to go into the details of what happened, and she vowed just then to never to tell Leon about Matthew. "I did pretty well actually. Became a kitchen maid."

Leon smiled. "You were lucky. Not many slaves end up with that kind of easy work."

"It wasn't that easy," Kale protested, remembering Anastasia.

Leon nodded. "Sure." He looked her up and down. "But from what I see, they still clothed and fed you. That is better than what I get here."

Kale had to acknowledge this. Leon was clothed only in a tattered tunic and shorts, and she could see that he was rail thin.

"So, what do you do down here?" she asked, breaking the awkward silence.

Leon grimaced. "Feed the prisoners, escort them places, take care of the jailor, run errands, and remove the prisoners that don't make it."

Kale was suddenly very thankful that she did not have that job, and she paled at the thought of what it might entail. Their conversation was suddenly interrupted, as footsteps echoed through the hallway. Leon immediately ducked his head to retrieve Kale's bowls. The large man that Kale had seen drag Leon off a year before came around the corner, a frown on his face.

"Hurry up, boy! What you doing anyways? Get a move on!" The large man came over and kicked Leon in the ribs, knocking him over. Leon scrambled to get up and step away.

The jailor came over and peered through the bars into Kale's cell. He suddenly chuckled. "A girl, huh? I know why you were hanging around here now." He gave Leon a friendly cuff on the shoulder that almost knocked him over again. "Well, if you finish up here early, I might just lock you in there tonight, too. Can't let her escape though."

Kale looked at Leon to see his response, but she saw no emotion on his face. "That would be nice, sir."

The jailor nodded, and then frowned again. "Well, hurry up! Finish up here!" he shouted again, continuing along the hall.

Leon pretended to be busy with the next cell's bowls as the jailor passed, and then he scooted back over to Kale's cell. She immediately whispered, concerned about the jailor's inference, "You wouldn't try anything, right?"

Leon chuckled quietly. "I am going to take him up on his offer."

Kale's eyes narrowed.

"Just to talk with you, of course," he assured her.

Kale nodded. She understood that a chance like this to talk was more than they could ask for.

"I should go now though. I could get any number of tortures for lagging," he admitted.

Kale's heart sunk. "He tortures you?"

Leon shook his head. "Thankfully, no. Though sometimes I'm sure he wishes to. He can make me go without food or lock me up in some cold cellar forever though." He managed a slim smile before getting up. "I should go now. See you tonight, if all goes well."

Kale nodded numbly, falling back against the wall as Leon walked away. Her mind was even more confused than when she arrived.

Leon is here! Leon is actually here... I haven't seen him in so long! He has changed, He is taller. . . and stronger. . . and more brave...

She reprimanded herself for thinking this way after she had fallen for Matthew.

Matthew, what would he think? Where is he now? Does he think of me?

CHAPTER

The day passed slowly, as Kale drifted into a listless sleep, full of haunting dreams that caused her to wake up in a sweat. Finally, she heard footsteps in the hallway, and Kale sat up with anticipation. To her horror, Leon didn't appear with the jailor.

The large man slunk up to her cell and unlocked it.

"Hasn't been a girl around here in awhile," he said with a strange light in his eyes. "Thought I might join you tonight." He began his approach. Kale paled and crawled away from the man until she hit a wall. The jailor inched closer; the torch in his hand was casting eerie shadows across his face.

Kale started to sweat, only fearing the man's intentions. She pressed herself against the wall, her heart pounding heavily. The jailor stretched out a hand to touch her cheek, and she panicked.

Unable to move, she screamed. This startled the jailor, and he stopped for a moment, just as Leon burst into the cell.

The jailor whirled around. "How did you get out, boy?"

Breathless, Leon couldn't answer. Kale trembled against the wall, her heart beating out of control. There was a long pause, but suddenly the jailor grinned in revelation.

"I see!" he chuckled. "You had your heart set on her, you dog!"

Kale sighed in relief, thanking God that the jailor found some humor in their situation.

"Well you worked enough for it, boy. I guess you can have her tonight." The jailor stepped out of the cell and rattled the keys in the lock.

"Enjoy your one night, for the rest are mine!" Whistling, he waltzed away down the hall. When the bobbing torchlight finally disappeared, Kale started crying from the stress. Leon knelt beside her.

"I am so sorry. I didn't know he would do this. He told me to get something from the cellar, and when I came back to the door, it was locked." He ran his hands through his hair, frustrated. "I knew suddenly that I had been tricked, and I tried to get out."

Kale was still crying, but Leon's whispering was comforting. "I finally broke the lock and ran as fast as I could." He looked at her—worried. "I wasn't too late, was I? I mean, he didn't hurt you or anything, right?"

Kale shook her head, very glad that Leon came when he had. Leon waited as she finally settled, leaning against the wall as she wiped the last of her tears away. Kale's brain was numb from the shock of what almost happened, but she tried to forget as she asked, "Does the jailor's mood often change that quickly?"

Leon smiled and looked up at the wall. "Yes, it can, but that is not always a good thing." He grimaced. "The first night was rough... actually the first week was." He paused and continued, "He must have been really upset about something, because he was never happy with what I did. Sometimes, at night, he would..."

Kale saw pain in Leon's eyes..

"Did he take it out on you?" she asked quietly, almost regretting the words the second she had said them. Leon turned slowly and showed her his back. A sick feeling grew in Kale's stomach, like something eating her from within. In the dim light she saw the jagged lines of many scars running up and down his back; long, painful ropes of skin. She pictured the jailor whipping Leon and the many nights of agony that would follow as the wounds tried to heal.

Kale almost completely forgot her own pain, for Leon's suffering was real, and her sympathy for him outweighed her grief. As he leaned back against the wall, Kale saw him shivering slightly. Untying her shawl from around her neck, she gingerly placed it on his shoulders. He smiled weakly at her. "Thank you." Quietly, he pulled her closer and held her gently. Kale wrapped her arm around his shoulder; she could feel him slowly stop shivering as her body heat warmed his bare skin.

"I guess we have been through a lot the past year," he admitted.

Kale was silent, as mental images of the last year plagued her conscience.

Leon continued, "But now that you are here, we can plan our escape."

Kale's heart started to pump faster. "Escape? Aren't we safe here together?"

Leon sighed and whispered to her, "Morning will come, and the jailor will try to come for you every night after that."

Kale hadn't forgotten, but she was desperately trying to push reality out of her mind.

"And then after that, you will be tried," Leon reminded her. "You could be hung for what you *did.*"

Kale sighed; she knew they had to leave. "So what can we do?"

Leon shook his head. "This place is pretty well guarded. It's designed so that people *don't* escape. It will be tough to come up with a plan."

Kale thought for a while. "Are you ever allowed to leave this place?"

"I only go out to help load the bodies."

"Bodies?" Kale asked, in disbelief.

"Yes, for those whose trials don't end well."

Kale sighed, despair clutching her gut. Then she thought of something, and her mood lightened for a moment.

Leon waited for an explanation. "Do you have an idea?"

"I don't know if it would work, but why can't *I* die?" she asked.

"Did you hear me, Kale?" Leon continued. "We don't want your trial to end badly! You would get a ride on the cart, alright, but as one of the dead!"

Kale smiled wider.

Leon looked confused for a second, and then realization washed over his face. "I could carry you outside, as though you were already dead, and dump you on the cart! I may even find a way to join you... as long as you can manage riding with the 'others'."

Kale nodded. She knew it was their slim but only hope.

"There is still the problem of making you look convincing, getting past the jailor and outside the gate; they always inspect the bodies at the gate."

Kale watched Leon intently. She could tell that he was working it through.

"Ok," Leon finally decided. "It might work, but we need to do it before tomorrow night, and there are only a couple more hours before dawn."

Kale nodded. "How do we start?"

"Well, it is just our luck that the man that carts out the bodies will come later in the evening tomorrow, giving us a little more time, and the cover of night for our escape. You probably shouldn't 'die' until later in the day. If the jailor comes back and you are dead only a couple hours after I was with you, he will suspect foul play." He scratched his head. "You should also start playing the sick role now, so that you have it down by tonight."

"Ok, I will try, but how will the jailor fall for it?"

Leon paused, and then nodding, continued, "I will smuggle some ash to try and make your skin white, and if I can, I might even be able to get some sleep syrup. The jailor's wife has a bottle for when her husband has really restless nights."

"Ew," said Kale. "He has a wife? Poor woman!" Then she remembered the plan. "How will that help?"

Leon smiled. "It will knock you out completely, so you will be as good as dead. It even slows your breathing."

Kale clarified. "Ok, so I will look dead and be unresponsive for a couple of hours while you drag me out of here?"

"Exactly."

"What if something goes wrong?"

"Something can always go wrong but this may go right, too. We only have one chance."

"So after we get a ride out of town, we are free, right?"

Leon breathed deeply. "Hopefully."

Kale nodded. "Just stay here with me for a while, okay? I like being like this, quiet and still, no running away."

Leon sighed. "Yes." He wrapped his arm around her again, and they held each other until the first light of dawn cracked through the spaces in the cold stone.

CHAPTER

T he jailor soon thumped down the hall again and jingled the keys in the lock, "Aw, such purty love birds. Come boy, hope you had enough, because that is all you are getting."

Kale unwrapped her arms from Leon's shoulders, and he stiffly rose to his feet. She shivered; the air had felt cold after she had been used to his warmth.

The jailor and Leon walked away, and Kale leaned back against the wall. Once she was sure no one was there, she remembered the plan.. Carefully, she practiced her cough, silencing at every sound that may be a footstep. Once she was satisfied with it, she coughed and wheezed continuously. The cough soon became a habit, and she started to wonder herself if she was in fact coming down with one.

Around lunch, Leon came with her water and bread. She moved to the bars and practiced a couple of coughs. Leon smiled, as he bent down to push her bowl under the gate. He ducked his head and whispered quietly, "Good job! The ash is under your bread. I don't have the sleep syrup yet, but I will have it when I come back for your bowls."

Kale nodded as she started to gobble up the bread. Leon stood up and left Kale to finish her meal. She found a good amount of ash at the bottom of the bowl as Leon promised.

Kale stared at it for a moment, realizing that there was no turning back after this. "Well, here goes nothing."

She dipped her fingers into the bowl and started to work the ash into her cheeks and forehead, making sure that there were no visible flakes on her face, ruining her potential disguise. She then rubbed ash onto her lower and upper arms and all over her hands. She used the rest of the ash to cover up any skin on her legs that was not already pale from recent hunger.

Then Kale focused on smoothing all her color out, reworking any spots missed. Once satisfied, she spread out any ash she spilled, and rubbed it into the dirt on the floor. Then, continuing to cough, she pretended to collapse on the floor, acting shaky and weak.

I like this acting stuff, she smiled to herself.

A couple of minutes later, Leon returned to collect her bowls. Kale crawled over to the gate, groveling on the floor, shaking weakly.

Leon saw her on the floor and gasped. "Are you sure you are not actually sick? You are starting to scare me."

Kale smiled. "That is the point, isn't it?"

Leon smiled back and shook his head in astonishment. He grabbed her bowls and checked to make sure no one was looking, then tossed her a piece of soggy bread.

"Eat that," he said. "It will knock you out until dusk. I soaked it in the syrup, because I couldn't find any bottle to bring that would be easy enough for you to hide."

Kale scooped up the bread and hid it in a fold of her dress.

Leon started to turn. "Do it quick. You need to be dead before the cart arrives. Well before, or it will look suspicious," he cautioned.

Kale nodded and crawled to the back of her cell. Just as Leon started to walk away, the jailor strutted into the hallway. Kale gave a couple of weak coughs just for effect.

The jailor started at the noise and came over to her cell. "Hey boy, what is wrong with the girl?" he asked suspiciously.

Leon froze and slowly walked back. Kale's heart raced uncontrollably, as she feared her cover was obvious.

Then she called out, in the most pathetic voice she could muster, "Water… please. I can't swallow. Please…" before breaking out into a coughing fit and falling to the ground, her body trembling.

The jailor turned to Leon. "Get her water boy! She's sick! What have you done?"

Leon obeyed and handed water to Kale. While Leon blocked the jailor's view of her, she quickly slipped the drugged bread into the water. Leon saw this, and he raised an eyebrow at her. She ignored him and started to sip the water as Leon stood up, diverting the jailer's attention. Kale quickly downed the bread before the jailor could spot it. She was not finished all of the water in the bowl when her head started to swim.

She choked on the liquid, her eyes getting heavy. Remembering her 'condition', she threw in a couple of moans. Soon the coughing was not an act. Kale started to panic, and she tried to get up. Her muscles grew weak, as gravity's force magnified. She collapsed on the stone, just as her world went black.

CHAPTER

The jailor watched Kale collapse, the water sloshing everywhere. When she went still, he hurriedly unlocked the gate and ran in. Leon momentarily forgot his part and watched from behind, surprised by her success.

Coming to, he ran to the jailor in a panic, falling to his knees in desperation. "What happened? How can this be? She was perfectly well last night!"

The jailor looked at Kale's pale skin and he poked her. When there was no response, he sighed. Leon almost started to panic, wondering if he had fed her the wrong serum, for her breathing was no longer evident.

The jailor stood up and stepped out of the cell, addressing Leon, "Another one gone. Better roll her out. The cart is coming in a couple of hours."

He looked back at Kale and continued, "Must have caught something before she got here—" Just then, the jailor stopped short.

Leon froze, his blood running cold. He had seen it; Kale's finger twitched. Dead people don't twitch, but sleeping ones do. Leon watched intently, hoping this was not what had stopped the jailor in his tracks.

The jailor finally shrugged and started to head back up the hallway, calling over his shoulder, "Wrap her up and load her on the cart. Then get back to work!"

Leon waited until the jailor left before he ran into the cell and gingerly scooped up Kale. He was surprised at how light she was, and he moved her to the storage room with ease. Laying her down on the floor carefully, he grabbed some bandages and knelt beside her.

Starting at her feet, he carefully but tightly wrapped her. When he reached her face, he bound loosely around her mouth, to allow for air to pass through, but still tightly enough for the bandages to hold. Once she was completely covered, Leon picked her up again and carried her outside. He made two more trips back in, for the other unlucky prisoners that had died in the night. When he finished, he only had to wait a couple of minutes before an old creaky cart pulled by a grey gauntly horse rolled into sight. The aged man driving nodded to Leon, who immediately started piling the bodies on top of the already full wagon. He carefully placed Kale on the cart bed, positioning another body partially on top of her, so as to make the pile look random.

The driver got down and walked into the jail to talk to his employer, and Leon frantically tried to find a place to hide among the bodies. He realized that there was no room in the cart, and he searched for somewhere to hide. He bent down to look at the underside of the cart and smirked. There was a thick, wide board across the middle of the bed of the cart, which could certainly hold his weight. The small space between the board and the cart became the perfect hiding place.

Just then, Leon heard the cart driver's voice in the distance. He scrambled to fit on top of the board, and his hands slipped from his own perspiration while he worked himself into the tight space. He had just pulled his legs up when the driver came out of the jail entrance. Leon could see the driver's shoes from where he was. He held his breath as the man approached the cart. The driver looked around, obviously confused as to where Leon went. When the driver finally climbed back into the cart and urged the horse on again, Leon breathed a heavy sigh of relief.

They rolled on a bit through the town, and Leon only started to relax when they were almost at the gate. The driver was just about to leave the city when Leon heard shouts among troupes of running feet. Guards. Soldiers.

Leon almost pounded the cart in frustration, but not letting it get the better of him, he remained silent. He strained his ears as the driver continued.

"Ho, there! Stop the cart!" a soldier yelled.

"What is the meaning of this?" the driver angrily questioned.

"There was an escaped slave, sir. We were ordered to search every party leaving the city."

The driver sounded indignant. "I only have the dead! The effort you put into one runaway slave. You would think someone killed the king!"

There was a slight chuckle, before the soldier insisted, "We are just carrying out orders. We must search each body and make sure they are indeed dead."

"What are you implying?" the driver said. "I would sneak off with a slave?"

"No, but they may have hidden in your cart," the soldier said, as Leon's heart pounded even louder, surely alerting them to his whereabouts.

The driver sighed. "Very well then."

Leon held his breath. He knew it would take a miracle to keep Kale asleep and unresponsive. He watched through the cart's wooden slats as they unloaded all the bodies and lined them up on the cobblestone. He saw a soldier unwrap each of the bodies' faces, and watched as each one was inspected. The soldiers were convinced and about to leave, when the general put up a hand.

Leon's heart started to pound. "Please. Don't let them find her," he silently begged.

The general walked past each body, looking intently at every one of them. This was the type of man others disliked immediately, one with a heart as solid as the stone beneath them.

The general stopped at Kale. Leon held himself back, though his muscles were tense and ready to fight. The general frowned. "Unwrap this body and dump some water on it," he said simply, his eyes not leaving Kale's face.

The driver grew angry. "Have you no honor for the dead?"

The general remained silent and watched as Kale was unwrapped and a pail of water was dragged over.

Leon held his breath.

As the water splashed over Kale, she sat up, spluttering and gasping. The driver and soldiers stepped back in utter disbelief, as if she had risen from the dead. The general just pointed at Kale.

"Get her!" he shouted, drawing his sword.

Kale quickly took in what happened, and she tried to get up and run.

Leon saw the two soldiers draw their swords and surround her. He looked around for a weapon, wishing he still had his sword. Spotting an iron rod a little way off by a smith's stall, Leon rolled from under the cart, sprinted to the rod, and stood on guard. When the soldiers saw this boy dressed in a tattered tunic and a women's shawl, roll from under the cart they were taken aback again. Leon knocked out two soldiers before they even knew what happened. Grabbing one of their swords for himself and passing the other to Kale, he backed up to defend her.

CHAPTER 26

They stood back to back as the soldiers advanced in a circle around them. Leon tried to hold the soldiers back, but they were closing in on Kale. She had never held a sword in her life, let alone used one, and so she was waving it about, arm's length in front of her. One brave soldier darted forward and Kale panicked, backing up. With the soldiers closing in, she knew it would be the end. Thinking of nothing but her survival, Kale closed her eyes and with all the power in her, she thrust the sword forward, trying to create space.

All the soldiers stopped in their tracks, as one of them fell to the ground with Kale's sword in his chest. She stared at the motionless soldier in disbelief. Leon turned to see what happened and he grinned a little bit when he realized Kale's success.

Taking advantage of the break in the soldiers' resolve, he grabbed Kale's arm and pulled her from her state of shock, sprinting from the gate and along the wall. The soldiers took only a couple of seconds to take up pursuit, but their equipment slowed their pace. Leon and Kale charged up some steps to the top of the wall. As they reached the edge, Leon kept the soldiers back momentarily until they found themselves forced against the very back corner of the upper wall.

One soldier scored a slash on Leon's right shoulder. Kale flinched at the sight of scarlet blood pouring down his chest.

"Jump!" Leon said to her through gritted teeth, trying to hold the soldiers back with his left arm now.

Kale looked out over the wall's edge, frantically scanning the dense forest below. The drop was far and there was little to offer protection.

"Jump, if you want to live!" Leon said again.

Kale stepped up onto the edge, closed her eyes, and let herself fall. For a few sickening seconds, there was nothing… just the wind in her hair, and she opened her eyes just as she slammed into the top branches of a tree. Sticks tore at her skin, but the fall continued. She grasped at branches to slow herself, but nothing held, until one outstretched hand grasped a narrow limb. Clinging to it with all her might, she swung down under the branch, swaying wildly at first before coming to a stop. From her spot, she saw Leon still fighting on the upper wall. Kale gasped as the soldiers gained on him.

Leon tired, and fast; he didn't stand a chance. The soldiers were fully clad in armor, and Leon's tunic was shredded to pieces. He was not used to the sword he stole from the dead soldier, and his enemies were well trained. Finally, a soldier dealt him a blow with the flat of his sword that knocked Leon off the edge. He fell like a ragdoll into the trees. She watched as Leon crashed to the forest floor. She prepared herself for the sprint, expecting him to jump up and join her.

But Leon's body was uncharacteristically still; his limbs seemed askew at broken angles in the darkness. Kale felt a blow to the chest, as if the sword had hit her. Fighting for air, she watched the soldiers yell at one another and point to where he fell. She heard someone shout, "He'd never live through that!" while another ordered, "Check the wall for the girl!" A bell went off somewhere in the city.

"Leon?" managed Kale.

She knew they had to get out of there—fast. Shaking, she climbed down from her perch and ran over to Leon's side. His blood was pooling on the leaves, but she pushed away the passing thought that the fall had killed him.

She couldn't just leave him. Kale knew she would probably get caught without him anyways. Running again would be lonely and scary without Leon.

Kale realized, suddenly, how dependent on him she had been since their first escape. Glancing wildly around for any soldiers, Kale rolled Leon onto his back and pressed her ear against his chest. She listened for one agonizingly long moment of truth, praying that she would detect the sound of his heart.

Finally, she heard something. Kale could barely catch the weak heart-beat, but she cried, "You're still alive!"

Kale heard a soldier shout, and she snapped back to reality.

OK, he's alive, but soon we will both be captured and then killed.

She shook her head incredulously. *Out of the frying pan and into the fire...*

Kale shook Leon. "Leon! You have to wake up! The soldiers will come to take us back. We have to go... now!"

Kale's eyes started to tear up; she didn't want to go back to that horrid jail. "Come on, Leon! Please!"

She was rewarded with a groan.

Leon shifted, and she realized that he was too weak to move. After a year of malnourishment, the fighting had done him in. This fall was the last straw.

Kale tenderly traced the gash in his shoulder, gasping at how deep it was. Realizing that she needed to stop the blood loss before anything else, Kale tore off part of her dress and wrapped it around his arm and neck.

Bracing her legs, Kale slipped her arms under his neck and legs and tried to stand. Leon was heavier than she assumed, and Kale couldn't get up. She tried slinging just his arm over her shoulder, finding she could finally stand with him. She was glad no one was around to see her futile attempts and smiled at the thought of her mother watching her now.

Oh mother, how I miss you! What would you say now? Kale shook her head.

She knew exactly what her mother would say, "Kale Sarah Barlow, you put that dirty boy down right now and go wash your hands!"

CHAPTER

L eon passed out, rendering him useless. Kale quickly grabbed his legs
and pulled him into her arms. She looked back at Bartleona and could
see that a group of soldiers had formed at the gate, discussing how
to proceed. Luckily for Kale and Leon, the new moon made it much harder
to see into the dense forest. Kale knew it was unlikely for the group to send
a search party into the dead of a night like this without proper equipment.
Hopefully, this would buy them a little time.

Kale made her way through the trees away from the castle, dragging
Leon as he remained unconsciously propped up beside her. She soon found
herself tripping more often, and her muscles started to burn. The cool
night wind helped to calm her and urge her on.

After half an hour, she was forced to slow down. Leon started slipping from her arms and the going got rough. A light rain began to fall just
as Kale started to think there was no use. She suddenly noticed that the
ground had grown rocky and the going more uphill. Kale realized they had
reached a long range of mountains known in those parts as the Fray. They
were the one rocky outcrop near the city, and she knew they stretched all
the way back to her home.

As a child, Kale remembered looking out at the distant mountains and
wishing to explore them someday. Now she was thankful for their shelter,
but she wished she could have found them under different circumstances. Exhausted, Kale looked around for some overhang or a large cliff for
shelter. In the dark, she found nothing until she almost fell right into the
mouth of a cave.

Kale couldn't believe her luck. Almost completely invisible, there was a little hole in the face of the mountain, just big enough to crawl into. A large rock jutted out over the low opening, sheltering the cave from the elements and potential prying eyes.

Fighting the urge to collapse, Kale placed Leon on the ground carefully and bent down to look inside the cave. The inside swelled out into a small cavern. Kale guessed it was about six paces wide. She gingerly felt around and found the floor dry. Guessing by the leaves on the ground, Kale knew that this cave was too perfect to be naturally made. It probably housed a hibernating bear at some point. Relieved to be safe and out of the rain, Kale slid herself into the cave and gently pulled Leon in after her, careful not to strain his shoulder. Once inside, Kale collapsed onto the soft floor, and exhaled a sigh of relief.

"We made it," she murmured to an unconscious Leon.

She knew she couldn't sleep for fear of Leon's survival, and she immediately tried to make him comfortable. When she looked at him closely, Kale was shocked by how pale he had become. He lost a lot of blood with the wound, and Kale realized she needed to get some food into him immediately. Back home, she was never good at scavenging, and Kale worried about whether or not she could find something edible. She quickly tore off some more of her dress and wound it around Leon's shoulder. Slipping outside the cave, Kale wandered back into the forest to search for food.

In the dark, it was hard to tell what type of plants there were, but Kale looked nevertheless. The rain thickened, clouding her vision, and drenching her to the skin. In the downpour, Kale worried about finding her way back to the cave, let alone finding edible plants. Hunching her shoulders in defeat, she quickly made her way back in the direction she came.

She ducked her head to protect her face against the rain, and scrambled to find the cave entrance. At last she came across the opening. She crawled back inside the cave beside Leon and hoped he would live through the night. She knew it would be risky to look for plants in the day, as the soldiers could spot her, or she could leave footprints in the mud, but Kale also knew she had to take the risk. Leon's life depended on it. Determining it was important for her to get some rest, Kale let her eyes droop.

Before she knew it, dawn broke, waking her from a deep sleep. It was still raining hard outside the cave, and Kale rejoiced. It provided a cover, as it would wash away her footprints. Leon was still unconscious, but the blood flowing out of his wound seemed to have slowed a little. Not wanting to be seen, Kale went into the forest while it was still shrouded in a thick mist. She looked for a while, and finally came across a bush of wild blueberries. Wiping a handful off in the dew-covered grass, she headed back to the cave, itching to be in its shelter.

Inside, she carefully laid the food on a little rock shelf in the wall of the cave. Cupping her hands under the trickle of water dripping in the mouth of the cave, Kale collected a good amount of it. Swallowing the first handful, she collected some more for Leon. Crawling on her knees, trying to avoid hitting her head on the roof of the cave, Kale made it over by his side before the water started to leak from her hands. His mouth was slightly open, and Kale slowly let the water trickle through his lips and down his throat. She hoped he would swallow by instinct, even though he was unconscious.

He let out a little choke as he started to swallow the water. Happy that he was responding, Kale got some more and let it run down his throat. This time, he swallowed immediately. When Kale was satisfied that Leon was hydrated, Kale crushed some blueberries in her hands. Adding a little water to them, she tried feeding the blue mush to Leon. When he spit it back out, like a protesting child, Kale didn't give up.

"Come on, they're good. I need to get some food in you, Leon," she coaxed.

When he refused to swallow the berries, Kale tipped his head back, opened his mouth and dropped some to the back of his throat. He was then forced to swallow. In this way, Kale managed to get almost half of the berries she had collected into him. When she was done, she was out of breath from holding him up and concentrating so intently. Kale leaned back against the cave's wall, her own exhaustion overcoming her.

"Good, see? That wasn't that bad," she said gently. "You really are a lot of trouble, you know?"

Kale stared at Leon. This was the first time she could actually look at him without embarrassment or reservation. His pale skin made his freckles stand out more, and his hair was a mess from her trying to drag him along. The sun lit up his face, causing her to notice that he had long golden eyelashes floating gently around his eyes. Her eyes traced the curves of his face, moving over his brow, down his high cheekbone, and across his angular jaw.

Kale thought about Matthew, and then she thought about Leon. She was confused inside, about her feelings for them both. Lying still on the leaves, Leon looked helpless and alone. Kale remembered Matthew's kisses and she suddenly wondered what it would be like to kiss Leon. She pushed away the thought, but it kept resurfacing. Kale debated with herself; since he was unconscious, and he would probably not remember, she determined it would be okay.

Looking at him intently, she leaned in and brushed her lips briefly with his. It was as if an electric charge pulsed through her entire body. Somehow this kiss, in this hidden cave in the rain, stirred her heart more than her first kiss on that moonlit night. There were birds trilling outside and the forest was filled with the noises of a spring day, but to Kale, it seemed as if the whole world had dropped away. All she could hear was Leon's slow breathing and the frantic beat of her own heart. Shivers ran up and down her spine.

Now more confused than ever, Kale leaned back against the cave wall and nibbled on a few of the remaining blueberries. She realized suddenly how hungry she was, as the last meal she ate was the drugged bread with water the morning before. Quietly she crept out of the cave and went back to the blueberry bush. Kale ate until she was satisfied and collected as much as she could carry back to the cave.

CHAPTER

The rain was slowing, and the fog had risen when she reached the mouth of the cave. Kale knew it was too risky to move by daylight. When she crawled back inside, she was surprised to see that Leon had propped himself up and was watching for her. Kale ignored him until she crawled over to her little shelf, placing the blueberries there.

Leon regarded her with mild interest. "How long was I out?" he asked slowly.

Kale's brow crinkled in thought. "Through the night, and maybe a couple hours after sunrise?"

Leon shook his head. "Where are we? How did I get here? What happened after I fell off the wall?"

Kale held up a finger. "I will tell you, but first, please eat some more. I don't think I fed you enough this morning."

Leon took the berries she handed him, but he was still looking at her intently. "You fed me?"

Kale nodded. "And gave you water, and dressed your wound. Now can you please eat something?"

Kale could see that Leon was trying to hide how hungry he was as he gobbled down the berries, but she smiled at the fact that he was recovering. While he ate, Kale recounted what had happened since he landed on the forest floor.

"I picked you up and carried you away from the city, and it started to rain. By then it was dark, and I could see nothing, but I knew I had to find someplace to hide for the night. I reached the foot of the mountains, the Fray range," at this Kale could see surprise cross Leon's face at the distance they had covered.

"And purely by accident," Kale continued, "I stumbled on this cave. You were bleeding pretty badly, so I bound your shoulder and tried to find food. There was nothing out there that I could see in the dark, so I came in here and fell asleep until dawn. Then I found the blueberries, and I fed them to you. I went back out to get more berries and finally just returned."

Leon shook his head, clearly dumbfounded by the story. Kale smirked at the thought that he couldn't believe she had done it. Leon shifted his weight and winced. Gingerly, he touched his shoulder. "Is it really that bad?"

Kale shrugged. "I haven't looked at it recently. Didn't want to re-open the wound."

"We will need to redress it. I'm no doctor, but I need something else on this wound beneath the cloth, so that my skin does not grow back attached to it."

Kale grew sick at the thought. Crawling to the edge of the cave, she grabbed some large, green leaves, "Will these do?"

Leon nodded. "They'll have to. Come help me undo this."

Kale crawled over to his side and Leon started to pull off the corner of the bandage. He winced and his hand dropped weakly. Kale realized that she would have to do most of the work. Carefully, she pulled at the bandage and a gasp escaped Leon's lips.

"Sorry," she apologized.

He shook his head. "Continue." Bracing himself against the wall, he gritted his teeth as Kale tried to gently pull the bandage away from the healing wound. She grimaced as the piece of dress started to pull away from his flesh.

"I can't do this! I am going to rip away your skin!" she gasped.

"You won't. It's just the scab. But do it quick. I can't last much longer…"

Kale nodded and pulled the bandage completely away. Leon bit his lip. Gently, Kale placed the leaves on his wound, and then bound it again.

"That feels better. Thanks," Leon said, trying to manage a smile.

Kale sighed. "I am glad it is over."

Leon nodded and relaxed against the wall. They both sat in silence for a while.

"You know," said Leon. "I have a confession to make."

"I can hardly imagine."

"I was awake when you were talking to that woman in the slave house," Leon said slowly.

Kale pursed her lips. "Oh that. I figured."

Leon looked over at her with his intense blue eyes. "I heard what you said about me. It was the last thing I heard from you for an entire year."

Kale looked down, embarrassed.

"When I went to the jail house, all I could think about was how miserable I had made you, how I had ruined your life," he said honestly.

Pain grew in his eyes, and Kale looked up at him. "It was bad timing, I was kind of depressed," she said simply.

Leon sighed and looked out towards the cave entrance. "That makes two of us."

Kale realized at that moment that she may have actually hurt Leon, too. The difference was that he never meant to hurt her, at least in the end.

"I'm sorry, Leon. I never could accept that you didn't realize what you were doing."

"I did realize it, and I was so stupid. I never should have made the deal."

He looked down and Kale touched his arm gently. "There is nothing we can do to change what happened now, though I wish there was." Kale remembered the hurt, pain, and anxiety that she had to go through, and now she knew Leon did too. They just sat in silence for a while, not knowing how to change the past.

Suddenly Leon looked back up at her. "I was also awake for that kiss."

There was a long pause as Kale's face reddened and her heart went to her throat.

"I didn't mind it, you know," he assured her, trying to ease the tension.

Kale smiled a little in embarrassment. "I thought you were knocked out."

Leon smiled, looking intently at her with his bright blue eyes. "I was. I would shift in and out of consciousness, but I was never strong enough to even open my eyes."

Kale was unsure what to think. "Oh, well I guess you were hurt pretty badly."

Leon nodded. "Yeah, and it will be a stretch to try to find food for both of us and still not get caught with me in this shape."

Kale grinned slyly, relieved that the topic had changed. "I did get us this far."

"I still don't understand how. No offense, but you weren't really good at the 'on the road' thing before."

"I know. But I also have been through a lot in the past year."

Leon shifted his weight. "About that. I told you about my year, but you never told me what happened to you." Kale shifted nervously, thinking about Matthew. "All I ever learned was that you were a kitchen maid."

Kale tried to think up a story that left out Matthew. It would be incredibly awkward to talk about him in front of Leon, right after she had kissed him. "Well, I was sold to that woman, and I mainly just cleaned the house and kitchen, took out the trash, washed clothes, and looked after her little niece, Anastasia." Kale grew dark at the memory of the girl.

"What?" Leon asked, noticing her face.

"That girl was a little terror. She ran away, and I was accused of taking her. I landed in jail, just because of her little prank."

Leon looked surprised. "Her parents actually believed that you abducted her?"

"Not really, but when my master became desperate, she needed someone to blame."

"So that is all you did for a year?"

Kale suddenly thought of Matthew, the dance, and their kisses…

When she looked up, there was interest behind Leon's eyes.

"You met someone?" he asked.

Kale shifted and looked down, wondering if her face was that obvious.

"You can tell me, you know. It doesn't matter," he insisted.

Kale still did not really want to talk about Matthew, but she felt her reserve depleting, "Well, I don't know *how* you guessed…"

Leon smiled a bit at this. "So, who was he?"

Kale bit her lip. "He was an aristocrat living next door." Leon listened intently, as she fumbled. "He was a friend, that's all."

"You really are a bad liar," Leon said.

Kale looked indignant, but Leon laughed. "Why don't you just tell me?"

She sighed, knowing he really wouldn't care, but Kale still wasn't sure whether or not she did. "Well, we went to a dance together and on a walk in the woods."

She smiled at the memory. "On that walk, actually, I couldn't help thinking about how you and I were in the very same place, just under very different circumstances." Catching herself, she admitted, "Well yeah, I think he liked me, and I might have liked him."

Leon looked up at her. "Were you together?" he asked quietly.

"What, you mean, in a relationship?" Kale asked, not sure what he was implying.

"Yes, well, were you in love? Did you kiss him?"

Kale paused, wondering how he read her so easily. "I won't see him again," she sighed before continuing, "on the walk in the woods, he kissed me."

Kale couldn't tell what emotion flit briefly across Leon's face, but she went on. "We were kind of in a relationship, but it was never made official. We went to that dance and kissed a couple of times there, but I hardly remember those," she admitted sadly.

"I guessed you had." He paused and then looked at her again. "Will you remember our kiss?" he asked gently.

Kale paused for a second, unsure of what his question was really asking. Finally she looked back at him. "Yes, I think I will."

CHAPTER

Somehow, Kale was relieved at her confession. They sat together for a while again, and Kale could tell that Leon suddenly looked nervous. Curious, Kale prodded for answers, "What is it?"

Leon jerked, and then shook his head. A muscle in his jaw clenched, and then he sighed. "I haven't told you everything." Kale wondered what he was talking about. "Now that we are officially both wanted, I guess I should tell you why we were running in the first place. It is only fair."

"What do you mean?"

Leon looked away and back again. "The secret."

Kale held her breath in disbelief. *Will he actually tell me?*

"It was by accident, actually. I found a letter from our king, King Zorack, addressed to the king of Brecken, the neighboring country. Curiosity got the best of me, as I broke the seal and scanned the message. It seemed just like a pleasant letter at first, until I read *'It is done'.*"

Kale listened intently, as Leon spoke more passionately now, "I read on, to find out that King Zorack admitted to killing his brother, our former king!"

Kale gasped, but Leon continued, "Here the letter became rushed, and the writing more scrawled, but the king went on to thank Brecken's king for his assistance and to say he hoped the 'situation' would work out. King Zorack then wrote that he was glad to have assisted Brecken's king as well. They were in it together."

He paused, to see if Kale was catching on. "The king went on to say that an heir to his brother's throne was discovered after all, and this heir deserved his crown. King Zorack then issued a decree for the heir to be eliminated. But at this point, I was caught with the letter. Then our king Zorack found out, and I have been running ever since."

Kale nodded. "I think you hinted at that before."

"But there is something else."

Kale could see mixed emotions flitting behind his down cast eyes, and she waited for him to continue.

After a long pause, he looked up at her, "King Zorack…."

Kale nodded, cutting him off, "Yes. He's terrible. I am hearing you!"

Leon nodded, but paused, clearly not wanting to go on, "King Zorack… is my father."

Kale was dumbfounded and sat in shocked silence. She could tell that Leon was watching to see her reaction. Thoughts ran across Kale's mind, memories that never made sense until now. She remembered wondering about why Leon wore the name of nobility and why he had to run. She remembered how The Shadow captured them, and how they were chased.

Maybe Leon was involved in the plot after all! Kale realized, all at once.

Kale edged away from Leon, but Leon stopped her. "I had no part in this murder. I did not even know anything about it until I read the letter! Clearly, my father wanted to keep this a dark secret."

Kale remembered something that didn't line up. "Why did The Shadow not kill us on the spot then?"

"I don't think even The Shadow knows who I am, which means the king may not be entirely under his control. But also, the king did not want me dead until I found out he was a murderer. I think he was fine with me being his heir when the time came. I am not convinced he really wants to hurt me."

"That makes sense, I guess."

Leon sighed. "I had known that my father was always jealous of his brother, but I had never thought it would drive him to what he did. Ever since I read that letter, I have felt terribly about myself, terribly that I descended from such a line. I have been searching for a way to make amends for my father's mistakes."

The boy in the barn was turning out to be more and more complex. There was clearly more to the story, but Kale felt badly for thinking his betrayal of her was purely for selfish reasons.

"I am sorry for being so horrible to you before," she said, feeling deeply shameful.

Leon smiled. "Thanks for saying sorry, but I deserved it, for being an idiot."

"Stop being so hard on yourself." She looked down. "I made mistakes, too, like all those horrible things I said about you to Marge."

Leon shifted his position on the wall. "So can we say we are even and forget the past?"

Kale met his gaze. "Yes, friends?" she asked slowly.

Smiling, he said, "Sure. Now what's our next move, friend?"

Kale laughed. "Well you need to get better, and we both need to eat."

Leon nodded in response. "We are hidden enough here to avoid detection for a couple of days, but we should find somewhere to stay in the mountains until I can travel again. We will be safe there, as no soldiers will venture into the Fray."

Kale thought nervously of the tales she had heard. "Are you sure it will be safe?" she asked nervously.

Leon looked at her intently. "No, but it's our best chance."

"Fine, but if I die, I am not going to speak to you ever again."

"Ok, I'll remember that." Leon laughed. Just then, he noticed the berries and looked at them longingly. "Hey, may I have some more of those?"

Kale handed him a bunch, which he immediately began devouring. She looked outside and noticed that the sun was well overhead. Kale realized suddenly how hungry she was as well. Grabbing the rest of the berries, they ate until there were no more. Leon fell asleep after their meal, and insisted on Kale resting too, but she had too much to think about to even shut her eyes.

CHAPTER

B y afternoon, Kale's tongue started to dry up, and her throat felt parched. "I wish there was still water dripping in the edge of our cave. I am so thirsty," she said.

Leon shifted back into a sitting position and thought out loud, "We are near a forest, you said. There should be a stream nearby."

Kale knew what he was asking and sighed. "Is it safe to go look right now?" She asked, thinking about the soldiers who would probably be on their way by now.

Leon touched his bandage and winced. "I don't know, but we won't live much longer without water…"

Kale was resigned. "Ok, ok, I'll go. Don't' get into trouble while I am gone," she warned.

Leon smiled. "I'll try not to."

Kale grabbed the sword they had taken, just to be safe. Sighing and trying to look obviously annoyed, she left the cave, with Leon chuckling behind her.

The spring sun was shining down through the trees, trees whose leaves were still dripping silently onto the freshly washed ground. Birds were abundant in this part of the woods, and their joyous singing masked the noise of Kale's footsteps. A small rabbit hopped across the trail, its nose and ears twitching. Kale watched it intently, wondering where it got water. *It has to drink, too.*

Kale wondered if it would lead her to its water source. When the rabbit hopped ahead, Kale followed closely behind. After a while, she heard the music of running water. Letting the rabbit venture deeper into the woods,

Kale found the small brook and thankfully drenched her parched throat. Kale glanced around for a way to carry the water back to the cave. Looking at the trees, she wondered if she could carve a wooden bowl with the sword Leon took from the soldier. She realized that that would take too long, and she didn't fancy sitting out in the open for hours. Kale searched for another option. She found a nice dry log that would hold water and decided to carve it once she got back inside the cave. Finding some moss, Kale felt confident that it would be sufficient to get a mouthful of water to Leon. Grabbing a handful, she soaked it with water and clutched her log.

On the way back, Kale left a trail to help her find the river again. It took her no time to get back to the cave, and she dumped the log and sword into the opening before crawling inside. She scanned the entire cave, but Leon was not there. There were marks in the dirt, as though his body had been dragged.

"Leon!" she cried, hoarsely. But there was no answer.

Kale felt herself panic. *Did the soldiers take him? Had they found them already?* Her mind raced, filling with all the terrible possibilities.

Just then, something grasped her leg, and she spun around in fright.

Leon looked up at her with a questioning face. "What's wrong, Kale?"

Kale's body slunk over her knees, as she worked to gain composure. "I-I- thought you were gone! I thought they found you. How could you..."

"Take a break?" Leon asked, with a smirk.

Kale was embarrassed. Of course he would need to. This was the only chance he could have had to drag himself out the entrance and find a private spot.

"I am sorry. That was just silly. I found the brook, and I brought this back to make a bowl. Here," she said, handing him the moss. "This is all I could find for now."

Leon took the dripping moss and sucked the water from it thoughtfully. "Well that's a start, but we will need that bowl carved soon, so if something happens, and we can't leave the cave, we will have a water source."

Kale nodded and sat cross-legged on the floor of the cave. She tried to start carving the wood, but the sword was clumsy in her hands. Leon grinned at her attempts. "Let me do it. It will give me something to pass the time." Kale nodded and gladly handed the wood and sword to him. He immediately began expertly chipping away the bark to peel back the soft wood beneath.

"We should try to leave here as soon as possible," he sighed. "It isn't really safe."

Kale fixed her gaze on him. "Are you strong enough to travel?"

Leon paused his chipping. "I will have to try to make it to the mountains. The soldiers will get here eventually, and even this cave won't go unnoticed."

"Do you want to try to stand up and walk now?" Kale asked, quietly.

"I guess I'll have to," he replied, putting the sword and chunk of wood to the side and placing his hands beneath him. When he tried to collect his feet underneath him, a gasp escaped his lips, and he collapsed against the wall. He bunched his muscles to try again, sweat beading on his brow. Kale saw that he was getting nowhere, and she gently placed an arm around his shoulders. Together they got Leon onto his feet, and from there he moved slowly into the opening. A warm breeze blew by, and a fluffy cloud floated, revealing the sun. Leon closed his eyes and smiled, savoring the sunlight pouring down on his face.

They stood together, Leon swaying a bit, but Kale steadied him. She found that he was still weak, but since only his shoulder was damaged, he could manage walking. Kale carefully led him to the berry patch, where the blueberries were ripe and falling off the branches, filled to the brim with savory juices. The dense green leaves on the bush blew in the wind, and the patterns on the forest floor shifted and danced.

Once they had eaten their fill of the berries, Kale led Leon to the stream. Here he laughed in pure joy, as he knelt beside the brook, scooping up the sparkling water in his hands. Leon splashed it on his face and drenched his tongue. Kale smiled and joined him; the water was clear, cold, and refreshing. Kale was bending over the brook when something hit her from behind. The frigid water ran down her back, chilling her to the bone.

"Oh!" she turned, scowling at Leon, who had a sly grin plastered on his face. "You wouldn't!"

She scooped up some water and tossed it in Leon's direction. It hit him in the chest, splattering him with water droplets. He tore off her now soaking shawl and tossed it on the bank.

"Hey." He splashed more towards Kale, drenching her further. "You!"

Kale laughed as a full on water war began. Drenched and soaking, Kale splashed water as fast as she could, laughing and giggling hysterically. Jumping up, she ran a short distance, before Leon pulled her onto the grass and splashed her right in the face. Kale reached over and shoved him playfully, but Leon groaned and collapsed on the grass, clutching his shoulder. Kale gasped and quickly came to his side. "Leon, I'm so sorry, I didn't realize…"

Leon rolled over, laughing, and threw a handful of grass in her face. "Got you."

Kale looked hurt, but Leon grinned. She gave in and they rolled together in the grass.

Suddenly a twig snapped, and Leon stiffened. The forest seemed too still, and even the birds stopped singing. Kale looked worriedly at Leon. Just then a small rabbit, the same one Kale followed to the stream, hopped out from behind a tree and sniffed around. Kale and Leon shared a nervous laugh. Together, with unspoken agreement, they headed back to the safety of the cave.

Once inside, Kale sighed. "That was too close."

Leon nodded. "Agreed." He glanced around the cave and announced, "Staying here has been good, but I think we should probably move on tomorrow."

"No way. You were pale, unconscious, and dying under my nose just this morning. Just because you survived some fun at the brook doesn't mean you are ready to travel. We cannot leave until you are stronger."

Leon closed his eyes. "I am strong, just tired." He leaned back against the wall of the cave, starting to nod off.

Kale shook her head; she could see that he tired too fast to try a trek through the mountains. "How about one more week?" she offered.

"One more day. That is all I will risk."

Kale was about to object when she realized that Leon was already asleep. Leaning her back against the hard wall, Kale wrapped her dress tight around herself. She briefly wondered if Leon was cold, with so little covering. The sun was still up, and yet somehow, Kale felt exhausted. She watched Leon's chest rise and fall, and slowly, she also nodded off.

CHAPTER

K ale dreamt that she was back home. She got some bread from Sake, but it engulfed into flames and burned her hands. Kale panicked, and she dropped it, screaming. Then her mind flashed to a different time, and she was letting the cows out into the field. They knocked over the fence and started running away. Kale frantically shouted for her mother's help. Suddenly, she was in a different spot in time. A hand covered her mouth, and a voice urged her to be quiet. Kale struggled, but the hand stayed, and Kale was surprised by how real it felt...

Kale's eyes snapped open. Leon was covering her mouth and gesturing frantically at her to be quiet. There was fear behind his eyes, and Kale wondered what was going on. Then she heard the hoof beats thundering across the ground and raised voices shouting to each other. Kale shared a look with Leon, and silently they retreated to the back of the cave, curling up together in the farthest recess. Kale's heart quickened as she realized the danger of the situation.

A horse pawed the ground so close to the entrance of the cave that Kale could see the detailed horseshoe. The animal's cropped hair was drenched in sweat, probably from galloping through the day.

A man shouted close by, "Those were their tracks into this forest. I know it!"

Another man stammered, "But weren't there two of them? We only found one set of tracks."

Kale remembered how she carried Leon and thanked God for it.

"The boy may have died. We must find the other!"

"Search the forest!"

"Look everywhere until we find them! Don't let one stone go unturned!" Kale and Leon listened to their shouts.

Kale gulped. She hoped that the cave was well enough hidden to avoid detection. Just then the voice stopped; the soldier dismounted his horse and stood by the cave entrance. Kale could tell that he was listening for something, and she held her breath.

The evening was silent, except for Kale's heart pounding against her rib cage. She could feel Leon tense beside her, and they waited for what felt like an hour before the guard sighed and stepped back on his horse. Kale exhaled, and she felt her shoulders sag. Leon relaxed too, but only after the soldiers had galloped away. Both knew that they were a hair's breadth away from discovery.

After waiting a little longer, to be sure the soldiers were gone, Leon started packing up what little they had.

Kale saw what he was doing and laid a hand on his arm. "Wait, we can't leave when they are so close by! We would get caught."

"So we stay here and wait until they find us?"

"I don't know, but don't you think we should wait until night fall at least?"

Leon glanced outside at the setting sun. "They may be back before then."

"They may," Kale agreed, "but since they didn't find us when they were right on top of us, I think we are better off here than on the run just now."

"Fine, but only until they have stopped searching for the night, then we move."

"Ok," Kale agreed. She stared out into the forest. "What just happened anyway?"

Leon looked at her, "You were sleeping when I heard the horses' hooves. You must have been having a nightmare because you were thrashing about and screaming for your mother. I was scared that they would hear us, so I tried to get you to be quiet. That's when you woke up."

Kale bit her lip, remembering the dream. "Sorry," she said, embarrassed.

"It's ok, and they didn't hear anything, thankfully."

Kale nodded numbly.

They sat in the dark for another couple of minutes until a crackling broke the silence. Kale watched as some orange sparks rose above the trees. She could distinctly hear pops and snaps, telltale signs of wood burning. Laughing and merry talk carried through the trees, and Kale briefly wished she were there and not here in the damp, dark cave.

"Sounds like they have made camp. Should we head out?" she asked hesitantly.

Leon looked down and then back towards the soldiers' fire. "Better now than never. Let's go."

Kale sighed and gathered up the half-finished bowl, sword, and their other belongings. She then helped Leon to his feet and they crawled out of the cave. Leon winced as he stood upright, and Kale shot him a worried glance. He waved her off and started trotting towards the mountains. Kale followed quickly, glancing one more time at the camp.

CHAPTER

L eon moved at a hurried pace and Kale struggled to keep up. She offered to carry everything, as Leon was not yet strong, but now that they were actually running, Kale regretted it. They moved on silently and swiftly, and before long, the trees thinned out and the road headed uphill. When Kale started to pant and slow down, Leon grabbed some of their stuff from her back and kept going, ignoring Kale's protest.

On either side of them, trees were replaced by shrubs and dry grasses, the soft dirt replaced by stones. When they reached a small overhang, Kale paused to look down on the valley. From there, she could plot where they walked, she could guess where their cave was, and she could see the small glow of the soldiers' campfire. She lingered there for a moment before continuing, turning her back on all she had ever known.

They headed into the heart of the mountains, and Kale lost sight of the trees all together. The air grew cold as they climbed higher, and the rocky path was hard on their feet. Kale could see her breath crystalize in the air in front of her, and she was amazed by the height of the Fray. Her fingers start to grow numb, and they turned a shade of dark purple-grey. Kale tried to fight the urge to stop and warm them.

All around her, the landscape was a dull gray, cold and forbidding. Leon's eyes were sharp, searching for somewhere to hide for the day. Kale plodded on tiredly and wished they had stayed in the cave. After a couple of hours, she started noticing frost on the grasses. When a snowflake landed on Kale's nose, she stared at it in shock for a couple of moments. She had never been to the mountains before, and thought it impossible for it to snow in the late spring. Leon stopped and turned to see why she hesitated. When he saw her staring at the light snow that was coming down, he laughed a bit and motioned for her to follow.

When they had made it to a relatively high altitude, Kale noticed that she was getting short of breath. She felt as if the air could not fill her lungs. She didn't question this, as she had heard many strange stories about the mountains.

Leon stopped suddenly and Kale peered over his shoulder. In front of them, filling the whole of the valley they needed to cross, was a large, frozen lake. Kale glanced across the icy blue water for a way around it. On all sides were steep cliff walls, devoid of handholds, proving that the only way to go was back or across. Kale couldn't fathom what their fate would be with the soldiers, so she immediately settled on trying to cross.

"Do you think the ice can hold us up?" she asked.

Leon scanned the frozen surface. "I guess there is only one way to find out."

Kale nodded and they advanced towards the icy bridge. Leon crossed onto the ice, and it held, so Kale followed. Hesitantly, she slid her foot from the snow-covered bank and onto the slippery sheets of ice. When no vein of splitting ice appeared, and there was no alarming sound of cracking, Kale grew in confidence. They crossed the ice carefully, but quickly, praying the ice would hold out. Kale watched where she placed her feet, as any bad step could cause a fatal slip, sending her crashing into an icy tomb.

They made it to the middle of the lake when a small cracking noise sent shivers up Kale's spine. Leon froze in mid step and checked the ground around him. Kale looked down at her feet and was horrified to see a split in the ice. She tried to shift her weight off the area, but the ice protested louder, groaning beneath her feet.

"Leon?" she cried, her panic rising.

"Try to take a big step away from that spot," Leon urged.

Kale's heart pounded inside her chest, and she carefully took a large step away, balancing on her toes to try and make herself lighter. The ice groaned even louder, and tiny slivers started to break through. Kale watched, horrified, as a crack split the ice and ran haphazardly beneath her feet. She paused for a second and the world seemed to stand still. Looking up at Leon, fear coursed through her veins as she braced herself. They locked eyes for a split second before the ice snapped and a silent scream escaped Kale's lips. She plunged into the depths, the cold stunning her body, so much so, that her brain didn't allow her to try and swim.

As if in slow motion, Kale watched the surface of the water grow farther and farther away, taking with it the precious air that her lungs cried out for. The water felt so cold on her skin, it almost burned. As more of the frigid water put distance between her and the air, her head started to grow fuzzy, and she saw red spots appear before her eyes.

Just as she was starting to black out, Kale distinctly heard a splash, somewhere far above her head. Then she felt a tug at the collar of her dress, and slowly, she began to rise. The dark waters swirled about her, willing her to sink back into their cold depths. Then her head broke the surface, and Kale snapped back into consciousness. She gulped up a lungful of air as she was dragged over the edge.

Kale then had to choke it back out, spitting out a stomach full of water with it. Leon lay gasping on the ice beside her, and Kale crawled weakly away from the hole. She choked on some more water, and then threw up her stomach contents onto the ice. When she could breathe normally again, she sighed, and rested her cheek against the cold pond surface, trying to stop her head from spinning.

"Thanks," was all she could manage, hardly enough under the circumstances.

Leon acknowledged her but shook from the exertion and the cold and Kale knew he risked his life for her in his weakened state. His bare chest caused her to shiver.

He must be freezing wearing nothing but that tattered tunic.

"Now we're even," he said weakly, coughing.

Kale smiled and nodded. "That was really close."

Leon looked at her questioning. "Close to what? The ice fell through. Pretty much, the worst happened."

Kale smiled weakly. "You know what I mean."

Leon grinned and gestured to the ice. "If we crawl to the other end like this, the ice may hold up better."

Kale nodded. She did not trust her legs anymore anyway; their sensation had remained in the deep, cold waters.

Slower than she could imagine, they started to inch across the ice, pausing whenever there was any indication of breakage. After what seemed like an eternity, Kale and Leon reached the end of the frozen lake.

Kale crawled off the ice and sprawled herself out on the solid ground. Her soaked body shook so badly, she feared she could not go on.

"I d-d-d-on't think I c-c-can make it," she managed. "I'm t-t-too c-c-cold,"

When she turned around, Leon was already trekking away from the lake. Kale pulled herself up slowly and reached out her frozen limb towards him.

"Wait!" she called. "C- c-c-can't we just rest here?"

Leon did not turn. "Look!" he said.

Kale followed where his finger directed and spotted an old, run-down shack. She stared at it warily, but there was no evidence that anyone had been there in years.

Leon headed towards the house. "We will freeze to death out here, especially now that we're wet. We can hopefully warm up and rest for the night."

Kale nodded and dragged herself away from the icy bed. She didn't really like the idea of hanging around an abandoned house longer than she had to, but the ground had only offered her a frozen grave.

CHAPTER 33

W hen they arrived at the shack, Leon hesitantly pushed open the door. It swayed inwards on rusty hinges, revealing a dark, but strangely tidy interior. The inside did not look at all like the outside. Leon stepped through the door, and Kale glanced nervously around the odd room. The interior of the shack was small but cozy, as snuggly fit boarding on the walls served to keep the frigid night winds out. The floor looked as if it was made of oak, dark, and colorful. The center was adorned with an old, faded rug, woven and tied in a spiral fashion. In one corner, there was a small bed. Kale gaped at it. Her whole life she had slept on hay pallets, so this was something of wonder. It had a small quilt over a sheet stuffed with mosses, and when Kale sat on it, she sank into it like a cloud.

On one wall, there was a hearth, with some dry logs piled next to it. Inside the chimney sat a small kettle and pot on the rod. A neatly carved table rested in the corner, alongside a small log rocker.

Leon spotted a sword leaned in the corner and he immediately replaced it with the soldier's sword, hanging the new one in his belt. He also adorned a long cloak he found hanging over the end of the bed and unwrapped Kale's shawl from his shoulders. Kale watched him for a couple of minutes as he threw some logs into the hearth to start a fire. When a warm glow arose from the tinder, Kale finally felt sensation return to her limbs. Then Kale's eyes began to droop from exhaustion and recent warmth. Before long, she dropped off into a deep sleep. She drifted in and out of a dreamless slumber, but did not wake once during the night.

Kale's eyes opened to morning sunlight. She sat up and yawned, thankful for the rest. Suddenly, a chill ran down Kale's spine, and she froze, her muscles tensing with fear. Something was not right. Kale leaned over and was about to wake up Leon, when a hand pressed over her mouth. Kale's heart quickened, her blood surging to her brain, as she felt sharp cold steel against her neck.

A voice whispered behind her. "You are going to wake up your buddy quietly. Any sudden movements from either of you, and I slit your throat."

Kale nodded slightly, straining her eyes around to try and see who it was. She could tell by the voice that the speaker was a young man. The hand was removed, but Kale could feel the knifepoint pricking into the side of her neck. Slowly, she bent towards Leon and tapped him on the shoulder. As she bent over, she noticed that a dead buck had been laid at the doorstep, an arrow wound in its head. Leon's eyes blinked open, and though he was still tired, it took him only a second to assess the situation.

Jumping to his feet, Leon grabbed his new sword from behind his cloak and trained it on the intruder. Kale still could not see who it was, but she could detect no fear behind Leon's eyes. Whoever this was, he was not The Shadow.

Her captor spoke. "Drop the sword or I kill her."

Kale looked to Leon, begging him to run and save himself, but he waved that off with a shake of his head.

"You kill her and I kill you. A small dagger is no match for a sword," Leon said.

"I do not care if I should die, but your friend here would die with me." He accentuated his point by driving the dagger a little harder into Kale's neck, causing her to gasp.

Leon scowled, his anger evident in his features. His pride stung from being forced to surrender. Without letting his gaze drift from the intruder, he placed his sword on the ground.

"Good man," the intruder admitted, "now we can talk." He let go of Kale, and striding over to Leon's dropped sword, added it to his belt, which, Kale noticed, also had the soldier's sword strung from it. The young man had dark brown hair and a tall, well-built figure. Kale was astounded by the youthful look of his features. He looked as if he may be 18, making him two years older than Leon, and three years older than she. Kale wondered what his story was, to be wandering around in the mountains like this, alone. Kale watched him carefully as he strode over to his buck and patted it on the shoulder.

"I left my shack to hunt, as I was running low on meat, and lo and behold, when I come back, you are here. Please explain why you invaded my house."

Leon was still tense, his eyes fixed on the unexpected guest. Kale could see that these two were not hitting it off well.

She was convinced that this youth meant no harm, and so she went into an account of their tale. "We were running from soldiers, when we nearly drowned in that lake while trying to cross it. Weak and frozen, we then stumbled across this cabin, which we thought was deserted, so we decided to stay the night," she paused, trying to look empathetic. "We truly are sorry if we disturbed your home."

Leon snorted, clearly not trusting the youth. Kale didn't blame him; he had reason to be wary, but she did wish he would loosen up.

The young man seemed to soften at Kale's sincere story, and he sighed. "It is no trouble. Sorry for using my dagger on you. It's just that I don't normally get visitors, especially armed ones."

Kale smiled. "No harm done. My name is Kale."

He smiled. "I'm Colum."

Leon huffed. And Kale grinned. "He's Leon." Kale thought she saw Colum tense at his name, but she waved it off as a trick of the light.

"So why are you out here, Colum?"

He brushed a lock of dark brown hair from his face. "Well, I don't see why I should lie to you. I am running, too."

Kale gasped. "From whom?"

Colum glanced into the fire. "My father, Brecken. He is king of the neighboring country to here. He went mad and thought his own sons were plotting against him, so he ordered to have us killed. Sadly, my younger brother didn't make it, but I escaped in time. That was almost two years ago, and I have been hiding in these mountains ever since."

Kale's heart was filled with sincere compassion. "I am truly sorry to hear this," she admitted.

Colum would not hear of it. "I can deal with it. I don't' mind the life of adventure, hunting and survival. It is quite exciting."

Kale shook her head. "I don't know how you can do that. We have only been running for a short time, and I don't know how you can bear it…"

Colum let out a sigh. "You are forced to like it after a while. So, why exactly are you running?"

Kale began, "We are running because we—"

Leon grunted loudly, and Kale shot him an annoyed glance.

Leon gave her the look. "We don't know if we can trust him." He glared at Colum, who returned the cold stare.

"Boys, calm down!" Kale interrupted. "Leon, I'm sure Colum means no harm," she said, glancing back at Colum with a smile on her face.

Colum smirked at this, but Leon boiled. "You know, you can't fall in love with every boy you meet in the woods."

The tactless comment stung. Kale bit her lip, fighting back the urge to lash out. Clearly Leon had not taken the news about Matthew as well as he had seemed to. Flushed, she faced Leon. "So that's what this is about?"

"It's not that. I'm sorry. I just learned from experience that you can't trust everyone you meet…"

Kale stared at him through narrow eyes. "What kind of girl do you think I am? Maybe I shouldn't have trusted you then, should I?" she said, her eyes brimming with tears.

She looked to him for a response. His lips parted, but no words came. Colum remained quiet too, feeling uncomfortable in the awkward situation.

Kale glanced once more at them both and ran from the house. Her bare feet slapped against the snowy, cold stones, and her dress whipped around her bare legs. She glanced blindly around the barren valley through her tears and headed towards a large boulder against the mountain wall.

Her hands scrabbled for a hold; the rough, frozen surface was hard on her feet. Near the top, her leg slipped, and her knee scraped against the rock, leaving a trail of blood. Her heart beat wildly, as she grabbed a nearby branch from a scraggly tree and pulled herself to the surface of the boulder. Lying with her cheek against the cold rock top, she let the tears roll from her lids. She waited there until the pounding in her heart resided.

Crawling farther away from the edge, she curled up and rested her chin on her knees. Her mind was numb, flowing with cold thoughts of injustice.

Humiliated beyond belief, Kale buried her face in her hands. She sucked in air and tried to scream, but only a sob escaped her lips. A lone bird trilled the solemn tune of winter, the rays of sun doing nothing to warm the bleak, cold peaks of the mountains.

"May I join you?" A voice carried up to her.

Kale glanced over the edge of the boulder and spotted Colum. His dark brown hair was whipping around his face in the gusty wind.

At least Colum came to try and make things right.

Normally Kale would have welcomed company, but at the moment she didn't want to be near anyone. When Colum saw her recede over the edge without any response, he began to climb the rock anyway.

CHAPTER

K ale heard him scaling the steep rock face, but paid him no attention when he appeared over the edge. Colum walked over to her and sat down, resting one arm over his knee. A million words ran through Kale's mind, but nothing came out.

Troubled, Colum glanced at her. "I am sorry for what happened. I guess I should not have asked about your past," he said.

Kale shook her head. "No, it's fine," she sighed. "I shouldn't have reacted like that."

Waiting for her to continue, Colum didn't say anything; watching her responses carefully.

"And I am sorry for Leon's behavior, too. We have been through a lot, and he is entitled to his opinion, I guess," Kale admitted.

Colum's lips tightened and he squeezed his eyes shut. "I was probably egging him on. I'm sorry." Kale knew this was part of it.

"I am someone you can trust though," he said hesitantly, and she nodded slowly.

Looking into his eyes, begging for agreed secrecy, Kale confessed, "We are running for the very same reason you are."

Colum looked at her, confused.

"Leon is the son of Zorack, the king of this country. He is running from him as well. We also have reason to believe that Zorack and your father have been working together on something."

Colum thought for a moment, and then said, "It's possible, but what?" He scratched his head and then mumbled more to himself than to Kale, "What are those two up to?" Then he glanced at her. "So why are you out here then?"

Kale sighed. "Long story, but to summarize it, I was kind of pulled into it unintentionally until I killed someone, by accident. Now I am in for the long run."

Colum raised a brow at her, but she just grinned.

"Tell you the story another time," Kale said.

He nodded and then motioned towards the cottage. "We should go. I locked your buddy in the house, so he wouldn't get out here before I did."

Kale was surprised at this, but Colum was already climbing down the rock face again. She briefly wondered what was going on between Colum and Leon.

When they were back on the ground again, Kale walked quickly to the cottage, eager to feel the warmth of the fire, for her fingers and nose were nearly frost bitten. She could hear pounding inside the house's walls, Leon's shouts just reaching her.

Colum took out a key and slid it into the lock. "It only locks from the outside," he explained. When the door clicked, Colum stepped back as it flew open, thrust on its hinges by Leon's pummeling fists. He charged out of the house and shoved Colum—hard.

Kale saw that he was fuming mad and she rushed between them. She placed a hand on each of their chests, trying to hold them apart. Leon brushed her aside and tried to get at Colum. Kale grabbed Leon's shoulders and pulled him back.

"Stop it!" she said through gritted teeth. "What has gotten into you?"

Leon turned and glared angrily into her pleading eyes for a long moment.

Slowly, he settled. "He locked me in the house, I thought he was going to run off with you, or go get the guards. Or leave me in there forever."

Colum laughed. "With the buck I just caught? No way."

Kale confronted Colum, defending Leon. "Apologize. You scared him."

Colum grinned. "Oh. I scared the little boy?" he chuckled.

Leon growled and tried to leap at him again, knocking Colum over. They started to pummel each other with their fists. Unsure of what else to do, Kale screamed—the highest, loudest shriek any girl could manage. Both boys froze, Leon with his teeth in Colum's arm, and Colum with his hand wrapped in Leon's hair.

"Stop it, right now! Both of you apologize, or I will lock you in that house together with a note on the front that says who you are, and why you are running, for when the guards catch up to us here!"

The boys could tell she was serious. They untangled themselves and stood side by side, looking as guilty as two boys that just stole their mother's fresh pie. She glanced at each of them with the air of a schoolteacher.

"Now say you're sorry," she prompted.

Neither boy moved.

"Say you're sorry!" she said sternly.

Leon and Colum turned to each other and sputtered sorry in unison.

"Now shake hands," she demanded, hands on hips.

Leon grabbed Colum's hand and they shook briefly.

"That's better. Now, let's go inside, and I'll see if I can't make a meal of that beautiful buck Colum just brought in, hmm?" Kale declared before strutting towards the cottage.

Colum and Leon shared a brief look, shrugged their shoulders, and followed her inside.

CHAPTER 36

They found Kale staring sadly at the dead buck. "As much as I would like to taste meat, I do not have the heart to skin such a beautiful creature," she sighed.

Taking the hint, Colum and Leon grabbed the buck and pulled it outside.

Kale looked over the shelves and found some vegetables and dried herbs to help flavor the stew. She set some water over the fire and stoked it to help it boil. When Leon and Colum came back in, their arms loaded with fresh meat, Kale smiled and directed them to appropriate piles. Organs and bones would be buried to keep the scavengers away. The fattiest meats would be eaten right away for energy.

They piled the leftover meat on another part of the table; it would be dried later, so they would have food for travel. The fat was stripped from the meat to be made into oil and a type of meal, or gruel. Kale dumped the meat set aside for their supper into the pot and began to stir.

"It will be best to use up as much as we can, so if we need to leave quickly, little will be wasted. We will hardly be able to bring all of it, so best to use it up. We should also try to dry as much as possible, so we can pack it," she pointed out.

Leon agreed. "Colum and I will make the meat into meal. We can set the other meat out to dry once the sun gets higher." Colum nodded in approval, and they all got to work.

After one long hour, a steam carrying a thick, sweet smell wafted from the pot. Kale's stomach growled as she lifted the cauldron from the fire. Setting it on the table beside a lump of newly ground meat, she grabbed some wooden bowls and began to dish out the food. She could see the boys drooling as the lumpy stew poured from the spoon into their bowls. Once everyone had gotten a serving, they immediately dug in. For an entire fifteen minutes, no one talked. There were only the satisfied sounds of hungry bellies being filled. Leon ate like a mad beast, much to Colum's disgust, but he guessed that Kale and he had not eaten for a while and ignored it.

When the pot was licked, they sat back in their chairs, patting their stomachs.

"That was amazing," Colum said, through half shut eyes. "Best I've had since home."

Leon nodded in agreement, and Kale smiled. "If we pack enough of this, I will make more once we are on the road."

Colum raised a hand. "Wait, I know you have been talking a lot about, 'on the road' but what makes you think I am going to give you my meat or actually go with you?"

Kale sat silent for a moment. She had only assumed he would join them.

"Well, the guards are at the foot of the mountains and you will probably be found," she said.

Colum shook his head and said, "The king will not lose more guards by sending them into the mountains. To him, that is a pointless and assured loss. They will wait at the foot of the Fray, in hopes that we will return."

Kale sighed. "Whew. That gives us a few more days to make preparations. I still feel antsy sitting around here like old ducks. We need to get going! There is a mystery to be solved," she stated, her finger in the air.

Colum and Leon stared at Kale strangely. "When did you become so chipper?" Leon asked.

Colum chuckled. "Yes, and what mystery?"

Kale looked at them and saw that they were serious. She took a deep breath and tried to calm down. "Sorry, it's just that this is the first time I haven't been scared for my life in a while, and it feels great. And as for mystery, I am trying to figure out what those two kings are really up to! There must be more."

She only got blank stares in return. "Don't either of you want to get your kingdoms back?"

Leon and Colum said nothing.

"Ugh, why are you boys so boring? What else would you have us do? Sit around here in the mountains until we grow grey and shriveled? Doesn't a mystery sound so much more exciting?"

Still, there was no response.

Then Leon broke the silence, "I think we should calm down and think rationally about this. We have just escaped from death." He glanced at Kale. "Numerous times, and you want to go back out there?" Leon asked incredulously. Then somewhat quieter he gestured to the cabin. "We are safe here. Our fathers are corrupted, but we cannot set things right. What can three kids do against two kings and their countries? We have to accept that this is the way things are."

Kale looked down. Something in the back of her mind said that it would be right to try and fix what was broken.

"You are two big strong boys. I am a girl—too weak to handle myself out here alone, remember? Why is it that only I now have the courage to do what I know is right?" Kale saw Colum shift uncomfortably, and she added in for good measure, "And I don't even have a kingdom to fight for!"

Leon looked down, and Colum tried to avoid eye contact.

Kale went on, "Why don't we disguise ourselves and do some snooping around the cities nearby? I mean, it can't hurt to try." She gestured around the room. "We can stay close to here, and if our cover is blown, we can disappear into the mountains again."

Leon sighed. "Well, if you insist, I don't think it would hurt to try it for a time…"

Kale clapped her hands together and smiled.

"Colum?" Leon asked, glancing over.

Colum nodded. "Sounds alright to me."

"Then it's settled," Kale said. "We can leave once the meat is dried."

Leon gave her a wry smile.

Colum grabbed a chunk of shredded meat, and Leon joined him. They headed outside to dry it. Kale gathered the meat they had ground and began to mush it together with some dried berries she found on the shelves. She then took the fat the boys had skinned off the animal and used her hands to work it into the mixture. Satisfied with her work, Kale then sealed the meal in cloth, wrapping it tightly for later use.

Sweating from her work, Kale stepped outside and found the boys laying out the last chunks of meat. They had pieces staked on bushes, tree branches, and stones. The day was growing old, and Kale could see that the work had taxed Leon. They headed inside together, and after stoking the fire, they sat and stared into its embers.

Coals were glowing in the depths of the fire, flickering like precious gems. The shifting and lilting orangey-red flames cast flickering shadows throughout the room, mesmerizing Kale. A deep thrum started beside her, and Kale realized that Colum had started to sing. His voice was deep, and rich, filled with a kind of mysterious quality that caused Kale to dream of epic battles long ago. His body vibrated beside her and she leaned against him, closing her eyes to listen. As the last rays of sun left, Colum's voice seemed to comfort her.

Over the mountains, and shallow plains,
We will travel, travel a far.
The glowing lanterns, they blazed with light,
And cast no shadows,
On our paths that night.

Here, Kale was surprised to pick up the higher and more melodious voice that could only belong to Leon. Together, Kale noted, they sounded mystic, haunting, beautiful.

The old wolf cried, to his friend the moon,
His broken voice, a lonely tune.
They carried to us, and broke the night.
The shadows grew long, and filled hearts with fright.
We scattered from, our way ahead.
I never found them, my friends again.
Now to this day, I tell this story
Of those misty mountains, and the lone wolf.

Kale's lids slowly closed as the last notes drifted away. She thought blissfully to herself how happy she was that this had all been a dream. She would wake up at home.

CHAPTER 36

W hen sunlight brought Kale to her senses, she shivered as she realized the quilt had slipped away. She spotted Colum sleeping in the rocker and Leon on the floor. She smiled briefly and then got quietly out of bed. Kale tossed a log on the evening's coals, and when a flame started, she put some water in a pot to boil. Searching through the shelves, she found some oats.

After the water warmed, Kale put the oats in the pot along with a small amount of honey, stirring the mixture slowly. As sweet smelling steam started to rise from the food, Kale collected bowls and placed them out on the table. Tipping the warm pot carefully, she dished out the oatmeal, scraping every clump out of the pot. When breakfast was ready, Kale gently shook Colum and Leon awake, and they sat down to eat. The boys were pleasantly surprised to find a good, warm meal on the table.

"By the looks of this, you've been up for a while," Leon started.

Kale shook her head. "It did not take long to make."

Colum smiled and downed his bowl. "Well, it is the best breakfast I've had in a while."

Kale smiled over her bowl. "Thank you."

In a couple of minutes, all the bowls were emptied and licked clean. When the dishes were put away, they went outside together and collected the dried meat to bring back inside. Carefully they started packing it in cases that would be easy to carry. These bundles were then added to the pile, along with the meal, and some other necessities. Besides food, they decided to bring a small cooking pot, a flint and steel, the weapons Colum had collected and stored in his cottage, some water canteens, and three of Colum's cloaks to shield against the weather.

Leon surveyed the pile with satisfaction. "I believe we have everything we need."

Colum nodded. "Yes, it looks like it. We have water and food to last us a while, cloaks to keep us warm, and weapons to protect us."

Kale smiled. "Now we just need a disguise."

Colum nodded. "I was thinking I could pose as your father, and you two could be brothers. I would be a widower, and we could be traveling through town looking for work."

Leon's brow crinkled in thought, but he eventually agreed, "I think that would work. Kale could cut her hair, and we both could find new clothes. You wouldn't be recognized anyway, Colum, if you have been living here for a while."

Colum nodded. "Just over a year, and I think time will have changed my appearance enough to avoid suspicion."

The boys smiled in satisfaction, but Kale was troubled. She had not cut her hair for as long as she could remember, and shaving it all off made her feel sentimental.

Colum shifted through his chest full of clothes and produced two outfits that looked about Kale and Leon's sizes. He also managed to find pairs of boots for each of them. Colum and Leon left the cottage to give Kale privacy as she changed. Kale shed her simple brown dress and scarf, looking at them sadly as she placed them on the floor. Binding her chest tightly with a strip of cloth, she then carefully slipped into the pants and shirt Colum had given her.

The fabric was tough and somewhat scratchy, but it was thick, and Kale knew she would be thankful for the protection it would provide from the cold night winds. She strapped a small leather pouch around her waist, which served to hold the loose shirt closer to her, while still holding her share of the coins she, Leon, and Colum possessed. Carefully, she slipped her sheathed dagger into the pouch strap. Looking at her reflection in the water basin, Kale briefly relished how bold she now looked. She glanced over the long, chestnut braid hanging down her shoulder, and her heart quickened at the thought of chopping it off. She stared at her reflection, trying to cement the image into her mind until Leon pounded on the door.

"You done in there? We are getting cold out here," he complained.

Kale muttered an apology and ran over to let them in. They rushed in, shivering, and Kale stepped outside to let them change.

After a couple of minutes, they opened the door. Kale surveyed the boys; both had new clothes, a big improvement for Leon, and this made them look astoundingly different. Each of them had a dagger, Leon had the sword strapped to his waist, and Colum had his bow over his shoulder. They stared at her too, wry smiles plastered on their faces.

Kale noticed them and blushed. "What?"

The boys chuckled.

"You would make a good boy." Leon smiled at her. "Now we just need to cut your hair."

Kale looked down while Colum got out his dagger. Knowing there was no way around it, Kale went over the water basin and wet her hair. Pulling her dripping braid from the bowl, she came over beside Colum and waited expectantly for what she should do.

Colum surveyed her dark, wet hair and stated, "Could you bend over and flip your hair over your head?" Kale obeyed, and Colum grabbed it up in his hand. He carefully placed the dagger edge near the nape of her neck and started to slice through the thick strands of wet hair. Kale winced as she felt her hair part beneath the dagger's edge. She closed her eyes until Colum was done. When she stood, she felt bare, as though she had lost her shawl, and not to mention lighter. Her head felt as if it would float away if it had not been attached to her neck.

She looked and saw a thick mat of wet hair in Colum's hand. Kale was partially stunned. It looked as if he was holding a small wet squirrel. He placed it on the table, and then worked at her hair some more, until it was all even. Kale rushed over to the water basin and looked in. She gasped; staring back at her with mild interest was a young boy. He had wet, chestnut hair and a strong look about him. His eyes said that he had seen much in the last couple of years. Kale looked for the innocence and delicacy of a young girl, but found neither. When she turned around, she found the two boys slack jawed.

She smiled a little, and Leon shook his head. "I would never have recognized you; this will definitely work as a disguise." Colum nodded in agreement.

Kale bowed. "Why, thank you." Grabbing a dark green cloak from the pile, she donned it and pulled up the hood. "I am ready for adventure!"

Leon chuckled and put on a dark blue cloak, handing the black one to Colum. They looked at each other in satisfaction and growing excitement for one more moment.

Then, checking that everything was ready, Colum said, "We need to get a good last night's rest here. Time for bed."

Kale reclined on the bed, pulling the comforting green fabric around her and watched sleepily as Leon and Colum settled down as well. They wanted to get an early start, so they went to bed ready to leave in a moment's notice. The sun grew red outside, and Kale's blood flowed in anticipation for the morning.

CHAPTER

They started the trek bright and early. Kale silently thanked God that the winds were not too rough. At high altitudes, there had been stories of travelers toppled from the peaks by the winds or lost forever in large, unexpected blizzards and fogs. Kale shuddered at what might lie beyond the clouds and was glad that Leon and Colum were there for protection. Even though it was unlikely they should come across other travelers, the threesome travelled with their hoods shadowing their faces.

As Kale watched, the peaks grew colder and more unfriendly with every step away from the cottage. Winds whipped around the stones and frozen ground, forbidding any life to exist. Kale shivered and drew her cloak closer to her for warmth. The path became icy, and the snow piles by the road they followed grew larger.

The air became thinner, and all three travelers found themselves short of breath. Gray clouds rolled over the skies, covering any visible blue. Mists swirled around the mountains, hiding the jagged peaks from view. Their forms began weaving lazily through the air. Kale didn't notice the vapors until they started to block the path from view. Kale looked worriedly around, pushing down the fear rising in her stomach.

The fog grew thicker until Kale could barely see her own hand in front of her face. Leon and Colum became only dim forms ahead of her, slowly drawing farther and farther from her. Growing worried, Kale ran to catch up with them, but they moved so quickly. When she finally reached their gloomy forms, instead of the boys, a large rock came into view. Its jagged surface so devoid of any life that it almost mocked Kale.

She panicked, her heart thumping in her chest. Thinking worriedly about the stories of lost souls, she swung her head around franticly, searching the clouded landscape, but to no avail. The fog had grown so thick she couldn't make out any form at all. It seemed as if everything she had ever known had been completely erased. She cried out, calling Leon and Colum over and over again, but her voice became lost to stones' deaf ears.

Kale ran onward, blindly, trying to catch up to them. Frozen rain started to fall, and it stung her face and eyes, causing her short hair to freeze and her face to redden. It was so cold that it burned her flesh on contact. Just then a blizzard started, one flake at first, but then buckets falling all at once, swirling in the growing wind.

The snow grew deep, and she became tired from trying to move through it. Holding an arm in front of her face, Kale pushed on until she felt that she could go no farther. To her, it seemed to have been hours since she first lost sight of the boys. The snow washed even the mountain walls from view, and in all directions Kale could only see a monotonous expanse of bleak white. Exhausted and hopeless, Kale leaned against a sole rock, sinking softly into the snow.

She could not even guess what direction to walk, if she could gather the energy to try. She looked up at the sky to find the sun, but even the sky had been washed out. The sun was totally blocked from view. She knew Leon and Colum must be far away by now, her blind path taking her farther from them. A single frozen tear trickled down her face, and she allowed her body to collapse silently onto the frozen ground. Overcome by a sudden exhaustion, she watched as the world slowly dimmed, and then went dark . . . not even noticing the lack of feeling in her limbs.

CHAPTER 38

E verything was warm and glowing red. Somewhere in the distance, wood was softly snapping and cracking. Someone was calling her name. It got louder and louder, as the pain in her skin grew stronger. Kale gasped and blinked open her eyes. She was lying on a cloak-covered ground by a small fire. On two sides and above them were walls of rock, lit up and orangey in the fire's glow. Kale recognized Colum's shape leaning over her. When he saw that she was alert, he sighed and smiled.

"Whew," he said, looking over at Leon. "She's alive. Frostbitten, but alive." Colum looked back at her, as Leon walked over. They both leaned over her; Kale's vision was blurry, and it distorted them. She blinked to clear her eyes.

"How did you . . . ?" she winced at the pain in her cracked lips, and sighing, she lied back.

Leon finished for her, "We saw that you had fallen back, so we searched for you. We had almost given up when the fog suddenly cleared, and we found you unconscious in the snow," Leon finished.

Colum continued, "We decided to make camp for the night and found an overhang to take shelter under. The blizzard missed this part of the mountain."

Kale nodded and looked over at the fire they had built. The warmth radiating from its glowing center was comforting, a nice change from the freezing temperatures in the mountains. Kale tried to shift into a sitting position, but Leon laid a hand on her shoulder. "Don't move. Your skin is not yet used to the warmer temperatures again."

She licked the inside of her dry mouth with distaste. "Water?" Kale asked, trying to use minimal words. Colum nodded and brought over a canteen. Lifting her head a bit, he let some trickle down her throat. She gulped it thankfully, trying to rid herself of the taste. When Kale was satisfied, she moved her face away from the nozzle, and Colum put the cap back on. Overcome with sleepiness, Kale started to nod off again.

THE BOYS WATCHED AS SHE SLOWLY WENT BACK TO SLEEP before they went to sit by the fire again. Colum threw a log on the pile, sending a cascade of sparks into the sky around the overhang as the wood snapped and popped in response. Leon sat by the fire solemnly, staring into the flames. Colum noticed that he was tense and tried to find something to say.

"I'm sorry for how I was earlier. I guess I was kind of jealous of you, being in a similar situation and yet not having loss like I have. My own brother. But it was wrong of me," Colum admitted.

Leon looked down at his hands. "Thanks, I guess. I'm sorry, too. It doesn't look good for us to be fighting the whole way, but don't expect us to be best friends."

"Of course." Colum nodded, offering a hand. "But we can be partners, right?"

Leon hesitated, and then smiled. "I guess so," he said, grasping the outstretched hand. "Partners."

CHAPTER

T he snow abated some since the night and Kale woke to a warm
sun on her face. The boys were packing up camp and preparing to
continue. Kale rolled onto her side and watched quietly.

Colum noticed that she was awake, and he smiled. "Hey sleepy head, it's
almost noon. Do you think you can keep moving?"

Kale was surprised at how long she slept and she tried to sit up. Her legs
protested from not being used for so long, so she stretched. The warmth
seeped back into her limbs. She was delighted to find that she still had a full
range of motion. After standing and moving around a bit, she grabbed her
pack. "I'm alive and well, so we should get moving. I'm pretty sure I can
walk alright."

She picked her cloak off the ground from where she was sleeping and
dusting it off, she put it around her shoulders.

Leon got a pack, and rummaging through it, pulled out a strip of dry
meat. Sticking it in his mouth, he tossed the pack to Colum, who expertly
caught it and pulled out another couple of strips. He tossed one to Kale,
who looked over it for a moment before she stuck it in her mouth. The
meat was tough and dry, but it was sweet. Kale admitted to herself that it
made a tolerable meal.

Without pausing to finish chewing the meat, the boys collected the
packs and started off. Kale was careful to stay close this time; she watched
the skies suspiciously for any signs of fog. Then she noticed that the boys
had taken all of the packs, and there was nothing for her to carry. She
worried about Leon tiring too quickly under the weight of their supplies.

"Leon, let me carry one of your bags," Kale said, coming up beside him.

Leon shook his head. "I'm fine. I don't want you getting lost again, *with* our food." He smiled, joking. "And just last night you were weak and unconscious."

Kale jogged a bit to keep up with his quick pace. "I am better now. What about your wound? Can you hold up much longer? I don't want to have to carry *you* again."

At this, Colum turned around. "You're injured?" he asked in surprise.

Leon started to deny it, but deciding better of it, he sighed and nodded. "It is not that bad."

Colum looked at him with interest. "And she *carried* you away?"

Leon smiled. "I couldn't believe it either."

Colum put his bags down and walked over. "Let me see it. I have not had much medical experience, but my mother was a healer, so I know something about the art."

Leon looked hesitant, but Kale came over. "Come on, put away your pride for a minute, please? It would be good if someone could help you with that. I mean, we don't know what else to do," she reminded him.

Leon shook his head. "I don't need help. Nature heals in her due course," he said stubbornly.

Kale stared at him in exasperation. "I don't need any more stress in my life, okay? Why can't you get some help, so I can stop worrying about you?"

Colum chuckled to himself, but Leon became frustrated.

"Fine, Fine! I'll get it looked at!" He walked over to Colum and plopped down on a stone. Pulling back his cloak and shirt, he revealed the bandage on his shoulder.

Colum knelt down beside him and unwrapped the fabric. When he reached the layer of leaves he grimaced, pulling the greenish brown mush away from Leon's flesh. "Whose idea was this? His arm could have rotted away with the leaves!" Colum rebuked.

Kale looked down in embarrassment. "We didn't want the wound to grow back attached to the fabric..." she started.

But Colum just shook his head. "Then you use a fabric with a tight weave."

He focused on the shoulder, which started bleeding again, and slinging a canteen from around his neck, he unscrewed the cap. Placing the nozzle near Leon's shoulder, he poured the water gently down the wounded area, cleaning it of the foul smelling leaves and new blood.

Leon sharply sucked in air and huffed as the water touched the wound. Colum went a little slower. When the wound was clear, he stared at it in awe. "I have never seen someone survive a gash this bad. And here I thought you were healthy . . . but just grumpy."

Kale smirked.

Colum looked over the six-inch slash and tried to guess how deep it was. Shaking his head, he sighed, "Must have been some fight. I guess it's still pretty sore,"

Leon nodded.

"It is too deep to close easily on its own, and it just reopened. Just removing the bandage causes it to bleed. Nature's not going to heal this one," Colum said sadly.

Leon stayed quiet, but Kale jumped in, with worry in her voice becoming evident, "What can we do then?"

"Well, we can leave it and see what happens, but he might lose his arm to infection from being open that long, or," he paused, "if Leon says it's okay, I could cauterize it to prevent infection and seal it up. It would be sore for the first couple of days, but after that it would heal faster than if it were left open..."

Leon stared at Colum, clearly not trusting him for such a procedure.

Kale paled at the thought. "Could you? I mean, it is better in the end, right?" she asked, nervously.

Leon chuckled a bit. "You sound as if he just gave me the death sentence. I am not worried about the pain involved. I am more worried that he will mess it up or something."

He stared pointedly at Colum who held up his hands in mock surrender. "Hey, it's your choice. I assure you, I will try my very best not to ruin your arm, but if you do nothing now, you are sure to have a bigger mess."

They stared at each other for a while until Leon finally nodded. "Fine, You can do it tonight when we make camp." He ripped a bit of fabric off their food sack and re-tied his shoulder. Shrugging his shirt back on and pulling his cloak into place, he tossed Kale one of the bags he had been carrying. "Here's the bag you sorely wanted. Hope you're happy."

Kale just missed being hit with the heavy sack and she retrieved it from the ground. Smiling, she picked it up and murmured to herself, "Immensely."

CHAPTER 40

They walked on through the mountains, reaching higher altitudes with each step. Kale, tiring from carrying the pack after only a few minutes, focused on the trail, determined not to complain. At around noon, they broke and stopped for lunch, only briefly to share some water and more dried meat. Then Colum led them on through the mountain pass. By late afternoon, Kale's muscles burned. Her arms and fingers cramped from holding up the bag. Her lungs felt as if they were on fire, trying to take in the thin air of the mountaintop.

Kale watched thankfully as the sun finally disappeared behind the peaks and the world grew dark. Colum found a small rock outcrop and plopped his bag down. Leon dumped his on the ground as well, and they went out to look for firewood. Kale stiffly set her bag down and sinking to the ground, she sighed. The boys were back in a couple of minutes, their arms loaded with wood. Wood was scarce at this altitude, and when they did find a lone tree, it was like gold.

It didn't take long to get a fire going. The wood was dry and soon a warm glow emanated from within. Kale took off her cloak and laid it by the fire. Thankfully, she flopped onto it, edging as close to the flames as she dared. Rubbing her hands together, she massaged warmth and life back into them. Stretching out on her side, she warmed her front, and then her back, relishing in the feeling she regained in her muscles. Her stomach rumbled, and grabbing the small cooking pot from their bags, she melted some snow in it. Seeing what she was doing, Leon passed her some of the meat and dried berries they brought.

Kale smiled and put them in the pot. Gently she placed the pot into the fire and watched as it began to boil. Carefully unsheathing her dagger, Kale used it to stir the stew. When she was satisfied, she used the dagger to pick up the hot kettle by the handle and placed it to the side. Leon and Colum edged closer, bowls in hand. Kale smiled and wrapped her shirt around the edge of the pot to pour some for each. Getting out her own bowl, she took a serving for herself. When they had finished firsts, the boys helped themselves to the rest while Kale cleaned the pot and her bowl.

After everything was packed, they sat around the fire for a couple of minutes in a satisfied silence.

Colum stood and walked over to the fire. "Kale, may I use your dagger?"

Kale nodded and handed it to him. He pushed the tip of the blade into the coals and left the dagger there.

"Kale, go get a bowl of snow," Leon said quietly.

Kale nodded, a knot twisting in her stomach at the realization of what was to be done. She scooped some of the cold white snow from the ground outside their shelter into a bowl and packed it in, adding as much as she could. Walking back into the cave, she placed the bowl beside Colum. Leon had undone his cape and laid it on the ground near the fire. He pulled his arm out of his shirt, and then shrugged it lower around his waist before undoing the bandage. Colum pulled out the dagger and glanced at it briefly before placing it back in the flames. He distractedly motioned for Kale to move the snow over beside Leon. Leon pressed a clump of the dripping ice to his shoulder, wincing a bit as the ice came in contact with his skin.

Colum moved closer to Leon, his seriousness intensifying. "Lie back and try not to move. Kale, be ready with more snow and give him something to bite on."

Leon did as he was told and leaned back on the cloak. Kale's heart raced as she filled the bowl with more snow. Grabbing a piece of cloth, she gave it to Leon who immediately clamped down on it. Colum pulled the dagger out of the coals. Its tip was bright yellow, a telltale sign of how hot it was. Coming over, he pulled Leon's injured arm farther from his body and braced it beneath one knee. Leon looked at him suspiciously but made no comment.

Colum looked up to Kale. "Get ready to grab his other arm, just in case."

Kale nodded and set the bowl aside. Colum pinched the skin around the wound, forcing it to close. He brought the dagger quickly to the end of the gash, searing one corner shut. Leon's muscles bunched beneath Colum's knee. He made a fist, digging his nails into his palm, his jaw locking on the cloth. Kale could see that he was trying hard to resist reaching over with the other arm, so she grabbed it firmly.

Colum pinched the wound again, but the break caused the glow in the dagger to diminish. He placed it in the embers again for a moment. They all waited expectantly for one long minute. Colum finally reached back to the knife, pulling it out white-hot. Leon eyed the dagger, knowing that the next part would be the worst.

Well aware of this, Colum knew he must be quick.

"Hold on tight, Kale," he warned. Kale tightened her grip on Leon's wrist, her gaze never leaving the dagger. Colum brought it down on Leon's shoulder, dragging it across the wound. The sickly sweet smell of burning flesh filled the air. Leon tried to reach the dagger, pulling with a sudden burst of strength. Kale had to grasp his arm with two hands to hold him still. Leon's back arched, and a sweat broke out on his brow as he bit hard onto the cloth to mute his shriek. Colum pulled the dagger away when he was finished, and Leon's muscles went limp.

"Kale, go get some snow!" Colum directed.

Obediently, Kale ran and grabbed a handful of snow. When she got back, she quickly placed the snow on Leon's shoulder. Steam rose from the burnt flesh as it cooled. Leon sighed and laid his head back against the ground, panting into the fabric from the trauma.

As Colum stepped back, Leon sat up, spitting out the cloth forcefully. Colum surveyed his work with satisfaction. "That will do. I would give it some air, and don't move it too much for the next little while."

Leon nodded and experimentally moved his elbow slowly around. He quickly stopped, wincing.

Pulling his shirt all the way off to prevent rubbing, he lied down and wrapped the cloak over himself, exhausted from the event. Kale put away the bowl and stuck her dagger in the snow to cool off before placing it back in its sheath at her hip. Colum added another log to the fire before he, too, retired on the ground. Kale sat on her cloak watching the flames as the pounding of her heart slowly subsided.

The smoke rising from their campfire floated into the air, creating swirling patterns in the dark grey-blue sky. The sparks danced above the wood like fireflies, climbing slowly before they disappeared. As Kale rested on her cloak, allowing herself to slowly drift off, she heard an eerie cry from somewhere in the mountain crags. She listened as the wolf howled again, and then a pack farther away responded in a chorus of haunting yips and howls.

CHAPTER

The next day looked promising, as the sky had cleared somewhat, and a warm breeze blew from the south. Kale woke to find a bowl of fresh berries near where she slept, and rubbing her eyes, she helped herself to some. Leon was walking around again, though Kale noticed that he was favoring his left arm.

Getting up, she walked over with the berries. "Where did you find these?" she asked.

Leon nodded towards Colum, who was tying up their packs again. "He found them growing on a bush not far from here. Colum and I have already eaten our fill, so have as many as you would like."

Thankful, Kale ate some more. "I didn't even realize we had finally started our descent. Does this mean we are almost out of these blasted mountains?" she asked hopefully.

Leon shook his head. "No, we are just coming to a pass in the middle of the Fray, Colum said there is a valley a day's walk up ahead where we can rest and restock our food. He said he would teach me to use his bow, so that I can hunt, too. We may even have time to make one for me."

Kale noted the excitement in his voice and smiled. "That would be nice. I am longing to see the grass and trees again; these cold peaks are rather forbidding," she said, glancing around at the mountains.

Colum walked up to them and handed them each a pack, saving two for himself. "If you want to see the valley at all, we had better get moving. It is a good walk away."

He started off in the direction of the path they were following, and Kale and Leon followed after him, quickly grabbing their cloaks and packs.

They caught up to Colum and worked to keep pace with his sizeable steps. A question plagued Kale's mind. "If this is only a valley and not the end of the mountain range, what comes after the valley?"

Colum looked back briefly. "The hardest part," he said lightheartedly, as if it were nothing. "What we crossed was maybe half the height of what is to come and not even half as dangerous."

Kale shuddered, and he continued, "Up in those mountains evil roams rampant. Large avalanches leave you buried under mountains of rock and snow, literally. Flash floods wash you right off the peaks. Strange noises drift through the stone. Animals seem to grow too large to be real; bears and wolves the size of houses. Many other strange stories have been told around campfires at night..." Then he laughed at the look on Kale's face.

"I doubt any of them are true. We will just have to watch out for blizzards and winds," he assured her.

Kale nodded, but what Colum said swam through her head accompanied by frightening visions of what the mountains might entail. In the sun and warmer weather, it was easier to trek across the rugged terrain.

After lunch, the travelers started to slow down even under the warmth of the sun. Kale's hands began to sweat, and she found it hard to hold on to her pack. Hiking the bag up higher, she kept moving, trying to keep up with the grueling pace. In the late afternoon, Kale noticed that grass grew on the sides of the road, and eventually some small trees. The sun started to disappear over the peaks, casting a rosy glow on the stone. Suddenly they reached a drop in the path; ahead of them was a large dish in the mountains, a splotch of color in the bleak Fray. The valley was lined with soft grass and shrubs, and a small river ran down the middle. Trees dotted the ground in places, their leaves sending dappled patterns onto the grass. A warm breeze blew through the valley, rippling through the grass and leaves. Kale laughed aloud and ran down the hill.

She was about half way when she realized that it was too steep to run down. Gravity pulled her faster and faster until her feet came out from under her and she slid on her stomach the rest of the way down. Rolling on to her back, she laughed as Colum and Leon jogged down the hill beside her. Looking up at them, a stupid smile plastered on her face, she asked, "What?"

Leon just shook his head and followed Colum who had started to walk on through the trees. Kale got up and brushed the grass and dirt from her clothing. She gently rubbed a sore spot on her cheek where she contacted the ground on her fall.

Jogging forwards, she followed the boys through a small grove of trees to the center of the valley. Birds trilled in the trees, and a few frightened rabbits hopped from nearby bushes. The small stream ran right through the grove, and lush grasses lined its banks.

"Fresh water!" Kale cried, undoing her cloak and letting it fall to the ground as she ran to the stream. Kneeling by it, she sipped some of the water from her cupped hands before splashing it on her face. Colum dropped his packs and joined her, filling up the canteens before actually drinking himself.

Leon joined them after arranging their stuff to make camp. When all three were refreshed and rejuvenated, they laid out their packs and cloaks and gathered some wood for a campfire at night. The sun was almost set, and Kale felt tired and peaceful. Too lazy to make a meal, she pulled out some dry meat and gnawed on it while lying on her cloak. The soft grass beneath her seemed like a bed of feathers compared to the stone they were camping on before. The warm summer air made a fire unneeded, and the logs were left untouched. As the final rays of sun disappeared, small pinpoints of light slowly shimmered into being in the vast night sky.

Soon the heavens were covered in many glittering stars, some shooting across the sky like arrows. Kale stared at them until she noticed a small band of color on the western horizon. She watched as the blue green ribbon writhed and then grew. Purples and blues soon joined in, and a fantastic light show brightened up the sky. Kale gasped in awe as the lights flowed across the sky, flickering and waving, like a strange, supernatural river.

"What are they?" she asked in admiration.

Colum, lying nearby looked up at the lights and smiled. "Some call them the Aurora Borealis, but no one really knows what they are."

Leon pulled his arm from behind his head and propped himself up on his elbow. "So they just appear like that?" he asked, mystified.

Colum nodded. "Yup, some believe they are a sign of good luck."

Smiling, Kale stared up at the lights, watching as they slowly started to fade again. A cool wind blew across her face, carrying the sweet smell of grass and spring flowers.

Bullfrogs and crickets took up their nightly chorus, breaking the silence while they sang their hearts out to the world. Kale heard Colum shift beside her, his soft, low breathing barely audible. Sighing, Kale rolled onto her side and laid her head on her arm. She didn't even remember falling asleep.

CHAPTER 42

They decided to stay in the valley for a few days, to hunt and rest before continuing on. Colum and Leon went out to hunt at first light. Kale could tell that Leon was excited to try out a bow and she let them go.

At camp, Kale sorted out their food stock and refilled the water canteens. She re-arranged the packs, then dusted off each of their cloaks, and re-laid them out in a new area where the grass grew thicker and moss padded the ground. Glancing around at her work, she smiled, satisfied. She sat on her cloak for a couple of minutes, wondering what to do. Pulling at the grass lazily, she noticed how dirty her hands were. She wondered how long it had been since she had bathed and grimaced at the thought.

Snatching her cloak, she followed the river until she found a bend where the current slowed and the water was deeper. Scanning around for any sign of the boys, she hung her cloak on a branch. She guessed that the boys wouldn't be back for a while and she was now a distance from them, so she shouldn't be spotted. Kale dumped her boots, shirt, and pants on the shore and dove quickly into the water. The waves hit her like a cool shock initially, but the summer sun helped warm the water, so after a couple of laps, Kale felt comfortable.

Swimming up to the shore, Kale grabbed some moss from the bank and began to rub her neck and arms with it. She sighed as she felt the dirt and sweat come off. Dunking her head under the water, she scrubbed her scalp with her hands. Breaking the surface again, she laughed aloud, shaking her head to release the water from her short hair.

Just then, Kale heard a noise in the bush, and she spun around, sliding deeper into the river. Then she heard someone calling her name, and by the sounds of it, they were getting closer. Kale went pale, as she frantically looked for her clothes. Seeing them out of reach, she sank into the water up to her chin and waited.

Leon and Colum burst around the river bend, shouting her name. They spotted her clothes on the bank first, and Kale could hear Colum mutter something about drowning. Then he noticed her in the water and paused for a second, until realization flit across his face and he went pale. Leon noticed her a second later, and his face went beet red.

Kale grew embarrassed under their surprised stare. "Well don't just stand there! Go back to camp. I will be there in a second!" she said crossly.

The boys hurried awkwardly around the corner, disappearing into the trees.

Kale surveyed the land cautiously and then swam quickly to the shore. Wading out of the water, she dried herself off with her cloak and slipped her clothes back on. She then walked briskly back to camp, trying to remove the memory of what just happened from her consciousness.

Leon was sitting by the unlit campfire, using his dagger to carve an old block of wood. Colum was skinning a rabbit that had an arrow wound in its head. Kale sat down on a log, slinging her damp cloak across it to dry.

No one mentioned the boys' discovery, but Leon piped up as he put down his stick. "Colum, I fancy a swim. Care to join me?"

Colum set aside the rabbit and nodded. Kale watched as the boys headed down to the spot she had found. When they disappeared around the bend, Kale pulled out her dagger and began to whittle on a piece of her own wood.

The day grew late and she became bored. The boys were still not back, but she didn't dare to go and find what was taking them so long, and this made her frustrated. Getting tired of the stick she had almost whittled away to nothing, Kale started the fire and hung a pot over it. Throwing in the ingredients needed for stew into the kettle, she waited for the water to boil. Instead of using the hard, dry venison, Kale used the fresh rabbit Colum had brought back. By the time the stew was almost overcooked, the boys came waltzing back around the bend. They were laughing, shirts in hand, and cloaks hung over their shoulders. Both had water streaming down their backs, soaking the hems of their pants, and their hair was still wet. Kale blushed and looked down when she realized that she had stared at them. She hastily got out the bowls and rinsing them in the stream first, she dished out supper.

Leon came and sat down. "So my nose was right. Supper was ready!"

Colum laughed. "We had almost lost track of time, we were having so much fun trying to drown each other," he said, playfully shoving Leon. Kale made no comment and just handed them their bowls. When Leon didn't take his bowl right away, she shoved it at him. He clutched it at his stomach and stared at her surprised for a moment.

Then his expression softened. "What is it, Kale?"

She looked at them. *I'm just totally humiliated by being walked in on while bathing, and then you leave me here to wait and to do the chores, while you go have fun...*

"Nothing," she said, harnessing her emotions.

Leon looked at her for a moment, clearly not believing her, but he didn't pry.

When supper was finished, everyone helped clean up. They reclined on their cloaks as the last embers of the cooking fire died.

Colum and Leon talked about the plans for the next couple of days, but Kale rested with her back to them. She wrested with her emotions, wondering why she snapped.

Tuning into their conversation about the obstacles ahead, Kale shuddered at the thought of what may be beyond the clouds. She pushed the thought from her mind as quickly as it came.

CHAPTER 13

The next day was the last of their stay in the valley before moving on. Everyone worked hard to make preparations. In the morning, Leon and Colum went hunting. They hoped to find some rabbit that would be easy to bring along without too much work with skinning and gutting. Kale stayed at the camp and packed up all of their equipment. She carefully cleaned their bowls and utensils with the cold water of the stream before tucking them snuggly into the packs. She noticed that their food pack was significantly lighter and hoped that they would have enough for the rest of the trip through the mountains. Refilling the water canteens, she added them to the pack before tying it up. She dusted off the cloaks before placing them carefully over their stuff. It was not too long before Leon and Colum appeared through the trees, four plump rabbits slung over their shoulders. Kale clapped her hands together thankfully and began preparing them to be packed immediately.

It didn't take long for her to get the meat secured in their packs. When the preparations were out of the way, there was a sudden pause in activity. The sun was warm, too warm to do anything vigorous. Kale sat sluggishly on her pack, blinking around the meadow. She suddenly realized she missed being on the run. She had never felt so alive when death was shoved in her face. Kale sighed, wishing she would be satisfied with the mundane, and she could forget the thrill of pure chaos. No matter how hard she tried, she could not shake the feeling, her lust for adventure.

Colum pulled out his dagger and began twirling it in his hands. Kale watched as the blade flashed in the sun, spinning and flipping too quickly for her eyes to follow. Pulling out her own dagger, she stared at it apprehensively. Colum noticed and walked over. He took his dagger and let it fall over his palm. It twisted once in the air before landing handle up into the soft dirt.

"You try," he said, showing her again.

Kale held the dagger, blade up, between her thumb and fingers. Letting go, she watched as it rolled over the back of her hand and landed in the dirt, next to Colum's.

She smiled triumphantly; surprised at the joy it brought her, and did it again.   Colum watched in admiration. "Wow, that took me at least a week to master, and you got it on the first try!" He smiled at her. "You're a natural."

Kale looked down, aware of the heat rushing to her face.

"Here," he said, as he got up and walked away a little. "Come try throwing it a bit."

Kale joined him, eager to learn something new.

Colum pulled his arm back, and then with lightning speed, flicked it forward again. The dagger flew from his hand and slid through the air, piercing a nearby tree. Kale attempted a throw, but her dagger sliced the sky in a high arc, spinning wildly before clattering harmlessly onto the dirt. Colum suppressed a chuckle and retrieved her dagger. He handed it to her, and this time, before she threw, he moved her hands and arm into a better position, while whispering encouraging words. Kale could feel his hot breath on her neck and shivers ran down her spine.

The next time she tried, the dagger flew straighter, but it hit the tree handle first. Kale's shoulders sagged as she retrieved her dagger. "This is too hard. I don't know how you do it."

Colum shifted his weight and helped her get into throwing stance. "Now flick your wrist when you throw it."

Kale tried again. Pulling her arm back and taking a deep breath, she flicked her arm forward, snapping her wrist. The dagger flew from her arm as if on its own, and spinning once, buried itself up to the handle in the tree. Colum exhaled in admiration and Leon whistled. Kale didn't even know he was watching.

"Bravo, I told you you're a natural!" Colum said, retrieving her dagger from the tree with a tug. "Now you will give your foes something to think about next time they get in your way."

Kale beamed, and taking up the dagger, flung it at the tree again. It hit the tree in the exact same spot as the last time, carving the groove deeper.

Colum gasped. "Ok, now you're scaring me. I don't know anyone who can do that."

Kale blushed and lowered her head, pulling the dagger out quickly. She drew her arm back once more and lined it up with the tree. Curious to see if her throw was just luck or good aim, she threw the dagger again, hard.

When she looked up, the dagger was again buried in the exact same place. Colum stood dumbfounded. When she looked back at him, he jolted awkwardly at being caught staring. She smiled, and pulling the dagger from the tree with a jerk, she swiftly sheathed it by her side. Kale patted it gently; happy with the sense of security it suddenly gave her, and the respect she gained in her throws.

She practiced for a couple of hours, working her way from a tree to a small leaf floating on the wind as a target. As she practiced, Leon worked with a bow beside her. Soon a competition started. Colum called out the mark, and Leon and Kale tried to be the first to hit it. By the end of the day, both had blisters covering their hands and a newfound confidence in their skills.

Leon shot his first rabbit with the bow, carrying it back to camp over his shoulder. Kale could have sworn that his grin reached his ears. Taking it, she got to work making supper. Walking back to the fire, she quickly stirred up a meat stew.

They ate in silence as the sun began to sink, casting rosy-orange patches across the valley. The worry in the air was almost tangible. Kale knew what they are all thinking.

Will we ever make it through those peaks?

CHAPTER

The following morning came all too soon. Kale's eyes blinked open to Leon shaking her shoulder. "Get up, we want to get through these mountains as quickly as possible." Kale nodded and yawned. Getting up slowly, she shouldered a pack and followed Leon. They walked in a single file towards the forbidding mountains. Kale remembered her experience only days ago and shivered; the valley seemed to have grown oddly cool. As they walked, the valley slowly disappeared, taking with it the warmth and the trees.

When the snow started falling, Leon looked back to check on her. Kale moved closer to him, not relishing the thought of getting lost again. Soon the winds swirled around them and the air grew thinner again. Kale pulled up her hood and hugged her pack closer to her, hoping to gain some warmth. The winds picked up, and Kale lost all hearing. Colum looked back constantly to make sure they were still following, glancing worriedly at the coming storm. The wind then grew so strong that Kale felt as if she were walking through water. She barely moved forward, for fear of being knocked over. Colum saw this and stopped; he tied a rope around his waist, passing it to Leon, who did the same. The end of the rope was handed to Kale, who tied it securely around her own waist. She knew this would be a lifeline if the wind grew even stronger. It would keep her on her feet and from losing sight of Leon and Colum.

Slowly plodding, Kale lost track of time. The snow blotted out the sun, and the wind blew ice into her face. Kale imagined that if she jumped, the wind would completely pick her off her feet and carry her away. Having lost sight of Leon and Colum completely, Kale kept checking her rope from time to time to procure the occasional distant tug from the other end. The snow piled higher; its glistening surface reflecting the light like diamonds.

Suddenly the rope went slack. Kale panicked and followed the rope quickly. Arm after arm she moved along the rope, trying hard to not pull it to herself. Then she saw a faint light and moved towards it, suddenly stumbling into a shallow cave along the mountain's wall. It was as if sound, warmth, and sight hit her at all the same time, as she exited the white-out. She was overwhelmed by the sounds of Leon and Colum talking. Her vision was blurred by colors, vibrant compared to the stark white. Collapsing by a newly started fire, she pulled off her hood, and undid the rope. Outside, there seemed to be a monotonous expanse of white, as snow fell thick from the night sky. Exhausted, Kale barely had time to lay out her cloak before she collapsed in exhaustion.

At the break of dawn, they headed out. Even though they were now higher into the mountains, they had not yet reached the peaks. Kale retied the safety rope around her waist, for the winds were still very strong. Outside of the small cave they sheltered in, the snow had slowed some-what, but the air was still frigid. Colum started climbing higher into the mountains. Kale and Leon swiftly followed, pulling their packs up higher on their backs for protection.

Around noon, they stopped at an overhang that jutted out from the mountainside. Kale slung her pack down onto the frozen ground, sitting tiredly on top of it. Colum sat down on a small boulder, taking out some of the rabbit meat they had caught in the valley. Leon slid to the ground cross-legged against his pack, nibbling the meat Colum tossed him. They shared the rabbit in silence, staring out over the edge of the overhang. The clouds were below them, their large fluffy forms drifting lazily across the sky. Kale stared at the strangely picturesque view. The sheer height of the mountains amazed her.

Eager to move on, they left their spot after only a few minutes and con-tinued their trek upwards.

By nightfall they were weary and sore. A higher group of clouds floated around them, making it very challenging to see. Kale knew that they must find shelter before they stopped to rest. She only hoped that the fog would roll away soon.

Finally, they located a small shelter against the mountain wall. Exhausted, Kale fell to the ground, choosing slumber over supper.

In the morning, the fog abated a bit, and Kale could just make out the jagged rocks of the mountains. The air was crisp, and it was too cold even for powdery snow to fall. Kale suddenly realized that they were in the very tops of the mountains.

"Now that we are in the peaks," Colum said, shouldering his pack, "we will have better weather until we get to the other side."

He donned his cloak, and pulling the hood up, headed outside. Kale and Leon followed suit, and the three began the hike. The wind was still strong, and fallen snow whistled around the rocks.

Suddenly Kale heard an eerie howl, causing the hair on the back of her neck to rise. She convinced herself that it was just the wind, so she said nothing. The going was slow, and Kale noticed that they must be higher than the last range they crossed by now, for clouds hugged the rocks, and there was little air. Kale scanned the area, hoping to see some plant life, something familiar in this desolate place. Her eyes brushed past a nearby rock, and her heart jumped into her throat.

Slowly looking back, she hoped it was just her imagination. Her eyes swept past it again, locking with two large, yellow orbs.

Something was watching them.

Kale fought the urge to scream, as she turned to warn Leon—the yellow orbs following her every movement. When she was just past the rock, she reached for Leon's shoulder. Suddenly, and inexplicably, a wave of cold fear washed over her.

"Leon!" she managed before a low growl picked up behind her. She turned just quickly enough to see the gigantic wolf spring airborne, gliding for a second with outstretched talons and ravenous jaws open, before it slammed into her chest.

CHAPTER 16

S uddenly the air was gone, as if sucked away.

I'm drowning; Kale assumed, and she tried to find the surface. Pain blurred Kale's vision, and she groped around trying to find the source of it. Finally her hands located a large furry paw, at least twice the size of her head. Four of the finger length claws were buried deep into her chest. Kale panicked, but her head started to grow fuzzy, and she gasped, trying to take in the non-existent air. Somewhere she could hear a yell, but it was fading fast. Everything was fading.

Then the paw was gone, leaving only a searing pain. The claws were wrenched from her ribs, and she was flung away from the beast. Kale vaguely felt herself crumple against the hard ground and slide until she hit a rock. The air was returning, slowly, but every breath she took felt as if someone was stabbing her again, sending burning pain throughout her body. She cried out in anguish. She could hold her breath and stop the pain, but lose the needed air, or she could keep breathing; every breath producing a scream.

Her eyes came into focus again, and the blackness faded away. The source of her pain, a towering wolf twice the height of any man, was growling, eyes alight with hunger. A few feet away, Colum stood with his feet planted and sword drawn, his brown hair was whipping around his face, his battle cry lost to the wind. Leon had a dagger in one hand and a sword in the other, his features set with determination. Kale had never seen his eyes so bright, so alive and burning with revenge.

It was a standoff, and the boys made the first move, charging at the wolf with a loud cry. Leon slashed the beast's leg, and it snapped back at

183

him, barely missing his arm. Colum jumped up on top of a small rock and onto the animal's back, raising his sword with both hands above his head for a deathblow. The wolf reached around and sunk its teeth into Colum's leg, tearing him from his back. Colum screamed in anguish, and Kale could hear the sickening sound of a bone snapping.

Colum's scream was joined by Kale's, and Leon began a frenzied attack on the animal. It was soon apparent who had the upper hand, as Kale could see Leon tiring. Colum was lying on the ground not far from her, struggling to get up. Kale tried to pull her arm from under her, but the effort it took caused her to cry out and sink back down. She managed to wiggle her other arm free, but she found that her dagger was beneath her. The effort it took for her to breathe had almost caused her to lose consciousness.

Kale tried to regulate her lungs, taking only the slow, small breaths that she could manage. She held her arm out to Colum.

"Dagger…" she tried, moaning at the new bout of pain that shot down her chest. Colum was looking at her strangely, and Kale held out her arm, begging him to understand. He put his hand on the hilt of his dagger, and Kale nodded. Colum stared at her, slowly sliding the dagger across the frozen ground.

Leon cried out, his scream sending needles down Kale's spine. The wolf had caught his hand with its claws, disarming him while carving deep rents down his forearm to his wrist. He fell against the ground, clutching his hand, and he feebly crawled back from the wolf just as Kale's fingers closed on the dagger's handle.

The wolf advanced quickly, a frenzied look in its eye. Kale pulled her shaking arm back and tried to aim. The wolf crouched on its haunches, swishing its tail once before leaping into the air. Leon covered his face, and Colum moaned. Kale threw the dagger with all her might, her heart beating out of control. She watched as the wolf flew through the air, as if in slow motion. Leon's eyes filled with fear, and he made a last desperate attempt to scramble out of the way. The wolf was stopped by the dagger mid leap and fell to the ground inches away from Leon's face, instantly lifeless. Kale fell back; the exertion from her throw did her in.

The world was starting to fade again and she grew weak. She could barely make out Colum and Leon lying on the ground. The wolf was not much farther away, the hilt of a dagger buried into its skull. She sighed, drawing a gasp form her lips. She watched as if in a dream while the sky began to grow dark. In the distance, she could hear the howls of a wolf pack, moaning at the loss of their leader. A chill ran down her spine as reality sunk in. *The wolves are growing closer.*

CHAPTER 46

Leon clutched his injured hand close to his chest. The image of an enraged wolf flying at his face was still ingrained in his mind. His breath was ragged, and he stumbled, trying to get to his feet. He watched as Kale collapsed after her throw, still incredulous as to how she was alive, let alone able to throw a dagger. Her form relaxed on the cold stone as she passed out.

A WOLF PACK CRIED EERILY AND LEON JUMPED UP, SWAYING for a moment. He strode quickly over to Colum, who was lying—partially stunned—on the ground. Leon offered him his good hand and Colum nodded, taking it. He could hop around, but with one leg bone shattered and poked at the skin, Leon could see that it would take more than a splint to fix it. They made their way slowly over to Kale. Leon's head snapped around when a wolf howled again.

They reached Kale's still form and Leon went pale at the amount of blood that had pooled beside her. Tearing off part of his shirt, he wound it around his injured hand so that he would be able to carry her. Colum braced himself against a rock with his good leg and helped to lift Kale onto Leon's shoulder. She moaned, but did not come to, and Leon was pleasantly surprised again at how light she was.

They hurriedly hobbled away, urged on by the wolf howls. It had only been a couple of minutes, when the pack began barking in frenzy.

Leon glanced at Colum.

"They found the one we killed," Colum explained grimly.

They sped up their pace as the mad howls of the wolves seemed to grab at their heels. Leon could not go more than a jog without leaving Colum behind, who was doing his best to hop along hastily.

Silent paws flew across the frozen ground, racing faster and faster as the wolves caught scent of their prey. Soon the wolf at the head of the pack spotted the hunted—the humans that killed the Alpha. The lead bared his fangs in anticipation. All three were injured, he smelled their blood; it should be an easy catch.

Leon glanced back in time to see a large wolf turn around a bend, racing right at them with jaws open and eyes glaring. Leon pushed his muscles as fast as they could go, pulling Kale into his arms. His instincts told him to drop Kale and run, but knowing he could not, he continued—dread rising in his stomach. Colum hopped faster, using his sword as a walking stick, not even looking back at the beasts swiftly closing in.

Colum stopped suddenly and teetered as if avoiding something unseen. Leon shouted at him to keep running, when he noticed that the path just disappeared. He bounced to a halt just before plummeting off the cliff edge. A sickening feeling rose in his stomach and throbbed through his head. He guessed that this was how an animal felt, when it realized its imminent death just before an arrow entered its skull. He glanced over the cliff edge again, but pulled away quickly, the sheer height of the drop making him dizzy. Colum and Leon shared a glance, nodding.

Solemnly Colum pulled out his sword. Leon set Kale on the ground.

"I'm sorry," Leon said gently, before unsheathing his own weapon. He joined Colum, his jaw set grimly, as he watched the wolves split and circle them. They stood and regarded each other for a long moment. Leon noticed a young wolf directing the others' movements. Assuming it was the new pack leader, Leon returned its fierce stare. They glared at each other until the wolf swung his head towards the two pack members by his side. As if by command, they advanced, baring their fangs and snarling.

Leon adjusted his grip on the sword and braced his legs. Colum held up his own weapon, hopping around on one leg to try and find his balance. The two wolves closed in, while the rest of the pack sat down in a semicircle. Leon glanced at the rest grimly, realizing his own death would be the pack's entertainment for the day.

The two wolves leaned back on their haunches, ready to pounce, and Leon knew what came next. He braced himself for the blow, just as something shifted in the corner of his eye. Leon looked warily over. A stone door had materialized in the face of the rock, and an old man was leaning around it, beckoning frantically. He put a finger to his lips, and then beckoned again. Leon nudged Colum gently, who looked over and spotted the man. His eyes lit with suspicion, but after glancing at the wolves once more, he nodded.

THE PACK LEADER ALMOST HOWLED IN TRIUMPH, AS HE watched the humans try desperately to escape his member's fangs. The humans edged away from the two wolves, locking their stares. The leader surveyed the humans with a cold eye. The dark one could barely stand, his eyes shrouded with pain. The wolf had smelled his blood on the body of the Alpha. Salivating with the anticipation of crunching the rest of his bones, the wolf glanced at the other human. It was younger and lighter colored, but its eyes were bright and challenging. Tilting his head in observation, he noticed this human's eyes change. It was just subtle, but the wolf took no chances. He yipped commandingly at his pack members to attack.

CHAPTER

L eon locked his eyes on the wolf. His face seemed expressionless, but
somehow the wolf noticed something. Leon looked inquiringly into
its eyes for a brief moment. But without further hesitation, he lifted
Kale and began to sprint to the door, just as the wolf yipped, and the whole
pack advanced. A mad race to the mountain wall began.

Leon's heart throbbed against his rib cage, Kale's body thumping
roughly against his shoulder. Colum hopped faster than Leon thought
humanly possible, sweat beading on his brow. Suddenly, Kale moaned, and
she was wrenched from Leon's arms. He turned back to see that one of the
wolves had grabbed her foot in its mouth and tugged her to the ground.
Leon watched helplessly as her limp body smacked the stone and got pulled
back by the wolf. Springing towards the wolf, he started after her, but a
hand grabbed his wrist. He turned to find the old man clutching his sleeve.
Colum was already in the safety of the doorway and he stared forlornly at
Leon. The man shook his head, trying to pull him into the tunnel. Leon
wrenched his arm away and charged after Kale.

The man shouted for him to come back, but Leon ignored him. With
one swift blow, Leon struck the beast that had Kale with all the power left
in him. All the animals froze in shock, as their leader struggled to rise again.
With this moment's reprieve, Leon lifted Kale and leaped through the door
before toppling inside, just as the thick stone door swung shut with a resounding bang. He could hear the wolves' frustrated cries through the stone
and he breathed an immense sigh of relief.

Exhausted, he followed the strange man without question. They made
their way through a long torch-lit tunnel until they reached a set of steps.

Though they were beneath miles of stone, Leon noticed that it was not damp or cold; instead, it was rather comfortable. The thick stonewalls offered a sense of security, and he relaxed.

Leon appraised the strange man walking ahead of him for the first time. He was old, his grey hair balding at the top. He wore a long blue cloak that swept the floor, giving him the appearance of a scholar or a monk. He looked strong and able as he carried Kale in his arms with ease. He had given Colum his staff, and Leon noticed that Colum was trying valiantly to walk along on one leg, using the stick for support. Every now and then, Colum's gaze shifted to the strange man, and he shared a look with Leon.

They turned a corner and the tunnel ended. Ahead of them stood an immense hall. Leon gasped. Huge stone pillars, seemingly taller even than some of the mountains they crossed, held up the massive ceiling. Rows upon rows of these pillars filled the hall. All of them were exactly the same, perfectly carved, smooth, blue-black stone. Once, it could have housed feasts where thousands of guests would attend. Whole cities could likely fit in this place. Leon couldn't even see to the other side, because it was so far away that it disappeared into the darkness. There was something eerie about the massive stone shapes, and they surely had a story.

The old man continued and Leon quickened to catch up. They stopped at a wall, where the man rapped twice, and the outline of a door appeared. Leon blinked incredulously, following the man into a large room that the door led into. A fire glowed in the hearth, and three large beds lined one wall. The stone floor was bare, but it was not at all cold when Leon removed his boots. It was smooth and comforting, much easier underfoot than the rocky paths of the mountains.

The man laid Kale on a bed and motioned for Colum to sit on the one next to it. Colum quickly obliged. Leon suddenly realized a sharp pain in his hand, and for the first time, he noticed just how bad of an injury the wolf inflicted. Wrapping it up hastily in his shirt stopped the blood but not the pain. He watched warily as the man bent over Kale, pulling back her shirt to examine her wounds. Somehow Leon instinctively knew he could trust this man—he just hoped that Kale would live.

CHAPTER 48

The man walked to the end of the room and grabbed a small box. He pulled out a silver instrument and returned to Kale. Leon guessed that these were some sort of tweezers. The man bent down and inserted them into one of Kale's puncture wounds. He was still for a moment and then he began to pull. Kale moaned and her back arched, her eyes fluttering as if in a dream. He yanked harder and Kale gasped into consciousness.

She looked weakly about the room. Leon and Colum sat on a bed beside her, as a strange man bent over her.

Where are we?

She stared at the man. "Who are you?" she forced a whisper.

He smiled. "You are awake." He put a hand on her shoulder when she attempted to rise. "Rest, I am a friend. My name is Bromir. You are safe."

He tugged again and Kale cried out in pain as the silver tongs slid from her chest, pulling at least two inches of wolf claw with them.

Kale stared at the black nail that was removed from her body and her eyes grew wide.

"How am I still alive?" she asked incredulously.

Leon gasped when he spotted the claw. No one should have survived a stab like that.

Bromir shook his head. "I do not know. The claw narrowly missed your lungs and your heart, sparing your life; even so, the amount of blood you lost should have killed you. By all rights, you should be dead," he said, pocketing the claw. He took out a jar from his box, and opening the lid, he rubbed some balm onto his hands. He then gently rubbed this over Kale's wounds before binding them.

Kale quickly fell asleep when her pain lessened, exhaustion taking over.

Bromir moved to Colum and bent beside his leg, reaching out to examine it. Colum moved his leg away and inched farther from Bromir. Leon could tell that he would not blindly trust Bromir and he was not surprised.

Bromir just smiled and spoke sincerely, "If I wanted to harm you, I would have left the wolves to do that. Instead, I saved you. Why would I kill you now? I just wish to help."

Colum eyed him suspiciously but did not move when Bromir reached out again. He ran his hand over Colum's leg and shook his head. "How you managed to walk on one leg, I can't imagine. This one is broken pretty badly. The bone has split completely and is in the wrong place."

He looked up at Colum. "I can splint it how it is, but you will not walk as well, or I can try to snap it back in place, which will cause you some… discomfort. It's your choice."

Colum looked indignant. "I'm not afraid of a little pain. I'm in quite a lot right now already. I can't afford to lose my leg either, so go ahead."

Bromir nodded and placed his hands on either side of Colum's shin. "Brace yourself and try to restrain from hurting me."

Colum grabbed the bed sheets just as Bromir pulled on the lower half of his bone. Colum cried out and balled the covers in his fists. Bromir pulled the bone farther down, and then started pushing it to the side. Colum bit his lip until it bled, and Leon's skin crawled at the grating sound of bone moving over bone. Finally, there was a snap, and Colum sighed, sweat covering his forehead. Bromir securely wrapped the leg and watched, satisfied, as Colum gingerly swung it experimentally.

Bromir moved over to Leon, who glared back at him, suddenly realizing that he fully intended to work on him too.

Leon shook his head. "I'm just fine," he said sincerely, "but thank you for helping my friends."

Bromir took one look at Leon's hand buried in his blood soaked shirt and shook his head disapprovingly. "No you are not, and now let me at least wrap that for you." Colum grinned at Leon from behind Bromir's back and pulled an exaggeratedly frightened expression. Leon scowled at him, but he could not hold it for long. Eventually he gave in, slowly pulling out his hand.

Bromir inspected his hand for a moment before speaking, "What is it with you three? That girl with the stabs should be dead from her wounds." Leon's head jerked in surprise that Bromir knew Kale was a girl. Bromir noticed and smiled. "It's okay. I only know because I had to move the wrappings over her chest to remove the claw. But your friend with the leg should have been caught by the wolves long ago. And you my friend, your hand should be missing, and you should be dead for loss of blood."

He shook his head and then said, "It seems your fate is too strong to allow you to die just yet. You must have great purpose."

Leon thought of their mission and wondered if this was what they were meant to do.

Bromir continued, "I will have to take back what I said about just binding it. Those wounds need to be closed."

Leon jerked at these words and he shook his head, remembering what Colum did to him by the fire.

"No, I have had enough cauterizing for one week," he said, pulling back his shirt to show Bromir the burn marks on his shoulder. Bromir stared at the long scar running across Leon's right shoulder, clearly expecting him to share his tale. When Leon did not continue, his eyes drifted back to the wounds on his arm.

He looked at the long gashes running from his mid outer forearm across the back of his wrist and onto his hand.

"I was actually just thinking of stitching it up. Would that be okay?" he asked, matter-of-factly.

Leon turned the idea over in his head before giving in. Bromir wasted no time in taking out a needle and some strange grass-like thread.

"This," he said, holding up the strand, "is something I made myself. It stays in as long as it takes for you to heal and then it dissolves. You never have to remove it." He threaded the needle and held Leon's arm with his other hand, pinching the skin together. Holding the needle poised above Leon's arm, he turned.

"If I were you, I'd look away," he said. "It makes it hurt less."

Leon turned his head just before he felt a sharp stab. The pain was blurred, as the gashes already seemed as if they were on fire. He felt the thread start to slide through his skin. It was rough, and the nerves in his skin were shot. Moaning, he bit his cheek and focused on a pattern in the bed sheet.

Bromir worked quickly and soon the wounds were closed. He tied the greenish thread and put away the needle. Leon grimaced, as he found five neat rows of green thread running down his arm. Bromir rubbed some salve on his skin, and immediately the burning cooled. Leon exhaled as it receded, suddenly grateful for the help. Bromir then bound his arm before standing. He placed his little box back on the shelf and walked over to Kale. Satisfied that she was sleeping, he looked up at Colum.

"Could I trouble you in my study for a moment?" he asked, suddenly more serious. Colum nodded and when Leon stood to join him, Bromir shook his head.

Leon watched puzzled as they left, and the door shut behind them. He noticed that the stone of the door matched the stone in the walls so exactly, that at a first glance, the door did not even look as if it was there at all. Leon shoved out the panic that assaulted him on instinct. He walked over to the wall, tracing his good hand across the door. He ran a finger along the hairline crack with awe. This was surely not the work of mere humans.

He glanced over at Kale who was sleeping peacefully on the bed, curled up with the blankets bunched around her. He smiled gently and realized suddenly that he was exhausted. He walked slowly back to his bed and crawled beneath the quilt. Sliding his hands across the sheets, Leon was surprised by how soft they were. He remembered how Kale used to sleep on a hay pallet and wondered what she thought of the beds.

Suddenly the door opened and Colum stepped through. Leon sat up, waiting for an explanation. Colum's brow was crinkled in thought, and he sat on his bed heavily. Leon watched carefully then asked, "What happened?"

Colum looked up at him, startled by his voice, as if he just noticed his presence. He stared at Leon strangely, running his eyes over his face as if meeting him for the first time. Leon looked down uncomfortably, wondering what Bromir told Colum to make him look at him like that.

Colum shook his head as if in disbelief and slid beneath his covers. There was a long pause before he turned over.

"Is it true, about Kale?" he whispered.

Leon flipped onto his side.

"What do you mean?" he asked, leaning his head on his good elbow.

Colum looked over at Kale—making sure that she was actually asleep.

"You know, about who she *actually* is?" he whispered quietly.

Leon wondered how Bromir knew anything about Kale. He thought he was the only one who knew about her past.

"Yeah, it's true," he admitted. "But she doesn't know and we must not tell her," he said, pausing, "for her safety."

Colum nodded. "Yeah, with a secret like that, no wonder Zorach wants her dead," he breathed. "It will be a lot harder than I thought to keep her alive."

"We have to try. Keeping her alive is one good thing I can do to stop the evil my father has been doing since the late king's death. I feel that by stopping him from killing her, somehow I will finally have made amends for my bloodline." He continued sadly, "Even if I don't live through this, I will make sure she does."

Colum shook his head in disbelief. "You really are something, Leon. I admire your courage." Then he met Leon's gaze, "I'm with you."

Leon nodded and Colum smiled, turning over. Colum's slow breathing soon joined Kale's, while the fire still flickered in the hearth, adding to the warm environment. Leon reclined back on his bed, staring up at the thick fabric canopy. His head was swirling with colorful thoughts, none of which made any sense. Leon slowly drifted off too, the sound of the dying fire lost to his ears.

CHAPTER 49

In the morning, everyone was up bright and early, refreshed and rejuvenated by a deep slumber. Colum was pleased to find that he could step on his leg gently. He experimented walking around with the staff all morning, the wood making queer thumping noises against the stone. Leon flexed his hand and arm and was excited to find it much improved.

Leon marveled at the speed of their healing and suspected that there was more to Bromir than he was telling them, or not telling him. Perhaps Colum had been told more. He balled his fist and winced when the stitches pulled slightly. Kale was awake, but he noticed that her face was still quite pale, and she only managed to sit up. He sympathized with her and shot her a sorry look. She returned it with a pathetic glance, to which he grinned.

Bromir walked into the room and noticed with satisfaction that they were recovering.

"Would you like to join me for a tour?" he asked. Leon and Colum immediately accepted, eager to explore. Kale tried to join them, but she fell weakly back against the cushions, the blood draining from her face.

Noticing her condition, Bromir shook his head. "I don't think it is a good idea for you to join us today."

Kale's face looked so depressed that Bromir had a hard time not smiling.

"Don't worry. Tomorrow, I'm sure you will be able to join me for a personal tour," he offered generously.

Leon pitied her; he would stay back to keep her company, but he was too antsy to see the rest of this place. Their chamber was very comfortable and roomy, but the stonewalls were repetitive and bleak.

They left with one last apologetic look to Kale and followed quickly after Bromir. He led them through the giant hall and up some steps at the end. The height of the ceiling never ceased to amaze Leon. Tapping on the wall, Bromir opened a large stone door. Leon watched in awe as strange runes appeared on the door, glowing for a few seconds before vanishing as swiftly as they had come. Bromir did not seem fazed by the fact that his door just did something unearthly, and he passed through with a swish of his robes. Leon followed after Colum, who trailed in Bromir's shadow.

They entered a dusky room, and when the door shut, the room went completely dark. Leon glanced around, and his eyes widened as they tried to gather non-existent light. There was a click and a glowing orb lit up in the middle of the room. Leon felt like a moth drawn to a flame as his attention focused on the light. Another click. The whole room lit up and started spinning. Stars and galaxies swirled across the room. Leon realized that the stars were coming from the orb.

It was a flawless, glass oval that was somehow glowing and reflecting the light across the dome shaped room. Leon reasoned with himself that the stars reflected on the circle, which bounced off the walls. Suddenly he remembered that there were no stars out to reflect during the day. He then deduced that the light must be trapped in the orb and then reflected somehow.

Bromir took his staff from Colum and swirled it. The stars moved with his staff as he turned it here and there until he was satisfied. Colum looked at Leon incredulously; Leon shook his head, bemused. Then Bromir tipped his staff forwards, and the stars lifted off the wall, floating into the air. The little circles of light were definitely three-dimensional. They looked like the lights of fireflies, but much larger.

Leon reached out a hand and cupped it under a glowing sphere near him. He marveled at the small ball of light. It was pure white, clearer than anything he had ever seen; so white that it seemed to have pale colors inside of it, small flashes of blues and pinks. His hand tingled in the heat the light gave off, and he gasped. Leon stared at the stars and then at Bromir. Bromir looked back and smiled a bit, causing Leon to realize that his jaw hung open. He quickly slammed it shut, looking to Bromir for answers. Bromir nodded towards the center, and Leon looked back. The stars were swimming again, and Bromir zoomed in on a small green planet in the center of the room. It revolved once, revealing its blue waters and lush green expanses. Bromir walked up to the globe and tapped it lightly with his staff, causing it to emit smoky swirls.

"This is where we live," he said.

Leon stared at the globe, then walked slowly up to it and gently placed his fingers on it. His skin tingled strangely and he fought the urge to pull away. The surface was warm, yet not totally tangible. Leon stared at it skeptically, stepping back from the globe as it began to spin again. Bromir tipped his staff once more, and the world began to grow larger. Soon it filled up most of the room and was still growing.

It sank into the floor until only the top half was visible, and still it kept growing. Soon it was so large that trees and rivers were visible. It began revolving so quickly that Leon thought it might overtake him, and yet he felt as though he floated over the surface of the earth. The sensation made him dizzy, and he almost fell over as the world continued to expand.

Suddenly, the revolving came to a stop, right in the center of a town. There were small farm shacks everywhere; they looked just the same as the one where he had first met Kale. People were milling about the town, laughing and talking. Leon could hear their voices and see their expressions. He stared at them, reminding himself of where he actually was.

A man walked towards him, as Leon tried to step out of the way, but he was too slow. The man stepped right through him, and Leon clutched his stomach, gasping. He looked up at Colum, but he just shook his head. The people in the town looked just like the stars. They, like everything else Bromir created, seemed to glow and shimmer. When two people collided, wisps of smoke brushed off them.

"Are they real?" Leon asked, not taking his eyes off the town's people.

Bromir nodded. "Yes, what you see is actually happening right now, somewhere in a town not far from here."

Leon stared at them in disbelief. "Can they see us?"

Bromir shook his head. "No, they aren't actually here. It is just like a looking glass; you can see and hear them, but they can't see you. This is actually how I knew where you were before we met. I saw you through this."

Leon's mind couldn't wrap around what this meant. If this was possible, any of the stories he heard as a child could be true. Stories about elves, and dragons, and worse…

Leon interrupted his own thoughts, "So you can see what is going on right now anywhere you want to?"

Bromir nodded. "Yes, but not just present day. I can also see what happened in the past."

With a swirl of his staff, the town disappeared, and the world began moving quickly beneath their feet again. Soon it slowed at a large, black mountain that was covered in charcoal colored smog. The shiny black ground was shaking, red lava running like rivers every which way. The flickering light cast eerie shadows on their faces.

"This is before humankind. Nothing grew; the world was desolate. It was a war zone," Bromir said solemnly.

Leon stared at the fire mountain, eyes dilated from the power evidenced in its raging tremors.

"So you can see the past," he stated, and then asked hesitantly, "Can you see the future?"

"This orb is like a history book. It can show you what is happening and what has happened. But nothing save Providence can reveal the future. The future is too uncertain to predict, because man has free will. You cannot know the conclusion of a story without reading the book."

He looked seriously at Leon and Colum. "In the same way, you cannot know the events to come until you have lived them."

Leon's mind flickered to their journey to come, and he wondered if Bromir was trying to hint at something.

"Although," Bromir interjected, "I can guess some of what is to come, by reading the chapters we are living right now. Sometimes life sends us subtle hints, and we can only guess by those." Then he continued solemnly and somewhat to himself, "Sometimes one does not want to see the future."

He twisted his staff again, and the world stopped spinning once more at a dark expanse. The ground was not nearly as lively as the volcano, but everything was dark and cold. Thick black fog hung around a single jagged mountain. The moon was behind the peak, making it look even darker than the rest of the land. Everything here spoke of desolation and despair. Leon shivered, and an inexplicable fear crept over him. A small black dot that was moving swiftly across the dark sands caught his attention. As if on cue, the world spun and zoomed towards the figure. It grew until it was life-size, and Leon almost screamed. Astride a large black horse sat a familiar figure, covered from head to foot in black robes.

"The Shadow," Leon whispered, fear causing him to stutter.

Colum was trembling visibly, and even Bromir showed signs of discomfort. As The Shadow urged his horse faster, he made a sharp turn, causing the animal to rear. Leon caught a quick glance of The Shadow's eyes, red and glowing beneath the hood. He seemed to stare right at Leon, and he laughed, a rasping cackle that danced along Leon's spine. Leon backed away from the figure as the horse started galloping again.

"Where is he going? What is that place?" Leon looked to Bromir, who was watching The Shadow carefully, as if afraid that he might step out of the light and attack them.

"That is Gonder Dohr..." Bromir uttered, as if the very name was a curse. "The Black Mountain in our language, and it holds nothing but evil. Abbedon, or The Shadow, as you call him, lives in that mountain. Some say he is an old man who works for the king, and he hides there from the grief of losing his wife." He paused and then continued, "Others say he is not of this world, only a wisp of a human being that once walked the earth. Chained here by the evil he has committed, part wraith, all evil... but no one really knows."

Leon thought about the subhuman red eyes he spotted under the hood, *surely no human could possess such evil looking eyes... could the stories be true?* "So why is he leaving?" Leon asked.

Bromir shook his head. "Something has stirred him. He is looking for something." The words chilled Leon to the bone. Suddenly, he wanted to be anywhere but near this hooded figure. His heart pounded against a hollow rib cage, and he groped around the wall for a door, his scar suddenly burning.

"Turn it off!" he cried. "Please, I don't want to see him!"

His mind filled with an image of The Shadow reaching down with a glowing weapon, reaching out to him, getting closer...

The room went dark again, and everyone breathed.

Bromir's voice picked up in the darkness, "I only wish you to see what you are facing."

"How did you—" Leon started.

"I know many things," he said, gesturing to the dying light in the orb.

"Come. Let us see the rest of this place." A door clicked open, and Bromir exited, followed quickly by Leon and Colum.

They walked on through a hall for a few minutes when Colum piped up, "How did you do that? I mean, with those stars and stuff back in that room?"

Bromir didn't even look back. "I have spent half of my life reading and studying the scrolls and runes that were left here by a dying species," he said, somewhat amused. "I have learned some of their ways." He paused thoughtfully. "But every day I am still learning." Sweeping his stick in a circle, he continued, "They were the ones that made this place, with the help of the dwarves."

Leon's eyes widened, and Colum gasped.

"Dwarves?" they said simultaneously.

Leon lurched closer to Bromir. "So they are real! All those stories that are told by firesides, about great dwarf kings and elves and fire breathing dragons?" he asked, feeling like an excited child again, begging that fairy-tales be real.

Colum joined him, "Yes, and heroes and wizards and sorcerers?"

Bromir laughed. "Well, I am classified as a wizard, so does that answer your question? As for dwarves and elves, they *were* real. As humans began to populate the earth, they were forced to move. Many were discriminated against, and wars were fought. Now they are all gone, this place alone left to testify of their existence."

"But dragons?" he continued. "No, they never existed; they are just an embellishment added to the stories to make them more exciting."

Leon turned the idea over in his head, *elves and dwarves and wizards! How can it all be true?* Some part of him believed, but it was like a fairytale. It seemed too strange to be real.

"What about the wolves?" Leon thought out loud. "They were real, and they were way too big to be normal wolves. Before we entered those mountains I never would have imagined they existed." He reasoned with himself. "And The Shadow. Isn't he a testimony to the reality of all of this?" He looked up abruptly when he noticed that they had stopped.

Two of the immense wolves stood in the hallway, facing them. Leon's heart jumped, but Bromir seemed to be at ease. Leon noticed that the wolves' silvery fur was well brushed, and the wolves looked muscular and well fed, unlike the ones they had encountered. Bromir patted one of them on the head.

"Are they gone?" he asked it. "And what news?"

The wolf nodded and dropped a scroll from his mouth, seemingly bowing to his master. Leon stopped at the realization that the wolves must have been tamed by Bromir, if they understood him when he spoke. Bromir unrolled the scroll and nodded as he scanned it.

"Good boy, you may retire and grab some supper from the kitchen."

The wolf bowed again, and the pair left, their thick shoulders rippling with muscles, and their long silky tails swinging gently.

"I found them when I found this place. Tamed twelve of them, but those two are the most loyal. They keep me company in this lonely place," Bromir said thoughtfully. "I am very close to understanding their language, but it was very complicated, because, unlike us who depend on sound to communicate, the wolves use subtle shifts in their expressions, and can even read the changes in each other's eyes."

Leon shook his head and piped up. "So that is how that lead wolf knew when to give the attack signal. He saw right through me!"

CHAPTER 60

They soon came to another wall, where Bromir rapped his staff, twice, and a door appeared. As the cracks broadened and the door opened, they stepped through into a room completely different from the first. Its intricate walls were covered in shelves upon shelves of scrolls and books. The room was well lit and many tables covered the floor. On the tables were all manners of trinkets and devices. Some were swinging or twirling in continuous patterns; others emitted smoke or strange noises.

Leon stared at a small vase that was sitting on a table by itself and watched as the liquid inside changed colors, bubbling slightly. His head jerked at a loud crash, and he laughed when he spotted Colum in front of a pile of strange metal rods, which used to be in some sort of formation. His finger was outstretched—frozen—as he stared at the mess he made.

Bromir looked back and sighed. "Please don't touch anything."

Colum tried to make the pile look neater before he scurried away sheepishly. Leon grinned and moved on from the strange little vial. Bromir floated to and fro, fixing something here, adjusting something there.

"This is my study," he said with pride. "I make all sorts of things here and spend my time studying those manuscripts on the wall." He picked up a small jar and examined it.

"I also invent new remedies for illnesses and potions for whatever needs doing. Take this jar, for an instance," he said, as he shook it gently. "If you take a pinch of the dust inside and blow it into any room, it will make everything perfectly clean in a matter of seconds."

Leon stared at the pearl-colored sand with interest.

"It is very helpful for last minute guests," Bromir admitted.

He moved to a vial of clear, shimmery liquid and said, "This one I am still working on." He held it up to the light. "Vanishing fluid. I tried it on a statue, and it *did* disappear," he said, groping around until he almost tripped over something large and seemingly nonexistent. "Here it is. Come, feel."

Leon stepped over and reached out his hand. His fingers bumped into something hard, and he felt the cold smooth surface of a stone being. He blinked his eyes to try to procure its form. Nothing.

Leon moved his fingers over the masterpiece. He felt it, as if he were blind, touching every crevice to try and get an image in his mind of the chubby cherub. Bromir shook his head.

"The problem with this one, is that it never wears off. I highly advise that you do not try it. You may tire of being invisible forever," he said sadly. "I hope to someday perfect it."

He moved over to another table on which lie two bundles of cloth. He picked them up reverently and said, "One night, many years ago, a piece of star fell to the earth. I happened to come across it and took it home with me, once the rock had cooled. I then worked day and night to forge it into a weapon—a great sword that had no equal, save, possibly, one. The star metal has a mysterious composition. It is harder than all metals, yet lighter than most. When I was done, I forged it a sister—a dagger out of the left over metals, lighter and quicker in the air than many say possible." He unwrapped the cloth, revealing the two weapons.

Both boys gasped and stepped closer. Neither had seen a better-made weapon, perfectly smooth, with impossibly sharp edges. Each seemed to glow softly, flickering like a dying coal; their light the color of pale tropical waters and a robin's eggshell. The light moved in slow ripples up and down the silvery surface. Leon suddenly remembered the glowing weapon The Shadow stabbed him with and he wondered they might be the same. These weapons were a different color than The Shadow's, but evidently filled with the same kind of power. Leon stretched out a hand to touch the sword handle, his fingers reaching eagerly like a child for candy.

"I wouldn't do that if I were you," Bromir cautioned. "Even I have not touched them without gloves. No one should until it is decided who they belong to. There are three of you and only two weapons," he said before re-wrapping the weapons and heading back towards the door with them in his arms.

Leon raised a brow and asked, "How on earth are we supposed to choose?"

Bromir opened the door and slipped through, barely giving the boys time to follow before the door shut again. "You won't have to decide; the weapons will. Being made of star, the weapon will only give its full potential for the bearer that will wield it best."

Colum shook his head. "How will we know who was chosen?"

Bromir smiled. "Oh, you'll know." He laughed quietly to himself as he moved quickly through the stone halls, and the boys jogged to keep up. They soon reached their room again, and Bromir opened the door. He let them through but did not join them, allowing the door to close on him after placing the weapons on the table.

They found Kale sitting up in her bed, watching them.

"How was it?" she asked.

Leon noted her quick recovery and wondered if, like everything else he had just experienced, there was some magic involved.

"It's a long story," Leon answered. "I think it would be best if Bromir explained it to you tomorrow." Leon was not ready to explain something he did not understand himself.

Kale looked at him bewildered but did not push the subject.

"So what is that?" she said, motioning to the weapons. "On the table?"

Colum gingerly picked up the bundle, allowing the cloth to fall away.

"Weapons, made from a fallen star. Bromir said they are for us," Colum said, his gaze not leaving the sword.

Kale watched, mesmerized, as the glowing blue light flickered inside the weapons. She stared at them incredulously, and Leon understood what she must be thinking. Colum picked up the dagger slowly, pausing as his fingers curled around the handle. He watched the light carefully for any shift or change, but the dagger's glow stayed constant. He passed it from hand to hand before shaking his head and picking up the sword.

There was no change in either weapon, and after a while Colum sighed. "It would seem that I am meant to stick to my bow. Nothing has happened."

Kale focused on the glowing weapons in Colum's hands.

"Were you expecting them to do something?" she asked.

Colum shook his head. "I don't know. Bromir said something might happen…"

He stopped as Leon interrupted, "No, he didn't. He just said we would know."

Colum shook his head. "Ok, well, seeing as Kale is so good with a knife, she's our best bet for the dagger." He handed it to her. "Here," he continued. "Let's see if something happens."

Kale let her fingers curl around the soft leather handle and gasped. The light in the dagger seemed to consume everything. Her focus was only on the weapon. She found her other hand drifting to the handle until she had it clenched in both hands and near her face. Warmth started to seep into her fingers. At first it was pleasant, but then the heat grew. Kale instinctively tried to drop the weapon, but she found that her fingers would not allow her to. She was fixed in place, staring into the burning, flickering light of the dagger.

Soon the heat in her fingers rose to a scorching fire. It spread up her arms and into her body. Kale tried to scream, but her body immobilized. Her eyes flicked to the pain in her arms and a gasp escaped her lips. Her arms were riddled with vibrant, flickering blue ropes of light, the very same light that filled the dagger. It seemed to pulse through her, into her very being.

Leon stared at Kale in shock, unsure of what to do. Kale's eyes widened, almost as if soaking in the light. Blue veins of light traveled up her arms and around her body until they reached her face. Now her hair shone slightly with a blue glow, and her eyes were the same color as the dagger. Colum's jaw dropped open and he shook his head, aghast.

Before either Colum or Leon regained their senses, the light vanished as quickly as it had come. Kale fell limply against the pillows, the dagger resting in her palm, its light flickering normally.

Colum smiled slightly as he shook his head. "We'll know, huh? He could have warned us."

Kale sat up again and stared at the dagger in her hand. She placed it on the bed gently and the light dimmed. Curious, Kale picked it up again. The light in the dagger immediately brightened.

210

"Is this some sort of magic?" Kale asked, dumbfounded.

Leon and Colum smiled at each other.

"I guess you could say that," said Leon, as he held out a hand. "Let me try."

Kale placed the handle gently in his palm. The second his fingers touched the weapon, the light died completely, fading like a fire put out. Leon stared at the silver weapon in his hand, noticing its resemblance to regular steel. Kale gasped and took the weapon from his palm again. Immediately it began glowing, and Leon noticed that her eyes began to slightly glow again as well.

"It would seem the weapon has chosen you," Colum stated, somewhat amused.

Leon's gaze drifted from the dagger and onto the sword. "May I?" he asked, reaching out a hand.

Colum nodded. "Probably yours anyway. It didn't react to me that way," he said, handing it over.

Leon grasped the weapon as Kale did and waited. Nothing seemed to happen for a long while as he turned the sword back and forth in the air, and he started to doubt. Suddenly he felt warmth enter his arms, and small tendrils of light crept up his wrists. His eyes drew back to the sword's blade as the burning started. He panicked when he realized that he couldn't move, and he tried to drop the sword, but it was too late.

KALE STARED AT LEON FROM ACROSS THE ROOM. HIS EYES were glowing bright blue, and his whole body radiated light. The sword's light started to grow brighter, and Kale had to look away.

Kale turned to Colum. "Did I look like that?"

"Somewhat, but your light never grew that much. It stayed as small vines on your arms, and your eyes only glowed blue, not that blinding light that Leon's sword and eyes have grown to," Colum said, avoiding staring directly at the light that had now consumed the room.

"Why is that, do you think?" Kale asked, a hint of jealousy in her voice.

Colum stuck his hands in his pockets. "It's probably because Leon's weapon has more star metal in it, and therefore, more light. Your dagger is just as powerful, but it is only made out of a small piece of the star. That would be my guess."

Kale nodded. "It makes sense, I guess, but it is still crazy that they glow at all."

LEON COULD BARELY HEAR THEIR CONVERSATION. THE burning in his flesh grew, as did the light of the weapon, and he suddenly realized that it was far brighter than Kale's dagger ever had become. His lungs and heart began to burn, and he wondered how much more he could stand before it killed him. The sword seemed to be molding itself to him, flowing into his innermost being.

Finally the light dimmed like a rushing wind, leaving him weak and breathless. He leaned against the bedpost, gasping. His hands trembled, but they still grasped the sword, which was now flickering normally. He looked around the room and realized that everything was suddenly very sharp and clear. His hearing was magnified, and he could hone in on the quiet sound of Kale breathing.

He recognized that his senses had all been sharpened, and he was pleasantly surprised. He placed the weapon on the bed experimentally, and the sensation dimmed but did not diminish. He got up and slowly walked away from the sword. The farther he walked, the more his senses returned to their normal ability. Kale noticed and stared at him inquisitively. He walked closer again, and the ability grew.

"Wow," he whispered. "Impossible."

He took out his old sword from its sheath and discarded it on the bed. Sliding the new sword into the sheath, he smiled when his senses reached their peak again, as the light weapon bumped against his hip. Leon's eyes still held a slight blue shine. The light was just a small change from the grey blue they were before, not even noticeable at first glance.

"What's wrong?" Kale asked.

Leon tapped his sword and scabbard. "The closer I am to this weapon, the better I can see, hear, and smell. The farther I walk from it, the more my senses return to their normal ability. It's like part of the power has been transferred to me," he explained, with astonishment.

Colum stared at the weapons with a newfound interest. "A shame it did not choose me. I guess I shall have to find myself a bow made of star metals," he said, half joking, half jealous.

***

Kale pulled her weapon out again, wondering if she got the same sensation. She placed it on the bed and walked slowly away. Sure enough, her senses diminished as she grew further from it. In only three steps, they were back to normal. She smiled happily, satisfied that her weapon was powerful as well.

I guess I had just overlooked my new senses in all the excitement, Kale reasoned. A nagging voice told her that she was jealous of Leon's sword, but she shoved it away, reminding herself that she could have gotten nothing.

Colum noticed her stop and pointed out. "It looks as if both of your weapons heighten your senses."

"The farther we walk away from them," Kale said, "the more both our and the weapon's power diminishes. It would seem that the only difference between the sword and dagger is that Leon's possesses more light, and so he can be farther from it before the power is disconnected."

"That would make sense. This means we have to be careful to stay close to our weapons, so the power lasts. Kale even more than me." Leon pointed out.

Kale agreed and slid her dagger into the sheath at her hip, slipping back into her bed, exhausted. Colum sighed and crawled under his covers as well.

As the firelight died, it sent warm glowing light across the floor and walls, the welcome heat soothing the electrified atmosphere. Kale sighed and reclined back on her bed staring up at the faded canopy.

"This world has become way too crazy," she sighed quietly to herself before drifting off.

CHAPTER

T hat night, a cool wind blew down from the mountains, carrying the strong scent of pine and snow. The trees in the rain shadow of the mountain were bare; their dead branches jutted out at sharp angles like many bleached and broken bones. In this graveyard, a shadowy figure turned his head towards the peaks and breathed in the wind. He picked up the predominant scent of his prey.

"They are near," he said to himself, satisfied.

His horse stomped beneath him, its black flank rippling with excitement. Abbedon put a firmer hand on the reins to stay the animal.

"They will come," he whispered. He had made sure of it, although he had not dared to confront one boy again; he carried a light sword now; Abbedon could feel its power. No, the other one would be useful. Soon the girl would be his, and he would have his reward.

"Yesss, they will come," he rasped before spinning his horse around and giving it its head, allowing it to gallop through the trees and into the night.

THE NEXT DAY, BROMIR CAME TO TAKE KALE ON THE TOUR HE promised. Leon and Colum watched them go before taking up their arms. Leon was itching to try out his new weapon and Colum had agreed to spar. They took up their stance, facing and circling each other. Colum made the first move and took a swipe at Leon's head. He missed the blow and jabbed his new sword at Colum's stomach. His effort was also countered, and the sword was knocked to the side.

Leon took a hard swipe towards Colum's sword arm, and Colum brought up his sword to meet it. There was a loud clang, and Colum's sword dropped from his hands, split neatly in two. Leon stared at the broken sword in surprise. His eyes flit over the two halves and then moved back to his own sword. It was still flickering and did not even have a scratch.

Colum smiled. "Well, that proves how hard it is."

Leon nodded and grabbed his old sword, handing it to him. "Use this. I will try and use less force," he said, amused.

The day passed quickly as both boys were immersed in their sword-play, and Kale was intrigued by all Bromir had to show her. When she returned to the boys, she found them playing with their swords—drenched in sweat—sporting boyish grins. Kale plopped on the bed, her mind swirling with new ideas and possibilities, many of which she refused to believe.

"How can it all be true?" she whispered. Her eyes moved across the room, to her dagger, and she picked it up. Pulling it out of her sheath, she smiled as her senses increased.

This dagger alone is proof of what Bromir told me... Kale pointed out to herself. Suddenly aware of Kale's presence, Leon re-sheathed his sword, and Colum did the same.

"So?" Leon said. "How was it?"

Kale looked up at them. "Well, do you believe all that Bromir said?"

Colum nodded. "I believe what I saw with my own eyes. Bromir can use some form of magic. How else could he have done those things? Granted, the elves and dwarves thing may not be real, but that room was and so are your weapons."

"And don't forget those wolves. They're definitely not normal..." Leon agreed, pausing. "And what about our recovery? We were all near dead only two days ago, and now we are as good as new, if not better." Leon looked back at Kale, "Surely that says something."

Kale was silent for a moment. "I know, but it's still hard to believe. I mean, two days ago, I would have thought you were crazy trying to tell me this stuff," she said skeptically. "Now I am suddenly supposed to believe all this?"

Leon sighed. "I know, it is hard for me, too." Then he paused, remembering his flashbacks of the glowing knife... and The Shadow. "Ok," he corrected, "I guess it may be easier for me than you. I have been wondering about these possibilities for a while. I knew The Shadow, or Abbedon, before any of you."

He looked at Kale sadly. "I made a deal with him, remember?"

At his words, Colum's eyes widened briefly.

"I disappointed him years ago. He came after me with a glowing knife, not very unlike the one I hold now. His was longer and cruel looking; its light was not even a light at all. It glowed black and mysteriously dark and cold. The Shadow stabbed me with it." Leon continued, wincing at the memory. "And I never fully healed. I have lived with painful flashbacks and constant nightmares of that moment ever since, and every time I see The Shadow, my scar begins to hurt."

Leon paused and then said, "It's strange though, I did not have a nightmare last night, and that says something."

Kale stared at him, suddenly feeling very sorry for him. "You mean you were plagued by nightmares until you touched that sword?" she wondered.

Realization spread across Leon's face. "Yes! Would it do that?" He didn't wait for an answer. "I hope the sword keeps them away forever..." he said.

Running his hands through his hair, Leon shook his head and huffed. "So, what is our next move?"

Colum leaned his elbows on his knees and clasped his hands together. "We should leave here tomorrow."

Kale shook her head. "So soon? We have only been here three days."

Leon nodded. "I agree, we have only been here for a short time, but I also agree with Colum in that we have no need to stay."

Colum continued, "Exactly, we are totally healed and rested, partially to the thanks of some magic, I suspect. We also have supplies; Bromir saw to that." He gestured to the pile on the table containing a vast variety of resources.

Leon nodded, his face serious. "And I don't fancy sitting around here waiting for anyone to catch up to us. I would rather be doing something to prevent our discovery."

Kale understood where they were coming from and nodded. "I guess we better move on. We should let Bromir know tonight."

Leon opened his mouth to show his disapproval, but Kale put up a hand and continued, "And get everything ready to leave at first light. Bromir has done so much for us, he at least deserves to be warned of when we leave him."

Colum agreed, and Leon paused before consenting as well, "Then it's settled."

Bromir chose that moment to walk in. "What's settled?"

Colum straightened, looked up at him and answered, "We are leaving tomorrow."

Bromir nodded. "I suspected as much. It is best for you to get moving as quickly as possible, as Abbedon will be looking for you." Then he smiled and spoke gently, "I wish you all the luck on your journey. I will provide my four strongest and fasted wolves to transport you and your equipment. At the foot of the mountains, they will leave you and return here."

Kale smiled at his kindhearted offer, although she could not imagine riding one of the very monsters that almost killed her three days ago.

"Thank you for everything," Colum said. "You have done so much to help us these past few days. I can't offer any payment for your troubles, since we have so little left…"

Bromir smiled. "Your company has been enough. It can get lonely here."

Kale smiled at the kindly man. She could not even fathom what would have happened if he had not saved them. "Thank you or your help and for everything you showed us. You have given us much to think about," she said sincerely.

"Yes, and for these weapons," Leon added.

Bromir smiled. "You should get some rest before tomorrow morning, especially if you plan to leave early. And as for the weapons, I think there are some things you should know."

Colum muttered under his breath, "*Now* you tell us."

Bromir ignored him. "These weapons are not ordinary, and as such, they will choose one bearer, and be loyal to him or her until death, or until they are broken. Once the weapon breaks, the light leaves it, and it is no more unique than a weapon made of steel. The only things that can break the weapons are the dark swords." He paused before continuing, "There were seven, forged in the heart of a black star. Their bearers were evil, and they went to all lengths to snuff out any light. That is when The Circle was formed. A few select knights wielding swords such as you carry now went out to conquer the evil."

Kale sat on her bed, her ears soaking up everything he said. She felt like a child listening to a fairytale.

"It took hundreds of years, but most of the evil was vanquished, their swords broken. It was not without loss, however. Only two of the original twelve of The Circle were left, and after providing peace and crushing evil across the land, they put their swords to rest and broke them, disconnecting their power. They lead normal lives together now in their old age."

Kale shook her head. "But they never conquered *all* of the evil! And it took them hundreds of years you said; no one lives that long!" she protested.

Bromir put a hand up, "Too many questions! Yes, they did not kill all evil. As long as this world exists, so will evil. You cannot have light without darkness. It is the same with cold and heat. If you only had heat, it would not be heat at all; it would be classified as normal, common. There would be no heat or cold. In the same way, you cannot have light without having darkness as well."

Kale interrupted. "Then what is the point? If the good men never win, then why do they try at all?"

Bromir shook his head and said, "They do win. Unlike good, evil is not content with what it has; it always wants more. If we just left evil to its own devices, this world would be in chaos and ruin. Instead, good keeps evil at bay, and sometimes, even wins a victory that sends it into hiding for a time."

He continued, solemnly, "But it always comes back. As long as there is evil, we must fight it. And your swords will help you with that. As I'm sure you have already discovered, some of the light is transferred to you. As long as you and your sword stay close, your weapon will supply you with strength, increase your senses, and heighten your reflexes. As you spend more time with it, the distance that you can be separated grows, until it does not matter how far you are parted. This power is what kept the knights alive long enough to vanquish much of the evil."

Leon's eyes brightened. "So it is like the sword is part of you? When the sword breaks, is it like your spirit breaks too—like you're half a being?

Bromir suddenly grew very serious. "No, definitely not. Do not even suggest something that evil. Our spirits are to remain in our bodies while on earth. Magic can heighten our God-given gifts, but never mess with the spiritual. It is far better to die with all of your soul, than to live with only half of one."

Bromir's sudden outburst cooled a bit and he sighed. "The reason Abbedon still lives is an example of that. He tampered with his soul, since he was afraid of death. When his wife outlived her years and her sword was broken, she died. Abbedon became mad with grief. He missed his wife, but even more than that, he feared death. To try and avoid it, he placed part of his soul into the sword. He was very powerful for a long time. That was until his sword was broken and that half of his soul died, leaving him not totally human, yet not totally dead. He was not heard of for years. I thought he died of his grief. But he found himself a new sword, mind you, and he has been growing stronger ever since."

He finished suddenly and left the room. They stared after him for a while, but it soon became apparent that he was done speaking.

Leon sighed softly. "Wow," he said, crawling into his bed.

No one had anything to say. They had too much going through their minds to speak.

Kale reclined back on her comforter and closed her eyes. She was determined to fall asleep quickly on her last night in a soft bed, without worry, despite all she had seen and heard that day, but strange images of a half-dead figure floated through her mind's eye.

Leon rested his head on his arm and stared at the dying fire in the small hearth in their room. His eyes grew heavy as the night went on, and Leon sighed, allowing himself to finally relax. He dreamt, but neither of The Shadow nor of a glowing knife. The sword at his hip continued to glow softly.

CHAPTER 62

hen morning finally came, everything was packed up and ready. Kale hung her cloak on her shoulders and picked up a sack. She carefully strapped her dagger around her waist, sliding the sheath to the back of her hip so it was hidden in the folds of her cloak. Bromir came to escort them outside the mountain, where they found four large wolves waiting. The horse-sized animals never ceased to amaze Kale, and she shrunk back a bit when one swung its large head towards her. Leon noted that there were saddles strapped to the wolves' backs, but there were no reins.

"I sure hope these animals know where they're going," he whispered.

One of the wolves turned and stared at him menacingly, and Leon paled. He had forgotten that they understood what was said. Bromir talked quietly to one of the wolves before stepping back again.

"They will take you to the foot of the mountains. You can each ride one, and the packs can sit on Whorl," he said, gesturing to one of the wolves that did not have a saddle on but just some strange basket-like contraption. Leon immediately took the packs over to the wolf and warily placed them into the baskets. Kale handed her pack to him, and he loaded it as well. Kale stayed as far as possible from the large wolves, her nerves on end.

Bromir smiled at her wary glance. "They will not hurt you, and they will protect you from anything else that may be out there," he said. Kale shivered at the memories that flooded her mind of frozen wastelands and strange noises. She nodded hesitantly, suddenly thankful for the protection they would provide, but she still kept her distance from the wolves.

Bromir walked up to one of the animals. "Who's first?" he asked. Colum walked up, much to Kale's relief. Bromir pulled down a stirrup and held it out. The stirrup was chest level for Colum, and he could not reach it. The saddle was just above his head, making the stirrups only just over a foot long.

"Aren't those stirrups too short?" Colum asked.

Bromir shook his head. "If you were riding a horse, yes, but on a wolf it is different. At full speed, their limbs need a lot of space; your legs would get in the way. This way your feet will not fall past their belly, and your knees will be able to help keep you on."

Colum swung himself up using Bromir's cupped hands as a stepping stool. He settled himself into the saddle and hooked his feet through the stirrups. Looking around, he noticed that there were no reins.

"What am I supposed to hold on to?" he asked, worried.

Bromir smiled and motioned to the scruff of the animal's neck. "Hold on to a large handful of fur. It is not sensitive, so don't worry about pulling on it."

Colum grabbed up a bulky handful of the long silky fir and wrapped his hand around it. Kale noted how his position made him look like a horse racing jockey.

"Ah-hem." Bromir coughed beside her. Kale jumped and blushed when she realized that she was caught staring. Her heart quickened when Bromir bent down, clearly ready to help her onto the nearest wolf. Kale stared from him to the animal, and her face visibly paled.

Leon chuckled. Walking up beside Bromir, he moved in front of Kale, and stepping on Bromir's hand, he quickly mounted the waiting wolf. Bromir walked over to the last saddled wolf and bent down. Kale slowly followed him, noticing that the animals were getting antsy. Colum's wolf was swishing its long tail, brushing the snow on the ground, and shifting its weight from paw to paw. The other wolf pawed the ground and sniffed the air, almost sitting down on its haunches, much to Leon's dismay.

The wolf beside Kale grew obviously tired of her standing there and staring, so it crouched onto its knees, making it easy for her to get on. Kale accepted the inevitable and clambered onto the animal's back. The saddle was made of smooth, soft leather, and the fur beneath helped to pad it. Kale gently ran her hands over the wolf's long, silky fur before pulling up her legs and hooking them into the stirrups. The wolf rose gracefully, its leg muscles rippling. Kale was shocked at how high up she was. The second she got in place, with her hand curled around some of the wolf's mane, Bromir nodded to the animals, and they took off. Kale felt as if she left her stomach behind.

Bromir waved as they moved on, calling after them, "Don't let your guard down in the mountain forests; they are strange places!" his words only faintly reaching Kale's ears.

The wind buffeted her face, causing her hair to whip around her ears. The wolves had amazingly long strides, and Kale felt as if she was floating in midair, then crushed against the animal when it pushed off the ground, only to float in the air again. Every time the wolf leapt over a rock or stone, the abnormally large stride got even larger, and Kale felt the saddle pull out from under her. She panicked for a split second before she was slammed back into the padded saddle by gravity. Rocks and snow whirled by, but only the other three wolves that were traveling alongside Kale were visible. Then she laughed with the exhilaration of speed, forgetting all about the possible dangers of the animals that she had imagined only a moment before.

Turning her head to the side, she could see Leon and Colum, both with immense smiles plastered on their faces as they leaned forward in the saddles. The wolves seemed to have brightened up as well, and they yipped and howled in excitement to each other. One of them even emitted a sound that Kale could only describe as a laugh. They loped in a V-formation, Leon's wolf taking the lead. The wolf carrying the packs was directly behind him, keeping up well. Colum and Kale's rides both flanked Leon's wolf, their ears tipped in his direction.

Kale noted with a wry smile that Leon's wolf appeared to be the leader, and Leon was relishing this fact. The ride was wild, as were their mounts, but Kale found she was not afraid. Every leap her wolf took, her heart jumped into her throat, but this only caused her to grow more excited. As the scenery flew by, so did the time, and Kale noted that there was a rosy glow radiating on all the stones. The sun was disappearing behind the horizon, and the breeze began to cool.

As cold set over the mountains, the shadows grew. The wolves slowed to a stop. Leon and Colum dismounted and slid off their animals' backs.

Kale unhooked her stiff limbs from the stirrups and slid off her mount as well. The wolves waited until the pack lead was unhitched before they disappeared into the woods.

Kale watched them go and a sick feeling grew in her stomach. Worriedly, she asked, "Where are they going? Will they just leave us here?"

Leon slung the packs onto the ground and laid out his cloak. "I'm sure they will come back," he assured. "They are probably just hunting."

The stones surrounding the sheltered overhang they had stopped in were bare, as the weather was warm enough here to keep the snow away. Even in this lower altitude, nothing grew. Kale laid out her cloak as well, struck by how stiff she was. All of them were too tired to start a fire, and they reclined immediately. It only took Kale a few moments before her eyelids grew too heavy to keep open.

The early morning sun woke Kale, and she was surprised to find the wolves sprawled and sleeping nearby. Kale stood up slowly, excited to find that she was not as stiff as yesterday but rather invigorated.

Must be the weapons, she reasoned, fingering the hilt of her dagger.

It only took a few minutes to get everyone up, and they were soon on their way again, speeding through the mountains. The wolves were swift; their limbs moving faster than a human eye could follow. A trip that should have taken weeks was accomplished in only two days.

By the evening, the country they were moving through was dotted with forests and creeks; they had come to the edge of the mountains. Soon the wolves had to constantly avoid animals on the path. Kale marveled at the speed in which they travelled, running freely through the grasses, seemingly without the restraints of time. She noticed that there was smoke in the distance, beyond a dense forest, marking a small town.

The wolves seemed to have noticed this too, for they slowed down, loping to a halt. Leon slipped gracefully off his animal and patted it gently. The wolf seemed to nod before it sprung off in the direction they had come. Kale and Colum followed suit, slinging their bags off the back of the pack wolf. Walking back over, Kale stroked her wolf's fur gently, marveling at its large golden eyes with flecks of brown—so majestic and forbidding, yet somehow warm and questioning.

"Thank you," Kale whispered.

The wolf twisted its massive head towards her and stared at her for a moment before dipping its velvety black nose and turning towards the mountains to join the other wolves. Kale swung her pack onto her back and surveyed the land before them. The woods were heavily forested and looked unfriendly. The thickly packed leaves let almost no late afternoon sun through to the padded ground, and shadows seemed to hang in the very air. Leon squinted into the black depths, clearly not trusting the forest either.

Nothing seemed to move; it all looked eerily deserted. Colum pulled his bow off his shoulder and walked towards the forest edge. Leon and Kale followed slowly, nerves on end. They stepped foot beneath the leafy canopy, and the world seemed to go dark. The trees' branches were gnarled and old. The silence was forbidding.

Kale found herself whispering to Leon, "I don't like this place," as she gingerly followed Colum deeper into the dark forest.

Leon shook his head. "Neither do I. There's something about it. Something evil," he said quietly.

Kale nodded. *The mountains were cold, but this is worse.* It was almost as if something foul was rotting in the shadows, like a carcass beneath a stone. She stared at the strange shapes that the trees made; they seemed to have a very human resemblance. Kale looked harder for a second and could just start to make out old, knobby faces on one of their trunks, and long, broken arms reaching out to her. Kale got the strange feeling that the trees were moving slowly, and a chill ran down her spine. She looked back the way they had come; trying to see the light, but where they had passed through was completely invisible, the entrance blocked out. Kale looked around, confused. They were not far enough into the forest to have lost sight of the light, yet it was as if the trees moved to replace their path.

These trees don't want us to leave! Kale realized. She stopped short and grabbed Leon by the shoulder.

"Stop!" she whispered. "Stop!"

Leon paused, and Colum turned to look.

"What now?" Colum asked.

Kale shook her head. "I don't think we are going to get out this way," she said slowly.

Leon looked at her quizzically. "Why? We have been traveling along a straight path."

Kale shook her head. "I don't think the trees want us to leave," she said, looking down sheepishly, realizing how ridiculous she sounded. "I don't know. It sounds crazy, but I think they moved over the way we came in, so we can't leave, and they look like they have... faces," she said, the fear now evident in her eyes.

Leon glanced around at the forest before looking back at her ruefully, and he said, "I still need to work out this magic thing. Don't talk to me about moving trees just yet."

Then he smiled. "Besides, I don't think a few trees can hurt us." Tapping one, he continued, "They're just old wood."

Behind Leon's back Kale watched as the surface of the tree that Leon had tapped moved and wrinkled to form a face—evil, old, and very angry. It seemed to have eyes that were like pits or dark holes into the very center of the tree.

Kale gasped and pointed. "There! Behind you!"

Leon spun around, but the tree had already moved back to its former shape.

"What?" he asked, confused.

Kale pointed. "The tree moved!" she insisted.

Colum shook his head. "Now is not the time to be playing games, Kale," he said sternly, before moving on.

Kale looked wounded, but Leon followed Colum. Kale did not want to be left behind in this strange place, and she was forced to follow, swallowing her growing reservations. Once she hurried after the boys, the tree behind her wrinkled until the face reappeared, watching her departure.

CHAPTER

T he three travelers walked on for some time, until Kale thought she could go on no longer. Her calves began to burn, and her breathing was heavy. Kale had lost all concept of time, and she wondered forlornly if the day would ever end.

"When are we going to stop for the night?" Kale asked hesitantly, hoping they were not still angry with her about the trees.

Colum sighed. "We can stop now, I guess. I did not even notice how long we had been going. I am just trying to get out of this place," he said, placing his sword against a tree.

Leon dumped his pack on the ground and unclipped his cloak. Kale sank wearily to the ground and pulled out some of the dry bread that Bromir provided for them. She noted that Colum did not even attempt to light a fire before lying down and wondered if he recognized the possibility of living trees. If they did exist, she guessed he did not want to be the one to chop one of their limbs off and burn it. Resting her head on her elbow, Kale lied down and looked over at Leon's still form across from her. His chest moved slowly up and down, but she could tell that he was not asleep yet. Colum was sitting against a tree, keeping a watchful eye on the forest. Kale did not like the idea of falling asleep in this place. She tried to keep her eyes open, but soon they grew so heavy, that she was forced to let them droop.

Kale's eyes snapped open, and she sat up. Something woke her. She looked frantically around for what might be wrong. A faint tickle on her ankle came to her attention, and Kale bent over, pulling up her pant leg. A thick tree branch seemingly from nowhere was coiling slowly around her foot like a large snake. Kale jerked her foot back and screamed, waking Colum and Leon. The tree branch immediately reacted, curling swiftly around her ankle, tightening almost to the point of cutting off her circulation.

Leon jumped up, trying to find the source of trouble. Kale's eyes were visibly frightened, but he could not tell why. Colum pulled out his bow and was pointing it in every which direction, searching for any sign of movement. The branch started to pull Kale away from the camp, and she clawed at the ground, trying to find a handhold. There was nothing to grab but dry leaves, and Kale panicked.

Leon spotted the large branch around her ankle too late. It started pulling her faster and faster into the forest. Kale felt herself bumping along the ground through the darkness, and she screamed, not even daring to look where she was headed, fearful of where she might end up.

Leon stared at the receding form in disbelief, hoping this was just another of his nightmares.

Colum clapped him on the back before he began running in the direction Kale disappeared.

"Come on, if you ever want to see her again!" Colum shouted.

Leon snapped out of his stupor and snatched up their cloaks and packs quickly before dashing after Colum.

CHAPTER 64

K ale could feel herself leaving the ground and being pulled up into the air. She flew into the leafy canopy, screaming the whole way. The branch suddenly stopped, leaving her swinging from her ankle. She could feel the blood rushing to her head, and she quickly scrambled around, reaching for her dagger. Wiggling as much as she could, Kale frantically tried to reach out to cut the branch with her knife. Another branch snaked out from nowhere and knocked her dagger to the ground before she could even get close. Kale noticed that her heightened senses diminished, and she felt a sudden wave of helplessness.

The trees seemed to move around her revealing their faces, their branches swaying slowly. She stared at their heavy brows and forbidding eyes and grew in panic. Kale began to scream again, and she frantically tried to wiggle away from the trees. They seemed to shrink back at her voice, their leaves rustling, even though there was no wind, just as if they were whispering to each other. Kale stopped short and strained her ears to listen. She picked out a few words in the weird whispering voices of the trees.

Intruder, knife, kill, suffocate.

Kale started to tremble at the conversation she was able to decipher, and she swung around.

"What do you want from me?" she screamed at the trees.

They seemed to recoil at her shrieking. A branch snaked out and curled around her mouth, silencing her. Kale wiggled and tried to bite the branch, but found it like chewing on dead wood.

A tree moved forwards and whispered to her, "Shhhhh, do not disturb the forest." It rustled at her angrily.

Kale stared into its strange black eyes with anger, and she shook her head violently, trying to rid herself of the branch. The tree seemed to regard her for a while.

"You are strange, little mouse. Why were you in our forest?" the tree whispered.

Kale tried to respond through the branch over her mouth, angry that the tree expected her response, yet it hindered it.

The tree suddenly seemed to notice this and it rustled quietly. The branch was immediately removed, much to Kale's surprise. She looked at the tree with a hesitant curiosity, trying to determine what the intentions of these weird tree beings actually were.

"We were passing through here, trying to get out of these mountains," Kale said simply, choosing her words carefully.

The tree frowned at her outspoken voice. "Quieter mouse, our ears were not made for noise," it said. "Why were you in the mountains? Who were you traveling with?"

Kale returned the tree's gaze openly. "I was traveling with my friends. We were running from soldiers and fled to the mountains," Kale explained, realizing there was no point in hiding anything from a tree.

The face moved closer to her. "Soldiers? Those shiny mice with swords?" The tree asked suspiciously.

Kale nodded, ignoring the fact that the trees called humans "mice". The trees recoiled, and they started whispering again—all at once—the noise sounded like a thunderstorm. The tree that confronted her groaned loud and long, like an old wooden door. Then the forest quickly grew quiet again.

The tree glared at his companions before turning back to look at her seriously. "You were running from these mice—with swords?" it asked.

Kale nodded vigorously, noting the hatred in the eyes of the trees when a sword was spoken of.

The tree seemed to pause, as if contemplating. "Then we will help you to the edge of our forest, because you are enemies with our foes, the sword bearers. They chop us down and burn us!" he said furiously, and Kale could suddenly understand their fear of the weapon. "But you must leave immediately, and don't return, or tell anyone of our forest!" he instructed.

Kale nodded enthusiastically and said, "We will! Don't worry; we were just passing through here. I promise, we will tell no one!"

CHAPTER 66

Leon and Colum dashed through the forest after Kale, following her frantic screams. When the noise stopped for a moment, Leon panicked and froze in his tracks. Then her screams picked up again, closer by. They tramped in her direction until she again stopped. They waited for a long while, but the forest was silent. Only the faint sound of rustling leaves could be heard.

Leon paled. "Do you think—"

Colum put up a hand. "No. We will keep searching until we find her," he said with determination.

They walked in the direction of Kale's voice until they stopped short at the edge of a clearing. The trees formed a perfect circle around the edge, as if they sat at a round table. Kale's voice could be heard softly floating from somewhere in the canopy. Colum started to jog into the ring, and Leon followed, his heart racing.

Kale smiled at the unexpectedly kind trees, and they turned her right side up, but did not remove a branch from around her waist.

"Thank you," she said.

The tree nodded. "Just remember to never come back once you are out of this forest," it said seriously.

Kale nodded vigorously. "I will—"

A crashing noise suddenly broke the silence. All the trees turned to stare at Leon and Colum who had come thundering into the gathering, swords drawn. Kale stared at them and bit her lip.

Just great, now the trees will kill us. We have swords, and they are making noise!

The trees around her swiftly changed to look like normal trees again, and

Kale glared down at the boys.

They stared up at her, jaws sagging.

"How did you get up there?" Leon shouted.

Kale waved her arms and called down in a hoarse whisper, "Shhhh! A tree brought me up here. Now put away your swords before they kill you!" noticing the branches that were slowly making their way to the boys, snaking towards them behind their backs.

Colum shook his head. "In this place? No way," he said, somewhat quieter.

Kale looked at them sadly; the branches had almost reached them.

"This is your last chance. Drop your weapons!" she whispered insistently.

The boys looked at her in disbelief, but it was too late. Branches snaked around the boys' ankles and wrists, hoisting them into the air. Kale watched helplessly as the boys shouted and yanked their limbs frantically, trying to rid themselves of the writhing wood. Leon cried out as a branch squeezed his wrist tighter, causing him to drop his sword. A nearby tree snagged Colum's weapons as well, and they fell to the ground with a clatter. Two more branches snaked out and wrapped around Leon and Colum's mouths, silencing them too. Kale clutched the thick branch encircling her waist with fear.

Are they going to kill us? She wondered as the trees' faces began to unravel again.

The main tree confronted Kale with its rustling voice, "You never told us your friends were sword bearers, little mouse," it whispered angrily, its branches shaking with fury.

Leon and Colum stared in shock at the face that had appeared on the tree, and when Kale started talking to it, Leon's eyes widened in surprise.

"We just carry these swords to defend ourselves from the sword bearers. You can't fight swords with your bare hands," Kale insisted.

The tree looked at her. "I am still not sure we should believe you," it whispered. "Sword bearers are never good."

"This time we are! We are just trying to defend ourselves, just as you could if you had a sword." Kale said, wanting to take back her words as soon as she had said them. *Since when do trees bear swords?*

The tree seemed to think for a moment, its old wood wrinkling above its eyes. "We could bear these weapons?" it rustled softly, questioning.

Kale nodded, looking for any possible escape route. "Of course, pick up one of ours off the ground and try it," Kale offered generously.

The large tree moved a branch gingerly towards Leon's sword lying on the ground. Kale felt a prickling on the back of her neck, and she turned to find Leon staring at her in astonished anger.

He jerked his head towards his sword, but Kale just shrugged her shoulders, turning back towards the tree. Carefully, the tree picked up the weapon and immediately its light grew dim. Swinging it around a few times, the tree gazed at the sword. Kale noted the enthralled faces of the other trees as they moved in closer, like moths drawn to a flame. The tree finally returned the weapon to the forest floor, much to Leon's relief.

The tree turned its dark eyes to Kale. "Where might I get one of these?"

Kale looked to the boys for help. "We may have an extra, but I would not know, so please release my friends so they may tell you," Kale begged sweetly.

The old tree lowered its outstretched limb, and the other branches slid away from their holds on Colum and Leon's mouths. Thick branches coiled around their waists, as the restraints on their wrists and ankles were removed.

Leon spit on the ground to remove the taste of old bark from his mouth, and he wiped his lips with the back of his hand.

"I'm sure we have an extra," he said, reinforcing Kale's statement, before turning to Colum.

"Where is that one I gave you?" he asked.

Colum's eyes never left the tree. "It is in my brown satchel there on the ground," he said softly.

The tree immediately wormed a branch into the pack and pulled out the old sword Leon had stolen from the soldiers back in Bartleona. The sword seemed to move through the air on its own accord, swooping and slashing with grace as the tree tested it.

The old face seemed to smile.

"I will accept this gift and will still help to get you where you were going," it said, and all the trees nodded slowly. Kale nodded as well, feeling that it was appropriate for this situation.

The tree rustled again, but this time Kale could not understand what was spoken. Branches surrounding them bent and twisted as they lifted the packs, cloaks and weapons off the ground. These items seemed to hover in the air around them.

The lead tree looked to Kale again after conversing with the other trees.

"We will pass you along from tree to tree's branches until you reach the edge of our forest," it whispered. "We will also carry your baggage behind you."

Kale agreed, a little apprehensive of the thought of being passed along by living trees.

The tree seemed to smile at Kale. "Thank you for your gift," it rustled, twirling its new sword, "and good luck on your journey, little mouse," it said somewhat fondly.

Kale suddenly felt the branch around her loosen, and she flew through the air, with one last glimpse in the corner of her eye of the tree's shiny bobbing sword in the distance.

CHAPTER

K ale tried not to scream, as she sailed through the leafy canopy. She felt herself falling and flailed her arms, trying to find something to grab onto. Another thick branch materialized in the darkness, and Kale slammed into it, the impact almost winding her. The branch held her for a moment before swinging her off its rough bark like a sling, and on through the forest.

From the corner of her eye, she could see Leon zooming along not far behind, his face clearly expressing both bewilderment and surprise. Colum, on the other hand, had his arms spread as if he was flying, and the wind whipped his hair around his face. The grin on his features was unmistakable; it seemed to stretch from ear to ear.

Kale hesitantly stretched her arms as well, getting used to the feeling of moving through the air and occasionally being lifted again by a nearby tree. She looked down at the ground whizzing by below them and got the sensation that she was flying. Lifting her head again, she watched as trees whirred by, their dark forms almost blurred completely together.

The darkness did not seem as unfriendly anymore—the shelter of the canopy almost welcoming. It was like a soft protective blanket over the forest, shielding it from scorching light rays and prying eyes. In only a couple of minutes, the trees stopped catapulting them through the air, and Kale found herself sliding down a long twisting branch towards the ground.

A field appeared below them—its grassy, yellowish carpet was a nice change from the dark olive colors of the forest. It provided a soft place to land as Kale thumped to a halt, spreading her hands over the clover and forget-me-nots and lavishing in the warm light. The summer afternoon sun showed just how much time had passed while they were in the forest. Time had stopped while in the forest among the trees. Kale's bag landed in her lap with a soft thud, and her cloak followed shortly after. One branch coiled downwards, carefully releasing Kale's dagger into her open palm. She looked up at the trees and just caught a glimpse of the writhing branches that had dropped her belongings, before they returned to their places and stiffened. Wrinkling her brow, Kale stared at the trees; they looked dormant and normal once more, as if they had never moved at all.

Behind the forest, in the distance, Kale saw the outlines of the mountain peaks where they journeyed. They seemed miles away now, and Kale wondered how they travelled so quickly. She turned back around and found Leon and Colum both staring at her. Leon jerked his head away and focused on the grass intently.

Kale looked at him, waiting.

"Yes?" she questioned.

Leon's eyes flashed up to her and then back down again. "You were right," he said quietly, shaking his head.

Colum sighed. "Sorry for not listening," he said sincerely.

Kale nodded. "And almost getting me killed?"

Leon looked at her worriedly and said, "I was so scared that we were too late."

Kale blushed. "It's nice to know that you're looking out for me."

Colum sighed and shook his head. "Talking trees with swords." He smiled amusedly at the ground before looking up. "I would not care to be the next traveler to pass through there."

Kale played with the buckle on her cloak. "I hope we didn't cause any trouble by arming a forest," she said, and they all laughed.

"What a trip! Who could ever imagine?" she sighed. "First riding on wolves faster than light itself…" she breathed, fondly.

Leon continued, "And then flying through a forest like birds, propelled by branches…"

"Well, we will sure have some stories to tell when we get back." Colum chuckled.

Kale nodded. "That's for sure." But then she paused and said, hesitantly, "*If* we get back…"

CHAPTER

It did not take long for the three travelers to reach a nearby town. It was a small community, with many huts and farms lining a long, communal road. The track was dusty, and in the yellow setting sun, it looked almost orange.

Kale stared in awe at the people passing from under her hood. A heifer on a rope followed a small pheasant girl nearby. As the girl passed, Kale met the girl's eyes and found that she was staring at what could be a younger version of herself. They looked at each other carefully before the girl's mother called her back. Kale felt a tear burn her eye, as she remembered her own mother back at home.

A boy walked by, tending a small flock of sheep with a stick, prodding them when they strayed from the path. Small shops were set up here and there, and Kale bought a loaf of bread from one cart, eating it reflectively.

She noted that Colum was out of place amongst the crowds, unlike Leon and Kale; he never had practice weaving through the moving bunch. He was constantly bumping shoulders with those passing by, some turning to glare at him before hurrying on. Kale smiled a bit, realizing how out of place even she felt among people. It had been almost two years since she walked the streets of a town, yet somehow it still felt as if it was part of her.

Or at least a part of my past, Kale corrected herself.

They made their way up to one of the houses, and Colum knocked on the door.

An old man answered it and scowled at them.

"What do you want?" he asked suspiciously.

Colum pulled off his hood and tried to smile. "We are traveling through this area, and my two sons and I," he said, motioning to Kale and Leon, "were hoping to find work in exchange for food."

The old man looked them up and down before shaking his head. "Sorry, don't have any work for you here," he gruffly said, shutting the door before Colum could say any more.

Colum shook his head dejectedly and walked to the next house, rapping on its door. A young woman opened it. She stopped herself, then looked again.

"May I help you?" she asked politely.

"My two sons and I are looking for work in exchange for some food," Colum said.

The girl seemed to think for a moment. "I do not know of any work for you at the moment, but I wish to advise you to move on from this town. I doubt anyone will hire you here."

Colum frowned. "Why would that be?"

Kale noted the girl's fascination with Colum, and a weird feeling grew in her stomach.

The woman fidgeted. "Well, we have all been warned to watch out for three criminals," she said, causing Kale's heart to drop. "Two boys and a girl, each about the age of your sons. They say they are dangerous."

Kale's mind raced. *How did they know that Colum had joined us?*

"Ok, we will move on… look for work elsewhere. Thank you for your help," he said, bending to kiss the woman's hand gallantly. Kale tried to hide her awkwardness as the young woman's face turned bright red.

She spun around and began briskly walking down the road, as the woman closed the door softly on them. Colum and Leon followed after her, puzzled by her rash response.

They walked through the town passing many more huts and people on their way. A filthy dog ran past them, carrying a bone in its mouth, with an angry butcher in hot pursuit. Soon they reached the end of the road, and only a lone inn remained – its old wood paneling shabby and bent in the setting sun. Leon stepped towards the door and looked at the rotting sign hanging above it.

"This should be a good place to stop and spend the night," he said, opening the door.

They stepped inside and found a well-lit tavern with only a few folks sitting at the tables and benches. Colum walked up to the bartender and slapped down three gold coins.

"Two rooms and suppers for all of us," he said definitively. The man nodded and slipped the coins into his pocket, walking out from behind the counter.

They followed him up some steep steps to the right until they reached the second floor of the building. Here, the tender led them through a narrow hallway to the end, where he pushed open two doors and left them. Both rooms looked exactly alike, consisting of only a small hay bed in the corner and a little wooden table to its right.

Colum and Leon dumped their packs and weapons in one room, and Kale set her stuff in the other. They closed the doors behind them and headed back downstairs for a meal.

Kale chose the table in the far left hand corner; it was right beside a small fireplace that sent unusual glowing patterns across the now darkened room. They sat down at the benches and waited for the food to be served. A woman soon walked over, balancing three plates and mugs on her right arm. She expertly set the plates in front of them before sliding the pewter mugs beside each. Colum nodded his thanks to the woman as she walked off. Kale stared at the meal in front of her, grimacing.

Leon noticed her face and chuckled. "Come on. It's better than what we get in the woods," he said, stuffing some in his mouth.

Kale poked at the mushy brown mess and said, "I wouldn't be so sure. It looks like they just dumped a bucket of ground leftovers on our plates… and forgot to cook them."

Kale cautiously tasted some but immediately regretted it and reached for her cup. The meat tasted exactly as it smelled; like long dead cow. She chugged down some of the liquid, and a burning sensation sparked in her throat. She spit the rest of the drink back in the cup and frantically tried to wipe her tongue on her shirt. Both boys burst out laughing.

Tears ran down Colum's face, as he tried to swallow his food without choking. "Have you seriously never drank mead before?" he asked cheerily.

Kale shook her head. "Not without a lot of water added. Why did you not tell me?" she asked, scrunching up her face at the foul taste still sitting

243

on her tongue.

Leon smiled. "We didn't know you hadn't had it like this before," he said, taking a swig of his own drink.

Kale tried to force down some of the meal, knowing that every bite food they had was precious. She even tried a tiny bit more of the mead, being careful not to drink too much of it at once, and found it at least tolerable and not as fiery as it was by the gulp.

An hour later, when they had all finished the food on their plates and their cups were empty, the trio headed back upstairs where they parted and entered their separate rooms. Kale shut the door after her and walked over to the hay pallet in the corner, shoving her pack and cloak off of it. She curled up on the hay and pulled her cloak over her, the mead and meal in her stomach giving her a warm fuzzy feeling. Her eyes soon drooped and she fell fast asleep, oblivious to the whispers in the next room.

CHAPTER 68

Leon and Colum lay out their cloaks on the floor; both felt that it would be selfish to be the one on the bed.

They reclined on them, and Colum whispered, "So they know I am with you."

Leon whispered in the darkness, "Yes, I don't think Kale's plan of scouting through the towns is going to work out so well. It's too risky."

Colum sighed. "That's for sure….I think we should start making the trip to Brecken's castle."

Leon sat up on one elbow. "Are you crazy? Head back to the person who wants to kill us both?" he whispered loudly. "We need information."

Colum shook his head. "Where will we get it? The town's people don't trust us," he reminded him.

Leon sighed exasperatedly. "That doesn't mean we walk into the mouth of the lion."

Colum sat up, frustrated. "I think we should go to the castle and try to work something out. Who knows? Time may have changed the way things were."

"What do you expect?" Leon said. "Your father will accept you with open arms right after he tried to kill you? It isn't a good idea."

Colum glared at him through the darkness. "Ever since you came to my home with that blasted girl, you think you can tell me what to do!" he said. "I am going to the castle whether you like it or not."

"Fine!" Leon hurled back. "Be that way. I'll stay in the towns and do what I know best. I'll figure out what is going on while you go get yourself killed, and I hope Kale hates you for it."

Colum sneered. "Kale *loves* me Leon. She'll follow me to the ends of the earth, whether you're with us or not," he said, driving the words home.

Leon paused. After a couple of seconds, he whispered quietly, "Fine, I will leave you to look through the towns, you can continue to the castle, and we will see who Kale follows."

Colum said, "Ok, but you must leave by noon tomorrow, and don't tell Kale."

"Deal, but you don't tell Kale either. I will be gone by twelve."

Colum put out a hand and asked, "Exactly at twelve?"

"Exactly at twelve."

They shook and lied back down. Facing the wall, Colum grinned into the darkness, unnoticed by Leon. Everything was working out just as planned.

CHAPTER

K ale woke up that morning and sat up on her mat. Everything was how she left it last night, piled up beside her. She stretched and then smoothed out her cloak before draping it over her shoulders again. Picking up her pack, she slipped it on her back and headed outside. Downstairs she found Leon and Colum already sitting at a table, talking in low whispers.

She walked over and looked at them expectantly.

"Ready to go?" she asked.

Leon looked up at her and nodded, standing.

Colum picked up his pack, and they headed outside. The bartender was wiping the counter, but he paused as they left, watching them go.

Kale blinked in the sunlight, surprised at how late it was. It was almost noon. They walked behind the inn and into the peaceful countryside. Passing through fields and by small forests, birds trilled their songs in the trees while farmers worked under the sun.

Before long, they reached another town; this one looked larger, and there was a wall around it. Kale noted that there were not any guards at the gates, and the city looked only about half the size of Bartleona. They walked through the gate, and Kale was greeted by the familiar noise of a market. She looked in the shop windows at all the pretty trinkets and smiled, carried back to another time and place.

She remembered her town, and how the last memory she had of it was an alarm bell ringing in the distance. She listened in her mind as it grew louder and closer.

It's louder than I remember it . . .

Kale snapped awake from her daydream, as soldiers came running from all directions. The alarm bell was real, and somehow, someone knew they were coming. They were trapped, with no chance of escape in a small fishbowl of a city.

Kale panicked. *They can't take us back!*

Colum whispered to Leon, unheard by Kale, "It's noon!"

Leon looked at the sun and then stared at Colum, "But—" he started, looking warily at the oncoming soldiers.

Colum looked back at him seriously. "You said exactly at noon. Don't tell me you're a liar as well as a coward."

The soldiers were almost upon them, swords drawn.

Kale backed up. "Leon..." she said, looking back, the panic rising in her chest.

Leon's gaze shifted to her and then Colum, as if deciding something.

"Um, I have to go," Leon said.

Colum nodded, but Kale glared at him. "What?"

Leon looked at her sadly before turning and disappearing around a bend. Kale put up a hand and tried to follow him, but soldiers closed out where he went, focused on their find. Colum smiled grimly at Leon's departure and grabbed Kale by the arm, pulling her around a nearby building, with the soldiers hot in pursuit. She stared the direction Leon went for a moment before running after Colum.

They sprinted to the end of the road and headed towards the gates. There were no guards there to block them, and they exited the stone barrier's mouth with not a moment to spare. Kale followed Colum as they dashed towards the woods, hoping for some cover in the trees—their feet pounding on the grass-covered ground and wind whipping around their faces as their packs bounced heavily on their backs.

They made it to the edge of the forest in only a few minutes, and Kale panted heavily from the sprint. They slowed a bit and looked back, surprised to find that the soldiers did not even follow them past the gate. Kale crouched with her hands on her knees, gasping for breath. She shook her head, trying to clear her mind of the mixed emotions flying around inside of her.

"What was that?" she asked. "Why did he leave us?"

Colum sighed, leaning against a tree. "Decided there was no point in helping us. He probably realized that they were going to catch us, so he left us while he could."

Kale shook her head, trying to stop the tears. "He wouldn't! Not after everything we've been through..."

Colum put a hand on her shoulder. "He's no hero, Kale. People get scared sometimes, and he probably thought he was best on his own. You know Leon. He's stubborn...and immature..." Then Colum paused and said tenderly, "At least we have each other, right?"

Kale nodded. "He left right when I needed him most..." she whispered. "Thank you for staying with me, Colum. Leon has been unpredictable," she paused, "many times." Colum nodded sympathetically as Kale continued.

"You have been the only one who has been dependable," she breathed.

Colum straightened stiffly after a while, and they started walking through the forest.

"We should find a place to camp before nightfall," he advised, observing the color of the sky. Kale nodded, and they walked together in silence for a couple of hours. Finally, the sun sank past the horizon, and they halted, dumping their packs on the ground.

Kale didn't even bother to lay out her cloak, but instead she sat with her back against a tree staring out into the forest.

"I'll take first watch," Kale offered, and Colum nodded, lying down on his cloak heavily.

She leaned her head back against the tree, a warm wind caressing her face and brushing through her short hair. She ran her hand through it, remembering how long it once was, and her mind went back to the day she first started out.

Leon was just a boy she found in the barn, a filthy runaway. He had brought adventure, a change from the repetitive life she was living. One day he pulled her on the escapade of a lifetime.

It was wonderful, she remembered.

They ran from home, and they were free, careless, until that fateful day when The Shadow caught up to them and captured them, bringing them to Bartleona to be sold as slaves.

He betrayed me, she recalled, a tear trickling down her face. *He set me up in exchange for money. Made a deal with The Shadow.*

She pictured the next year, her life as a kitchen maid.

But then I found love! She smiled, fondly remembering Matthew. She tried to remember his face and was disturbed to find that she only had a vague image of him.

Then that little rat got me back in jail, Kale remembered, recalling her time in jail, where she had met Leon again.

He saved me. Kale reminded herself, as a tear travelled over her cheekbone and down her neck. An image flashed in her mind of the time they spent in the cave. Then of the journey into the mountains, where they met Colum, and then Bromir. Kale smiled a bit when she thought of the weird tree people and Bromir's wolves.

And now I am here, she said to herself.

Abandoned by Leon… again. She blinked back tears and looked up at the sky.

How can I ever trust Leon again? She asked. *After all I went through!*

Kale began to sob. *This is too much!* She wrapped her arms around her knees and cried herself through the night.

The next day, Kale and Colum walked silently side by side, each wrapped up in their own thoughts. At lunchtime, they stopped for a brief break. Colum left for an hour and came back with a rabbit, which they skinned and ate. After hiding the bones, they continued on again. The pain in Kale's heart about Leon's choice distracted her from the beautiful scenery of the forest. She did not even notice the animals that they passed by or the distance they had gone; it was though she was in a deep fog trudging along blindly. The day seemed to fly by more quickly than normal, and all too soon Kale was lying down on her cloak again, her heart again aching as she thought of Leon before falling asleep.

Late into the night, when both Colum and Kale were fast asleep, a dark form crept towards the campers; its presence chilling the air. It moved silently over to Colum and the tip of its cloak touched his sleeping form. Colum jerked awake, trying to strain his eyes in the dark.

"Shhh, the girl is sssleeping," the form said.

Colum said, "But why are you here? You said tomorrow."

Abbedon's head moved slowly in his dark, heavy cloak. "Yesss, bring her tomorrow. I will be there. I am just making sure we are still agreed on the plan?" he hissed.

Colum nodded and said, "Of course. Just bring your money and the letter from my father."

Abbedon seemed to grin through the darkness. "Of courssse," he rasped, gliding away from the camp. When he was too far for Colum to hear, he whispered to himself, "Humans, they are all too easily persuaded."

CHAPTER 60

Colum tapped Kale on the shoulder and she jerked awake. The sun was up, and birds were singing again. She yawned and grabbed her pack from the ground, slinging it over her shoulder. They walked through the woods for a while, and soon the forest grew monotonous. Kale felt as if she was seeing the same trees and plants over and over again. It seemed like hours before they finally reached the forest edge and entered a field. Rabbits were eating the clover, and swallows swooped through the air.

Kale smiled up at the blue sky, and her heart jumped at the peaceful sight of the meadow. It was a large field, and it dipped slightly in the middle, giving it the appearance of a valley. She looked over at Colum and noticed that he seemed to be fidgety. His eyes scanned the field, as if searching for something.

Kale looked at him and asked, "Is everything okay?"

Colum jolted, as if just noticing that she was there.

"Yeah, it's fine," he said, running a hand through his hair, tousling it.

Kale frowned, uncertain, but she left him alone. They walked on for only a short while longer when Kale heard a noise like thunder. Glancing up at the clear blue sky, she scanned the horizon for any signs of rain clouds. The thundering grew louder and more persistent.

Suddenly, Kale noticed something reflecting the sunlight on the edge of the valley. She squinted and looked closer, trying to make out what it was. The form drew nearer and nearer until she could just make out its outline.

Kale gasped and grabbed Colum's sleeve.

"Colum…" she yelped in disbelief.

"I know," Colum said and stared ahead.

Kale backed up, her mouth hanging open, taking in what her eyes could not alone hold. Surrounding them, on all sides, was an army. Not just ten or twenty soldiers, but legions. Their bodies like a human wall formed around them. Kale frantically scanned the ranks, looking for any way of escape. Her eyes passed over the forest. There the soldiers were fewer, as their horses could not fit between tightly packed trees.

Kale nudged Colum and cried, "We can run to the forest!"

Colum shook his head. "There's no point. The bowmen would shoot us before we got there."

The soldiers stopped, trapping them in the valley. Three soldiers parted from the ranks, their places quickly taken by others. They advanced, riding swiftly towards them, with swords drawn. Kale's heart pounded in her chest, and her palms grew clammy.

"Colum?" she said, the soldiers growing closer. "Colum, please! What do we do?" she asked frantically, but Colum just shook his head.

The lead soldier got within shouting distance, and he called out to them, "Give us the girl and get out of the way, then no one will be harmed." Colum stood rigid beside Kale, and she clung to him.

Why do they want me? She wondered, wanting anything more than to be taken by these soldiers.

The man on the horse got even closer, and he called out again, "Get out of the way boy! Remember the deal?"

Kale spun towards Colum, her face overcome by disbelief. "A deal? *You* made a deal with *them?*" Oblivious to the advancing soldier, Kale began to shout, "You betrayed me, too?"

The soldier was upon them, and he reached out to pull Kale onto his horse.

Colum seemed to pause, and then as if waking from a trance, he jumped up and whipped out his sword, killing the man with one stab. The other two soldiers advanced, swords drawn, and Colum gripped his own weapon in readiness.

He put a hand out to shield Kale. "Stay behind me!"

The soldiers charged and Colum yelled a battle cry, swinging his sword at the two men. He killed one on the first blow, and the other fell from his horse. Colum walked over in three steps and swiftly slew him as well. Kale stared at the blood on the ground, and she almost grew faint. She had never seen Colum so determined before, a fire alight his eyes.

Seeing that their comrades were dead, the first rank of soldiers advanced with a harsh cry. Kale was no soldier, but she could tell right away that Colum would not be able to fight alone for long. She did not know what else to do but squeezed her eyes shut tight.

We're going to die, she realized, as the soldiers urged their horses forward, the hooves on the ground pounding like drums.

Suddenly, a loud yell burst out from the direction of the woods and a lone figure came running towards them, sword drawn. It took Kale only a few seconds to recognize him, with his blue sword. He ran up to join them and stood beside Colum.

Kale stared at him in disbelief, muttering, "Leon?"

He looked over.

"Yes?" a small smile curled at the edges of his lips.

She couldn't take her eyes from him. "But, you…left us," she said.

Leon looked at her sadly and shook his head.

Colum regarded him as well, and he nodded. "Thank—" Leon put a hand on his shoulder and smiled, nodding.

They turned to face the oncoming soldiers with determination. As the first ranks drew close, some soldiers started shooting at them. Kale ducked on impulse as an arrow flew by, just above her head. Soon the soldiers were close enough for skirmishing. Kale could make out the angry features on their faces.

They grew closer, and she backed between the boys.

Closer.

Kale pulled out her dagger and held it in front of her, shaking with fear.

The soldiers closed in, and there was a resounding clash of steel against steel as the combat began. Kale watched in horror as the scene unfolded before her. Kale heard of battles like this, and even knew some of the young men who returned from them, but witnessing one herself was different.

The soldiers were so close that Kale had to avoid being stepped on by the horses' massive hooves. Beside her, Leon's muscles flexed as he prepared to take a swing at a soldier. On her other side, Colum dodged a blow from a mace man and thrust upwards, impaling the soldier through his neck. A soldier's helmet toppled past her feet, and his body flopped lifelessly against his horse. Kale gagged and tried to look away from the decapitated figure. When she turned, she found a soldier had gotten past Leon and Colum and was holding his sword above her head, ready to deliver a deathblow. Kale reacted and let her dagger fly. It drove home, and the soldier's sword fell from his hands. Kale dodged it and swiftly retrieved her dagger, yanking it from the body. In a few minutes it was apparent who had the upper hand in this battle against the group of first rank; the soldiers' steel weapons were no match for Leon's sword.

Soon only two soldiers were left—a foot soldier, and a bowman on a horse. Leon quickly dueled the foot soldier and dispatched him. The bowman backed his horse up and notched an arrow onto the bowstring. He pointed it feverishly at Colum and Leon, trying to guess who would advance first.

Leon started walking towards him, and the arrow directed at his head. Kale watched worriedly as Leon walked slowly towards the bowman, his eyes not leaving the arrow shaft. The bowman watched him too, pulling back on the string—his eyes clearly giving away his fear. Leon suddenly lunged and stabbed the man through his heart. The soldier fell against his horse, releasing the string on his bow which let the arrow fly harmlessly past Leon . . . and bury itself into Colum's chest.

CHAPTER

Colum gasped and stumbled backwards, grasping the arrow shaft in both of his hands. His mouth was open, trying to gasp in air. Kale stared at the wound in shock, her mind not believing what her eyes could see. Colum fell backwards against the ground and moaned, his head relaxing onto the dirt. Leon turned around and recognized what had happened, his eyes surveying the scene in only a couple of seconds. His look of victory suddenly vanished.

Kale startled, as if breaking out of a frozen state, and she ran to Colum's side. Ripping away his cloak, she was horrified to see the dark patch of blood that had soaked through the center of his shirt. Tearing off some of her own shirt, she frantically tried to wrap it around the shaft and stop the blood.

"It's not that bad!" she said. "We can get you to a doctor. I'm sure there's one nearby," she insisted, her voice shaking.

Colum lifted his head and put a hand over hers, stilling her frantic attempts. "Let it be," he whispered.

Kale kept trying to shield the blood from her view, covering up the fact that she did not want to believe was really true.

"No!" she cried. "You will be okay! We can still fix this."

Colum shook his head. "Stop it, Kale. You won't make it better."

Hot tears rushed to Kale's eyes as she said, "But you have to get better! How will we continue without you?"

Colum smiled weakly. "You'll find a way. You must," he said coughing, "For me." He squeezed her hand and fell back again, fighting for breath.

Kale tried to fight back the tears that pooled in her eyes. Leon came over and knelt beside them. Colum blinked open his eyes once again and managed, "I am so sorry. For everything."

Leon nodded. "Hey," he said softly, "I was no better, remember?" Leon's face was strangely devoid of emotion.

Colum nodded. "Thank you." He closed his eyes and paused, before continuing. "Leon?" he whispered.

Leon looked back at him. "Yes?"

Colum coughed. "I'm sorry I never told you. I wasn't sure myself until I talked with Bromir that night."

Leon waited for him to continue.

"You must get our kingdom back…" Colum paused. "Little brother."

Colum smiled faintly and reached out a hand to Leon. Leon grasped it, shaking his head, trying to deny the tears that were suddenly coming to his eyes.

Colum coughed violently and then sighed, his final breath leaving him. Kale let Colum's hand slip from her fingers as his body went limp. She didn't even try to stop the tears streaming from her eyes. Carefully picking up Colum's head, she placed it in her lap and shutting his eyes one last time, she rocked him gently back and forth.

Leon stood up and faced away from them, raking a hand through his hair. Kale could tell that he was crying. She looked back down at Colum, her tears dripping onto his still features, running down his neck. His brown hair was tousled from the battle, and he had a smudge of dirt across his face. Kale gently wiped it off with her hand, and he suddenly looked peaceful.

Kale tried to believe that everything was all right, that Colum was just sleeping. The rest of the army had now caught up and was closing in, but that did not matter to Kale anymore.

Leon suddenly woke from his grief, and he turned with worry in his eyes.

"Come on Kale, we have to go," he said, his voice broken.

The soldiers were closing the gap between them and the forest. Kale ignored him, her small frame hunched over Colum's body. Leon walked over. "Come on Kale, they will kill us all if we do not leave!"

Kale spun around, lashing out with her hand, knocking him back. "Go away! He's dead because of you! If you hadn't left…" Kale sobbed loudly.

"You," Kale cried, "only care about yourself!"

Leon shook his head. "You don't understand, Kale. Colum..." he paused, not wanting to say something just yet. "I'll explain later, but you have to come now!" he urged. Now the soldiers were almost completely blocking their route of escape.

Kale screamed at him with tear stained eyes, "I can't just leave him here!"

"He's dead, Kale!" Tears filled his eyes. "Dead!"

Kale stared up at him, a bewildered expression on her face—shocked that he had yelled at her. Leon immediately regretted it, and he sighed, watching as their last chance of escape disappeared.

He knelt back down beside her, and putting an arm around her, he whispered, "I'm sorry. We can stay."

The soldiers drew closer; at their head was a large black horse. It ran a full two lengths ahead of the rest of them. Its muscles rippling as it galloped towards them. On its back, the rider spurred it forwards, his shadowy black cape billowing in the wind.

CHAPTER

bbedon grinned roguishly down at them from his mount. He circled them and surveyed their grief-stricken forms. Such joy did it give him, to see them suffer. Leon looked up at him through shrouded eyes.

The Shadow laughed. "We meet again, boy. Too bad your new friend wasss not able to join usss," he mocked. Leon did not answer, but he continued to stare at The Shadow, who motioned to the soldiers. "Lock them up."

Leon didn't even resist as shackles were roughly clapped around his wrists and ankles. The soldiers grabbed the weapons, tossing them in a bag, which The Shadow then tied to his horse. Leon was dragged off the ground by the soldiers and forced to walk away from Colum's body, which was soon lost among the many horses' hooves. Kale and Leon were hooked together behind Abbedon's horse.

The army soon scattered and headed off along a large road, likely to a nearby city. The Shadow, however, started walking away from the company and through another part of the forest. Leon and Kale were forced to keep up with his horse, or the chains yanked on their ankles and they fell on top of each other, dragging across the rough ground. The silence was hostile, as they did not even whisper to each other, too caught up in their grief.

They made their way through the forest and on through the night. Kale grew tired and lagged behind. Leon noticed and put her arm over his shoulder, helping her along in spite of his own exhaustion.

She leaned her head against his shoulder and whispered, "Thank you," into his ear.

Leon just nodded and focused on the path ahead.

Soon the forest became sparse, and they entered what seemed to be a wasteland. As far as the eye could see, there were dark sands and shadowy clouds. A lone mountain was almost visible in the distance; its black form spoke of death and despair.

Leon recognized it immediately from Bromir's light stone, and he repeated the name, "Gonder Dohr." Even the speaking of the name brought a heaviness over them.

Kale removed her arm from around his shoulder and stared at the ghastly sight.

They jerked back into reality when their chains snapped tight, and they were forced to keep moving. The black sands were not fine and silky; instead, they were many pieces of sharp rock and broken shell, stained black by some past volcano. Kale winced as the rough ground cut through her shoes, shredding them to pieces, leaving her feet bare. She tried to stop, but the horse pulled them forward. The jagged rocks soon shredded the soles of her feet as well, and she noticed that between her and Leon, they left two sets of bloodied footprints on the sand.

A cold wind whistled over the sands, blowing pieces of dirt and grit into their eyes. Kale coughed violently as she tried to choke up the dust that had entered her lungs.

After what seemed like hours, the mountain did not look any closer, and Kale felt that she would not be able to continue much longer. Neither of them had had any food or water, and they had been walking all through the night. Kale could not even fathom the pain of being dragged across the sharp ground, so she tried to stay upright, for the sake of Leon. They were forced to keep walking, even though their bodies could not carry them.

Three agonizing hours later, they finally entered the cool shadows of the mountain. A large, stone door opened in front of them, clicking as it locked in place. The horse entered first and Kale noticed that apart from a few torches lining the walls, the interior of this place was completely dark. The large stone gates slammed shut on them again, causing the dark interior to grow even blacker.

Their chains clanking against each other created a cold and eerie echo through the halls. A chill ran down Kale's spine, and an unwelcome feeling of dread entered her stomach.

The Shadow dismounted his horse, his cape-covered form barely visible in the dark lighting. He unhooked their chains from the saddle and allowed his horse to wander off. As the animal disappeared, the hollow sounds of its hooves on the stone drifted off as well.

Yanking on their manacles, The Shadow dragged them to a darker part of the hall, where they started descending a steep, spiral staircase. Kale stumbled blindly after Leon, glad that he was between her and The Shadow. The air grew colder, and it became damp and smelly. They reached the bottom of the staircase and started walking down a long hallway. Leon suddenly stopped in front of her, listening as the sound of keys jingling together broke the silence.

A rusty creek of an old door pierced Kale's ears, and she suddenly felt herself being shoved roughly. Blindly falling, Kale scrabbled around to find where she was. She felt the cold, wet stone, two seconds before she crashed into it, beside Leon. The rusty door swung shut again and the keys clattered in the lock. She did not hear The Shadow leave, but somehow the cell felt a tiny bit warmer. Kale groped around in the darkness until she found Leon's arm. His skin felt hot compared to the cold stone floor. Kale edged closer to him for warmth and comfort. Leon fidgeted, trying to think of what to say.

Struggling to overcome her grief, Kale finally broke the silence, "So he was your brother?"

Leon nodded in the darkness, and Kale realized that her eyes were adjusting.

"I guess so," he paused. "I don't know how I didn't see it before."

Kale shook her head. "It makes sense. You looked so similar, and you never got along."

Leon nodded. "And we both made the same mistake."

Kale looked at him, confused. "What was that?"

"We both betrayed you."

Kale's heart weakened at the hurt and repentance she saw in Leon's eyes. Then she shook her head. "But that is what I don't understand. Of all people, why are they after me?" she asked quietly.

"Don't ask me. The Shadow will undoubtedly be back to try and get you and I to talk. If he found out that I told you, he would surely kill you, but if he learns you know nothing..." he paused. "Well, it may be better for you."

Kale was itching with curiosity, but knew better than to push. Her eyes were fully adjusting to the dark now, and Kale noticed that there were some bowls near the base of the door. She crawled over to them and brought them back. Crouching beside Leon, she handed him one and tentatively felt the mush inside.

Leon tasted it and immediately began gobbling the rest down.

"Gruel," he said, between mouthfuls. "Not the greatest taste, but a great energy builder."

Kale ate the watery porridge in her bowl without complaining. When they were done, Leon set his bowl back down and leaned against the wall. "It would seem that The Shadow wants healthy victims to torture," he said softly.

Kale's heart flopped at his words, and her fear grew.

CHAPTER 63

When Kale's eyes had completely adjusted to the dark, she immediately tried to pull out the sharp pieces of stone that were imbedded in the soles of her feet. She managed to pick out six large pieces and a numerous amount of small, glasslike shards. Finally, satisfied that her feet were not as sore, she leaned back against the wall beside Leon and tried to get some sleep.

They were left alone in the cell for two more days, or that was what Leon assumed according to when the bowls arrived. The gruel soon had them back to their former shape; even their feet had mostly scabbed over. This only caused Kale's worry to grow, knowing that soon The Shadow would be back.

Kale had imagined his rasping breath drawing closer so many times, that when he actually came back and unlocked their door, she was convinced that she was dreaming.

The Shadow yanked on their chains and forced them to their feet, pulling them through the door. They followed him through more hallways, and what Kale saw now that her eyes were completely adjusted to the gloom, horrified her. Lining the walls were all manners of rusty forms, sharp and hostile. Kale's skin crawled as she imagined what they were for. She noticed that a skeleton was strapped to one, its shape grossly bent, and she quickly looked the other way.

They soon entered a stone room; its only embellishments were a row of rings hooked low to the floor, a fireplace in one wall, and a lone chair in the middle of the room—its legs attached to the stone floor. The Shadow separated Kale and Leon's chains, hooking Leon up to one of the rings on the wall, and sitting Kale down in the chair, her arms chained around the back.

The Shadow hissed to her, moving closer to the fire and picking up a poker. "I am to find out what you know," he said, poking the fire with the metal rod. Kale stared at him warily. She noticed that Leon looked strangely worried; he was watching The Shadow's every movement, his eyes wavering over the poker. "What did Leon tell you?" he hissed.

Kale looked at him—where she believed his eyes should be—and answered as bravely as possible, "Nothing."

The Shadow pulled the rod out of the fire, its tip glowing from the heat. "I wasss hoping you would answer me honestly. Doing things the hard way is... tediousss," he said, sliding closer to Kale. "Tell me what you know."

Kale looked at him blankly, without any words.

The Shadow seemed to smirk, and his red eyes flashed beneath the hood.

"Very well." He reached out a hand and ran it through her hair. "A pity you cut it short."

He scraped by, moving beside her. The hot iron grew closer and closer. Kale squirmed away from its glowing orange tip, fear coursing through her veins.

Leon was straining at his chains, perspiration beading on his forehead. His eyes were full of sorrow and fear. Kale knew he was dealing with the situation worse than she was. His eyes flitted from the ceiling to the wall to the floor; he was trying to look anywhere but at her. Shooting pain seared up and down Kales arm, and she could smell the sickly sweet odor of burning flesh. A gasp escaped her lips, and Leon's eyes snapped back to her. But she had nothing to say, and this did not satisfy The Shadow.

"Looksss like your friend should have a turn. If I can't break you like this, I will break you the hard way." The Shadow yanked on Kale's chains and pulled her to the wall. He hooked her up there and then pulled Leon to the chair.

Sitting him down, he attached the cuffs. Fear widened Kale's eyes. Her pain was small, and she would much rather bear it than have to watch while Leon was subject to The Shadow's games. Her heart pulsated painfully, and she cried out, begging The Shadow to stop. The black figure ignored her and leaned close to Leon's ear, whispering,

"My ordersss do not say I must keep you alive, so I will just skip to the best part," he hissed, almost crooning.

Leon's skin crawled, and he shivered as he felt The Shadow's cold, bony fingers trace along his neckline.

Kale watched The Shadow caress Leon's neck, and she remembered what he did to Sam a year ago. Her hands grew clammy, and her brow lifted with fear. Kale and Leon locked eyes for a second, and Leon seemed to say, 'It's all right'.

THEN, THE SHADOW BENT HIS FINGER EVER SO SLIGHTLY, AND instantly Leon's whole body went rigid, and he cried out. He writhed and squirmed beneath his chains, but The Shadow stayed perfectly still. Leon moaned, his muscles clustering as his back arched. His chest was heaving, working extra hard to take in air. He tried desperately to get away from The Shadow's hand, as his scar burned worse than it ever had.

Leon seemed to suddenly be overcome with visions. He fought them, The Shadow, and for his own life.

KALE SCREAMED, HER MIND NUMB WITH THE SHOCK OF THE pain she was witnessing. Leon's body started to spasm, and Kale's eyes flooded with tears. She sat, totally helpless. Tears streamed down her face, and she sobbed brokenly. The Shadow seemed to grin from beneath his cloak.

"I can stop now, and he will wake up, so I can finish him. Or I can hold on for just a little longer and put him out of his misery."

Kale's tears filled her eyes, and sobs wracked her lungs, but she did not know what to say.

"Just a little longer…" The Shadow continued.

Leon was still writhing under the chains.

"Almost there…"

Kale watched dumbfounded as the spasms stopped, and he lay still, his head falling limply against his chest. Kale cried out and yanked on her chains once more, a frenzied scream filling the air. The Shadow dropped his hand to silence her. "Silly girl, it's too late, he'sss dead."

CHAPTER 64

Kale stared through her tears in disbelief at Leon's still form slumped in the chair. The Shadow moved carelessly past Leon and came up beside her. "So, is there anything you wish to tell me now?" he asked softly.

Kale stared at him brokenly, her eyes clearly developing a fury towards the dark figure.

"No! I know nothing! Curse you, Abbedon, He never told me anything! He said it would be better that way, and now you killed him! For nothing!" she screamed at him, jerking on her chains, trying to get to The Shadow, tears streaming down her face.

The Shadow grinned. "You can't curssse a demon," he rasped. "Well, if you have nothing to tell, I can have you join the boy," he said softly, as if he wanted to see her reaction to his offer.

Kale did not respond. She was numb, now that her two closest companions were dead.

The Shadow cackled. "Too bad the king wantsss that honor."

Kale looked at him strangely. The Shadow reached out and stroked a piece of her hair, and Kale recoiled.

"You will be transported by one of my servantsss to the king's castle. I'm sure he has something planned just for you," he hissed, grabbing her chains from the wall and pulling her towards the hall they came through. Kale watched forlornly as the slumped figure in the chair disappeared around a bend, and a lone tear ran down her cheek.

Just as The Shadow promised, Kale found herself chained in a cart the next day, along with a bag containing their weapons and Leon's lifeless body. The cart rolled off into the hard, dark sands, pulled along slowly by a grimy old donkey. A deformed man sat at the front with the reins—his milky blind eyes a stark contrast to the black desert. Kale wondered how he could maneuver the cart with two blind eyes, but she was almost glad he couldn't see her, for it gave her a slim hope of escape. She decided to wait until they had reached a forest, so that she did not have to walk endlessly through the desert again.

They rolled on, over the sand, bumping along on the rough ground for hours. Kale hated the pitiful sight of Leon bouncing around like a ragdoll, and she wished there was some way to hold him still. His face was turned away from her, and she was glad of this.

Kale lost track of time completely, as everything in this desert spoke darkness; the sky blotted out by large charcoal colored clouds. Finally, the cart reached the end of the desert, and small trees came in sight. Kale started to wiggle around, and she tried to reach the bag.

The clanking of her chains caused the driver to halt the donkey.

"What are you doing girl?" he asked suspiciously.

Kale's heart pounded, and she scrambled for an excuse. "Um, I was uncomfortable and trying to find a better position," she said innocently.

The driver just huffed and continued on.

Soon they were completely beneath a forest canopy, and Kale noticed that the driver was following a well-beaten path. She scrambled around again, trying to reach the weapon bag, but this time, she was careful to be quiet. Her middle finger just brushed the sack, and she strained against her chains, trying to gain even a half-inch. Her nail caught in the loose weave of the sackcloth, allowing her to pull the piece within her reach. Kale carefully slid the bag closer and silently opened it up. She looked around frantically for her dagger and spotted it at the bottom of the pile. Reaching in carefully, Kale grasped the handle and started to pull it out. The blade made a scraping sound, and Kale winced, hoping the driver did not notice. Kale started singing a crude tune loudly to mask the noise, and she quickly pulled the dagger out.

The driver spun around, and Kale almost forgot that he was blind beneath his furious gaze. "Be quiet girl! My old ears don't like noise," he said roughly.

Kale nodded. "I'm sorry, I won't sing anymore."

She tucked her dagger into the folds of her shirt and leaned back, relieved, against the wood of the cart.

Suddenly, the driver stopped the cart and jumped down. He walked to the side and picked up the weapons. Kale's heart skipped a beat.

I forgot to close the bag!

She bit her lip, hoping the driver would not notice.

Luckily for her, the driver just swung the bag into the forest, where it fell with a clatter among some bushes. He then scooped up Leon and walked over to the bushes, dumping him beside the bag. The old man sightlessly scrounged around for leaves along the forest floor to cover Leon's body.

Kale tried to stop the panic rising in her chest when she saw Leon buried, something triggering inside her head the reality that he was gone.

When the driver got back onto the cart and it started moving again, Kale immediately went to work on the wood securing her shackles. She dug at the rotting wood around the hook that her chains were attached to until she had blisters on her fingers.

Kale could tell that the sun was setting by the color of the light filtering through the trees. She tried desperately to loosen the peg, but it was still firmly inserted into the wood. Eventually, Kale was forced to put away her dagger and try to sleep off her exhaustion. She only rested for a few minutes when the cart jostled her awake again.

CHAPTER 66

The night had not yet passed as a thick mist hung over the forest. Kale pulled out her dagger from the folds of her cloak and immediately started working on the peg again. She could slide it around now, but the hole she made was still not big enough to pull out the peg. Kale chiseled at the wood continuously, only stopping to check if the peg would slide through. She worked at it, pulling with all her might on the peg. She muttered a simple prayer, and the wood gave way a little, the peg sliding halfway through the hole. Kale's heart pounded, and she carefully tugged at it a little more, twisting and turning it. Finally, the peg came out, and she sighed thankfully.

The driver stared blindly straight ahead, seemingly undisturbed. Kale tucked the chains into her cloak and held them tightly to her stomach to muffle the noise. She then wiggled to the back of the cart and carefully slid off, landing noiselessly on the dirt track.

She watched in satisfaction as the cart kept rolling ahead without her, the driver not even blinking an eye. Kale guessed that it would not be long before the driver noticed that she was gone, and he would come back for her.

Kale slunk into the forest and immediately began running back the direction she had travelled in the cart, never straying too far from the road. Her eyes scanned the foliage, looking for a particular bag near some leaves. She estimated that since she was moving twice the speed of the cart, she should reach the spot that Leon was left in a couple of hours. Kale plodded on, the weight of the chains still attached to her wrists slowing her down somewhat. Nevertheless, she kept moving, with keen determination.

At last, Kale slowed a little, scanning the area for any sign of the bag. It had been three hours of gruesome plodding, and her breath came in short heaves. Kale guessed that this was about the right area, and she anxiously started searching. She looked behind bush after bush that looked similar to the ones that Leon and the bag were hidden behind, but to no avail.

The day had gotten old by the time Kale finished scouring the whole area. She had almost given up, her heart growing heavier. She sat wearily down on a nearby stump. Running a hand through her hair, Kale looked down and noticed a piece of brown sackcloth beneath her foot. Kale gasped and tugged it out from under the bush. Sure enough, it was the bag that was dumped, but now it was empty.

Kale sprung to her feet and hesitantly looked around the bushes for Leon's body, squeezing her eyes shut tightly for a moment, not ultimately wanting to see his long dead form. Reminding herself of why she was there, she scoured the area carefully.

But Leon was gone.

Kale sat back on the stump with the empty sack in her hands and stared at it.

What if someone found his body and took it?

Then she paused for a moment and looked around.

What if he actually wasn't really dead, and he just left, taking the weapons with him?

Kale shook her head at that thought. *That's impossible*, she said to herself. *An animal must have come and carried him off. Oh Leon, I'm so sorry. You said we should run. I ignored you, and now you're dead!*

Tears collected in her eyes, as Kale put her face in her hands and wept. She remembered suddenly how Bromir had told her that life was like a book. She realized painfully that Colum, and now Leon, had just lived out their last pages. Something in her did not want to believe that Leon was actually dead. It kept saying again and again that he *must* be alive, yet it just was not possible. It was like the hope in her was battling despair. Neither could gain the upper hand.

The daylight had long gone when Kale finally got up again. Fireflies started their dance among the grasses, their cheerful blinking lights a stark contrast with Kale's state. She began moving through the forest away from the trail, the sackcloth still clutched in her hand. The shadows were long, but Kale put as much distance as she could between herself and the road before resting. She did not even bother collecting wood for a fire. Numb and cold, Kale settled down on her cloak alone, remembering how only a week ago, Colum and Leon would have been beside her.

Kale's mind painted pictures of their journey, recalling everything they had gone through since Leon and she first met. Her thoughts drifted back to days before when she had asked him why everyone wanted to capture her. His voice drifted back to her through her memories.

"*I can't tell you. It is better if you didn't know,*" he had said.

Kale wondered what he had known that she did not, and why he wanted to keep it from her.

He died to keep me safe, Kale remembered sorrowfully. *Why was he willing to give up his life?*

Then that voice in her head picked up again.

No! He can't be dead, she argued with herself. *I refuse to believe it.*

She looked up at the stars and shouted out to the world, "I will go to that castle, and I will find out why they tried to kill us. I will keep looking for Leon until I find him!"

Then she vowed to herself quietly, "And I will make them pay for what they did."

TO BE CONTINUED
in Book 2 of the series

Did you enjoy The Last Pages?
Please support the author by leaving a
review on Amazon, Barnes and Noble,
GoodReads, and/or iTunes.

Made in the USA
San Bernardino, CA
19 June 2014